What the critics are saying…

"Madison Hayes is an admirable writer who manages to stroke the funny button, the libido and jerk the heartstrings at the same time, a feat I cannot take for granted." ~ *Maitress Enchanted in Romance*

"Kingdom of Khal: Redeeming Davik is a powerful, fascinating book…Petra remains a mystery throughout most of the story, but this air of mystery helps set up some surprising twists, which are revealed at the end. This well-written book is highly entertaining." ~*Renee Burnette The Romance Studio*

"I definitely recommend Redeeming Davik for its fresh, rousing love scenes and strong plot." ~ *Barb Chan Just Erotic Romance Reviews*

"Madison Hayes has a hit on her hands with these sexy and exciting Gryffins! If you're a fantasy lover, this is one book you can't miss." ~ *Susan Biliter ECataRomance*

"An erotic masterpiece! A daring fantasy romance that explodes with amazing colourful imagery and teases with an unforgettable couple…readers of Gryffin Strain: His Female will find this erotic tale far superior to many others." ~ *Naomi Fallen Angel Reviews*

Prized Possession

By Madison Hayes

PRIZED POSSESSION
An Ellora's Cave Publication, January 2005

Ellora's Cave Publishing, Inc.
1337 Commerce Drive Suite #13
Stow, Ohio 44224

ISBN #1419951505

Edited by: *Mary Moran*
Cover art by: *Syneca*

Warning:

The following material contains graphic sexual content meant for mature readers. *Prized Possession* has been rated *E-rotic* by a minimum of three independent reviewers.

Ellora's Cave Publishing offers three levels of Romantica™ reading entertainment: S (S-ensuous), E (E-rotic), and X (X-treme).

S-ensuous love scenes are explicit and leave nothing to the imagination.

E-rotic love scenes are explicit, leave nothing to the imagination, and are high in volume per the overall word count. In addition, some E-rated titles might contain fantasy material that some readers find objectionable, such as bondage, submission, same sex encounters, forced seductions, etc. E-rated titles are the most graphic titles we carry; it is common, for instance, for an author to use words such as "fucking", "cock", "pussy", etc., within their work of literature.

X-treme titles differ from E-rated titles only in plot premise and storyline execution. Unlike E-rated titles, stories designated with the letter X tend to contain controversial subject matter not for the faint of heart.

Contents

Gryffin Strain: His Female

Chapter One

Jarrk threw himself backward and twisted to avoid Grat's sledgehammer right, knowing Grat would follow up with a low left. Then jumped back another step to avoid the hammering left. He could have come back with a rounding blow to Grat's stomach, but didn't want to make the golden Gryffin angry.

He just wanted to win.

An angry Grat would be hard to beat. And he had to win. A quick glance at the human female reinforced his opinion, along with his resolve. Jarrk squinted against the afternoon sun, bursting through the trees that ringed the clearing, and almost missed Grat's next barrage.

Chiarra watched the golden Gryffin as his fist shot out to swipe viciously at his opponent. On his head, a ruff of spiky hair rose in angry menace. The silver male was fast, agile. As he threw himself backward, Chiarra noted at least a glimmer of intelligence in his eyes.

She didn't hold out much hope for either of them, however. Gryffins were nothing more than animals—at least that's what she'd been taught and there was no evidence here to convince her otherwise.

Jerking against strong hands that gripped her, Chiarra sneered at what she considered pure, ugly, male barbarism. She couldn't help but see her position as a lose/lose situation. The two males circled each other, hand hackles raised, barbs out, as they fought for the right to include her in their fold. The creatures' upper bodies glimmered with a sheen of sweat as they paced out a circle on the trampled grass, each of them searching for the opening that would assure success, each of them reluctant to commit to an action that would threaten failure.

Chiarra's eyes followed the silver male. Although the Gryffin had had openings, opportunities to injure, he hadn't immediately pressed his advantage. Instead, he appeared to hold in rein a leashed power not yet released. His behavior implied he would not be satisfied with injury and waited for his opportunity to destroy. As though he had a *strategy*. Now she frowned at the man.

Male!

Male, she corrected herself, quickly.

Barbs thrust forward on a huge fist, Grat made his next lunge. Jarrk's head snapped back as he took the barbs high on his cheek, felt Grat's barbs tear into his skin. As he slanted toward the ground, Jarrk punched the top of his left hand with his right fist. A jet of blue liquid shot into Grat's eyes and the Gryffin howled. Jarrk's hand snaked around Grat's neck and pulled the heavier Gryffin earthward with him as a twisting motion put Jarrk on top. With his knee between Grat's shoulder blades and a fist in his hair, Jarrk yanked his head back and pressed his barbs tight against Grat's scalp at the base of his ruff.

There were a few panting seconds as Grat glared up at Chiarra with violence. "Take the bitch!"

As Jarrk released Grat, Chiarra watched the golden Gryffin hop to his feet, swift to demonstrate his defeat as merely temporary. With curled lip, Chiarra snorted at what she considered a pathetic display of male assertiveness.

Or re-assertiveness, in Grat's case.

She returned her attention to the champion. When he slid her a look from under white eyelashes, she hurried to meet it with a haughty stare meant to inform the Gryffin she was nobody's prize. She expected gloating satisfaction from the male. Instead, she was surprised to find his expression held only relief. She gritted her teeth. Evidently, the creature considered her a prize of some importance.

As Jarrk started toward her, the hands that had gripped her pushed her forward to face her new master. She elbowed herself free, wiping her hands distastefully on the simple linen wrap that hugged her hips. When the silver Gryffin stopped in front of her, she glared into his neon eyes and spat full in his face. Coldly, she watched his reaction as his eyes jerked to hers with a flash of pain, pain that had been entirely absent—earlier—when Grat had ripped into his face.

Grat let out a hoot of derision. "Thanks for sparing me that, Jarrk! Take the girl and welcome to her."

Chiarra watched her spittle sag on the Gryffin's cheek to mix with the blood he'd shed for her. His gaze darkened as he raised a hand to wipe his face. "You'll live to regret that," he told her, just before he turned and walked away.

Chapter Two

Jeering catcalls followed Jarrk while Chiarra stood watching his back. The Gryffin, having apparently lost interest in her, moved out of the clearing and melted into the forest as they disappeared into their lodges. With sudden realization, Chiarra accelerated after Jarrk. Just catching a glimpse of silver between two thick trunks, she followed him out of the clearing. It was an old forest with widely spaced birch and elm along with chestnut. Underfoot, the path was clear of the jumble of low growth found in younger forests. Small geyser pools sprang up in unexpected places to feed fences of willows. Chiarra saw Jarrk disappear behind a mass of green vine. She followed.

Parting a curtain of periwinkle, Chiarra slipped through the opening, straightened and blinked. She found herself within a long, low structure constructed of live willow, bowed into an arch and woven together. Turning, she frowned at the lodge opening, which, from the outside, was a perfectly camouflaged part of the forest. Several females were active in the long open dwelling.

At least, she assumed they were females and not boys.

Female Gryffins were straight-waisted and flat-chested. Chiarra pressed back a smile; for once in her life, she felt on the generous side of well endowed. Not that the women weren't without their own beauty. For although they couldn't boast about the size of their chests, Gryffin females had her beat all-to-hell in the color department. Each female sported a ruffled V-shaped fan above her shallow breasts, similar to the males' chest fans but in colors—vivid colors—varying from iridescent greens, to opalescent blues, pearly purples and every glowing, fiery shade of orange and red produced in the flickering depths of hearth-fire.

A female passed, her loose shorts riding low on her hips. Low enough that Chiarra could see brilliant crescents of color that started just below her pelvic wings and continued downward into the low-slung shorts.

But Chiarra wasn't there to guess how far the color dipped between a Gryffin's legs. She looked for the male, Jarrk. And found him across the room. He watched her from the corner of one eye, while one of his women painted a thin, clear substance over his wound. Chiarra opened her mouth...and held the words back with a curled tongue.

Like the shovel jaw Beejer, the Gryffin were a magnificent strain—you couldn't help but admire them. Jarrk's spiking curls framed an angular face dominated by a strong nose that started at his eyebrows and slanted down from there, in a long line, to just above his mouth. And the mouth curved boldly, wide above a strong but narrow chin. The eyes were neon—always neon—in Jarrk's case, an inner circle of brilliant purple ringed with a wide band of dark silver. And yet, the sum of these features is not what made Jarrk a striking animal, instead, it was the bushy white eyebrows that arched high and fierce over his neon eyes. They gave the creature an air of intelligence that she would never have credited—

"It's impolite to stare," he told her. His tenor voice graveled and rasped like stones in a jar.

She smiled at him indulgently. "I only returned yours."

He grunted. "You're supposed to be better than I," he reminded her. "Mind the example you set."

Her mind reeled backward across the room, across space and time, across misconceptions and unfounded prejudice. She'd heard of animals, like the Gryffin, that used tools, that could communicate. Some birds used thorns to spear grubs. Small apes used leaves to collect drinking water. Certain sea animals communicated amongst themselves with rudimentary language. Dogs could be playful and even teasing.

She could not recall one report of an animal with a sense of humor.

Let alone a cynical sense of humor.

And yet...humor is what she saw in Jarrk's neon eyes as he turned his face toward her.

It set her back a bit. Her lips parted. They stared at each other several moments before Jarrk finally pulled his gaze from hers. "Thank you, Akela," he told the woman who had painted his wound.

"You told me I'd live to regret—"

"You will."

"That's a threat?"

He shook his head. "That's a fact."

She snorted at him, pityingly. She could have walked away from the clearing and lost herself in the forest. "What's to stop my escape from your...fold?"

"The maelstrom, mostly, although you're welcome to escape if you can manage it. You might try the forest. Mind the dragons." He stood and started across the room.

"You'll stop me."

He flicked a glance her way. "No."

She almost decided the male might be simpleminded after all. Why had he fought to include her in his fold?

"I don't give a—fuck—what you do."

Chiarra started.

"Did I use the word correctly?" he inquired, politely.

Eyes narrowed, she gave him a curt nod.

"You may stay here if you choose, try the forest or attempt a crossing on your own. No one from the clan will try to stop you. And after your recent display of gratitude—"

"Gratitude!"

"—I doubt any will try to help you. If you stay, my females will show you how you can make yourself useful."

"Useful!" she sputtered. "To you? If you plan to use me—"

"Only if you force yourself on me."

"—I won't require instruction!" Chiarra took an angry breath.

Jarrk stared back at her, the beginnings of a smile on his face as his final words made some headway through the thick bunker that was her skull.

Only if you force yourself on me?

"I'll keep that in mind," he said, "although with eight females, *I* won't require a ninth."

"Why did you fight for me," she snapped, "if you don't plan to use me?"

"I thought I'd made that clear," he informed her brusquely. Then smiled slowly. "You needn't sound so disappointed." Long strides on lean legs carried him to the door.

"When will you make the next crossing?" she demanded, before he could escape. "When will it be safe to cross to the north side of the maelstrom?"

"Not until the next meteorological phase...several weeks in your language."

"You'll permit me to cross — then?"

"Nothing would please me more," he told her, "other than your earlier departure." He ducked through the door and was gone.

Scowling, Chiarra turned to find the female Akela glaring at her. Her ruff was up. "What!"

"You're slow," she said unkindly, "even for a human."

Chiarra made a gesture of impatience.

"You humiliated Jarrk in front of our clan. When you spat at him. You made him lose face."

"Why should I care?!"

"You're every kind of fool, human! Jarrk only fought for you to save you. When he told you that you'd live to regret your action, he meant it literally. You'll *live*! You'd have died in Grat's fold, inside a week."

"You don't give me much credit."

"Credit wouldn't help you when Grat set his barbs into you."

Chiarra felt the blood drain from her cheeks.

"The poison won't kill a Gryffin, unless it's delivered at the ruff. It did, however, kill the last human Grat mated."

Reaching out blindly for something to steady her, Chiarra dropped into a chair. Several revelations assailed her at once and she felt her forehead crumple like a battered shield as she reconsidered — the relief she had seen in Jarrk's eyes immediately following the fight — the pain when she spat on him.

"Tar's Pit," she muttered under her breath.

Chapter Three

By the time the meal was prepared, Chiarra was dragging. Akela had put her directly to work, skinning shanks. Chiarra carried a trencher to the pit and set it on a low table. Her legs folded beneath her as she dropped to the floor.

It had been a long day, a day begun with running interspersed with hiding. She'd lain, face down, heart galloping, in a narrow ditch while a column of men tramped to within a few feet of her hiding place. One of the soldiers had spat into the ditch.

Up again, a hasty glance behind her and more running. A glimpse of yellow uniforms between two trees. A frantic dash across the deep, smooth chasm while the maelstrom winds sucked at her with growing force. Knowing if she could make The Spit, she'd be safe—for a time.

Chiarra's eyes glazed with fatigue as she recalled the wild, swirling winds as they picked up velocity then increased with alarming violence—one foot had slipped—the maelstrom tugged then dragged her down the smooth, bare floor of the chasm, dragged her fighting for one more foothold, one more step.

Clutching upward to climb the chasm walls—Chiarra opened her hands to blink down at her skinned palms—coming face-to-face with the tall, golden Gryffin.

Grat.

But she was safe for the time being, for as long as the winds were up, isolating the spit of land that split the maelstrom.

Located about ten leagues inland, The Spit was created when the easterly winds swept across the ocean and pushed into the wide fjords at the sea's edge. The high mountains that bracketed one of these fjords channeled the winds into an ever-narrowing valley. At certain times of the year, when the winds were fierce and trending into the valley, the maelstrom was created, rushing through the valley with the tumbling force of a mountain stream. Within the valley was a shallower chasm on either side of The Spit. Originally created by water, this chasm was now empty and scoured bare by the maelstrom winds. At the height of the maelstrom, there was no way to cross the chasm.

Yes, she was safe for the time being. And after that?

She'd have to make the north crossing before the uniforms returned for her.

Jarrk's females turned to watch him enter the lodge. Swinging a bundle off his shoulder, he threw several rabbits down just inside the door and joined his females for dinner.

Like the females, Jarrk wore nothing on his chest. Loose dragon-skin pants hung low on his hips, revealing his belly and a good deal of skin below that—skin that gradually gave way to fringed scales that disappeared into his pants. A sporran of dragon spines hung to cover and protect his groin triangle. He wore nothing on his feet, which were calloused and spurred at the heels.

Blinking hard to keep awake, Chiarra picked through the crisped hide and cracked bones for bits of meat. Eyes glazing again, she found herself staring at the skin stretched taut across Jarrk's flanks. When he moved, she tipped her head as her eyes tried to follow the silver crescents into his pants. She stopped, holding her breath, and stared, captivated by a warm desire — to smooth her hands over the taut skin, the fringed scales — to slide her hands down between dragon skin and Gryffin skin, over the flat male stomach — to follow the riff of crescents and discover…what that would lead to.

He leaned forward. Almost absently, she noted the very thick, very male mound beneath his sporran. Whatever the crescents lead to, there was a lot of it. She blinked with a start and raised her eyes — and met Jarrk's intent gaze.

He adjusted his pants upward with an impatient jerk. Slowly, the ruff on his head lifted his curling hair. Tension sprang from him to his females as they all stared at him. Tension as thick as Tar's dick.

Chiarra lowered her eyes.

"Akela," he said. "It would seem my new female hungers for something other than what she's been offered." His tone was clipped and Chiarra bit her lip as her cheeks warmed. "Are there any knuckles left?"

Akela left to return with a jar, which she emptied into a bowl. Reaching for one of the meaty joints, Chiarra didn't stop until the bone was clean. When her head drooped, she jumped suddenly, realizing she was almost asleep. She needed to apologize to Jarrk, she thought. And that was the last thing she remembered.

* * * * *

She woke to murmurings of erotic pleasure. Rolling toward the sound, Chiarra could make out the female named Shani on hands and knees in the center of the sleeping pit, the dim form of Jarrk as he knelt behind her, groin firm against her bottom. With fingers spread, he worked them into the ruff on her head, which appeared to intensify the woman's pleasure. As he tugged his fingers through her ruff, Shani's neck arched backward and she jerked against him a few short spasms then collapsed.

That didn't last long, Chiarra thought briefly, then realized one of the other females now knelt behind Jarrk, her arms wrapped around him; her hands moving up his torso to caress the fan on his chest. Chiarra watched Akela's hands as they ran into the silvery crescents that spanned Jarrk's chest in the same place a human male would grow hair. Tiny, fringed scales lifted when she pulled her hands upward and flattened when she pulled her hands down.

Jarrk turned to face Akela and Chiarra's eyes widened on his erection—thick, hard and scandalously long—rising from a ruffled bed of silver, and suffering not the least for having serviced Shani. Leaning back on his heels, he turned Akela's back to him, lifted her and put her on his cock. As Jarrk speared between Akela's cheeks, Chiarra's body answered with an unexpected spike of lustful craving that took her at the core. She found herself breathless as she watched Jarrk hold his female on his cock, watched breathless while Akela sat impaled on his shaft, knees bent, legs spread outside his, perfectly still. The woman's hands were clamped just above her own thighs, tugging her cheeks apart to receive Jarrk's full penetration.

Again, it was over in moments and Chiarra—finally breathing again—was stunned. She watched Akela fall away from the male, seemingly content. Jarrk had never moved—never so much as flexed his lower body. Mesmerized, Chiarra raised herself on her elbows, eyes on Jarrk's impressive erection. His dick was as hard and full as when he'd started.

How could that be?

She'd learned a little about Gryffins during her lifetime. Although most people considered them animals, they weren't that much different from humans. Their sex was placed slightly further back between their legs—on both sexes—with the result that the male's erection strained, not so much parallel as perpendicular to his body. When threatened, their hackles rose on their knuckles, exposing—on the males—dangerous poison barbs. Similarly, the ruffed ridge on their heads lifted when they were provoked. Only one in five Gryffins was born a male. Accommodatingly, each male took on several females.

Which didn't explain why Jarrk had eight females in his fold, she thought wryly. At eight, he was beating the odds. Of course, Grat was such an asshole, maybe Jarrk had three females that otherwise would have belonged to Grat.

She was suddenly aware that he returned her stare. Pulling her gaze from his thoroughly captivating erection, she found his ruff up and his gaze heated, apparently angry that she watched. His eyes brimmed with violent passion and she stared back, unable to drag her eyes from the owner of that to-beg-for cock. Her heart racketed in her chest and she tried to quiet it—by reminding herself the male was angry with her—by telling herself she should be ashamed of herself for watching without candor.

Lowering her eyes, she dropped back onto her bedding, closed her eyes and struggled with her feelings—as well as her lack of them. Yes, she was aroused. No, Jarrk's anger didn't frighten her. And no, she really couldn't scrape up much guilt either. She shrugged. She'd planned a full apology in the morning. She'd just throw this indiscretion in with the rest of her mistakes and cover it with a blanket apology. Closing her eyes, she tried to rid herself of that image.

The image of Jarrk.

Jarrk on his knees.

An unruly twinge of desire came out of nowhere and crawled over skin, alive with sparking nerve endings. A little shiver of excitement originated at the nape of her neck and traveled to accumulate at the base of her spine where her back was inclined to arch in its zeal to accommodate the man on his knees in the pit. Arching her back, Chiarra stretched. The twinge made the leap from the small of her back to the depths of her very accommodating sex, which throbbed with intent interest. Desire twisted into her gut with warm clenching fingers that grabbed at her womb. A strong thrumming pulse sprang to life between her legs and shot upward through her body to squeeze her lungs and snatch at her heart. She could not erase the image of Jarrk wedged firmly in her mind.

Jarrk on his knees.

Jarrk. Out in his full glory.

He might not be a man, exactly. But he was *definitely* all male.

Chapter Four

"I'm sorry, Jarrk. I apologize for my behavior."

The human, Chiarra, extended her hand toward him, palm up. With bold trust, eyes the warm green of forest lakes held his.

The little human's abrupt reversal of attitude was unexpected. He'd understood humans were reluctant to admit error, yet here the female stood with hand out and palm up, her action an expression of apology and...submittal, if he understood the gesture. Jarrk hesitated, reluctant to touch the woman.

"I put myself in your hands," she said, without faltering, "and accept your protection while in your country."

He didn't want to touch her, but his refusal would be received as an insult. And then it would be open season again, he was sure, where this female was concerned. Raking one hand into his ruff, he reached out for her with the other and laid it, palm down, on hers.

It was worse than he'd anticipated. And better. Her skin was smooth, soft and invitingly warm. Excited nerve endings channeled conflicting messages from his hand to various parts of his body, with predictable results. Thank Tar she couldn't see his cock stiffen beneath his sporran, but she would see that same reaction mirrored in his lifting ruff. Again, he attempted to stroke his ruff into submission, which was rather like throwing fuel on the fire, as the stiff ridge of hair responded to the stimulus of his hand.

Excusing himself, he pushed out of the door. His ruff continued to lift as he stalked away from the lodge. Minutes later he was plunging into a large geyser pool, shaking the water from his hair as he surfaced.

Chiarra!

The haughty little human had his ridge up.

Tar! He pulled himself out of the pool and onto the flat, warm rock surrounding the pool. What a combination of conflicting attributes the woman was. Proud to begin with — too proud — insulting and rude as a spark. Jarrk smiled slowly. But he had seen the honest regret in her eyes. He'd met humans who would hold tightly to their proud opinions, foolish judgments and carry them to their graves. But, unlike others of her race, the girl, Chiarra, had revised her opinion in an instant. She'd apologized, afterward, unflinchingly, and at the first opportunity.

He'd predicted her regret — he couldn't have known it would come so quickly.

With such a rush of warmth.

Tar, the woman was warmth. Warmth. Jarrk held his hand before his face and stared at it as his smile evaporated. Too bad humans considered Gryffins little more than animals.

He'd heard stories of human females. Of the things they could do with their bodies. He'd heard about the rumored length of their orgasms and the...the *number* of orgasms, if he understood correctly. Frowning painfully, Jarrk continued to stare at his hand as every muscle in his body tensed and his cock jerked to life in unison with the ridge on his skull. Closing his eyes, he let his hand drop onto his ruffled groin. With the palm of his hand, he smoothed the fringed scales downward then fingered one upward.

Chiarra.

"Why did you fight for me, if you don't plan to use me?"

He could use her now.

Tar, human women were shapely. They were all in-and-out, as opposed to the women of his own race, who were straight-up-and-down. He closed his eyes and saw Chiarra, her small, female, curving form. He wished he could get a look under all that clothing she wore. Why did humans cover their chests! Were they ashamed they had no fans? With breasts like Chiarra's, a woman had no need of a fan. Her short, sleeveless jerkin did nothing to conceal the fact that her breasts would fill his hands...and nicely. The short wrap that hugged her hips didn't obscure any portion of her rounded derriere. His hands ached to travel those curves just as his fingers longed to stroke into her crease and follow it to the pool of warmth between her legs.

He turned his wounded cheek into the sun.

And her hair! Masses of thick waves that curled on her shoulders. Her hair was an unusual color, red mixed with brown. Red and orange were common in Gryffin females, but brown! It was as rich and dark and deep as the forest. Her eyes were long and wide. Her pupils—a continuous, uninterrupted lake of warm, peaceful green. A man could fall into that lake and never resurface.

Chiarra.

"If you plan to use me — I won't require instruction!"

Slowly, his hand smoothed downward then crept up against the pubic scales. He held his breath as he dragged his hand up against the lay of the fringed scales — they rose under his hand. At the same time, the fingers of his other hand slid into his scalp to dig into his ruff. With a groan, he pulled his fingers through his ridge. A moment later, both hands were smoothing and riffling the thick bed that surrounded his shaft, as his dick strained straight up from his body.

He clamped both hands around his erection and tightened his fists. What would it be like inside a woman? A human woman. What would it be like inside Chiarra? Would it last long? Would Chiarra? Last long? Would she last long enough to satisfy him? His hands loosened then compressed his pulsing length. Would he find release inside Chiarra's warmth?

"Need help with that?"

Jerking upright, he found Chiarra on the other side of the pool. Her lips were quirked in a smile while her eyes rested between his legs.

Startled by her intrusion, angry at his own indiscretion, he hid his annoyance and gave her a heated smile. "I think I've got a handle on the situation."

"Actually, you've got a hand on it. But you do have one hell of a handle."

"Do you like to watch, then, little human?" He stroked his dick languidly, boldly.

She made a face. "As a matter of fact, I wanted to apologize for my behavior last night."

He gave her a questioning look.

"For watching you with your females."

It took a moment for his eyes to register understanding. He shrugged. "You're one of my females, now. You're welcome to watch...or take part for that matter." His voice feigned disinterest but a smile of evil mischief accompanied his words.

Her eyes lit with a spark of her own mischief. "I wouldn't want to force myself on you."

He thought about that. About positioning her over his cock and letting her force herself onto his dick. "No. I wouldn't want that, either," he lied. "But we could ease into it slowly."

Her lips parted in pleased surprise.

"At any rate, an apology isn't required. Don't lose any sleep over it, and...watch as much as you like."

She snorted. "It hardly lasted long enough for me to lose any sleep." She cocked her head. "I *could* take part..." she ruminated.

Jarrk held his breath.

She smiled suddenly. "If I took part, I imagine there'd be a lot more to watch."

Jarrk sucked in his cheeks as his mouth dried and his dick surged painfully. A single iridescent tear spat from the tip of his aching cock.

Chiarra raised a finger to point at his erection. "How's it coming?"

It's probably coming under my own hand, he thought, and wished for it to be buried between Chiarra's legs. "It's coming along nicely, thank you."

Her laugh was a silvery sparkle. "Well, if you're looking for satisfaction from *me*, don't hold your breath."

"It wasn't my breath I was holding."

"That's right," she laughed again. She shot him a final grin before turning into the forest. "I like a man who can hold his own. Hope everything comes out alright," she threw over her shoulder.

For several moments, he watched the place where she stood as he pumped his cock in his fist.

"If I took part, I imagine there'd be a lot more to watch."

Jarrk's back stiffened. His eyes closed and he groaned just before he erupted onto his hands.

Chapter Five

"What! I don't think so," she stated vehemently.

Chiarra watched Jarrk as his hackles rose on his knuckles. He pressed the heel of one palm above the knuckles of his other hand milking downward on blue veins. Phosphorescent drops of deadly poison dripped into the cup of water.

"You'll drink it," he stated with determination. "It may save your life. It isn't common knowledge, but you can build up an immunity to Gryffin poison, by taking it in gradually increasing amounts. Just two drops today, three tomorrow." He slid the cup across the table. "Try it."

She pushed herself away from the table, gave him a wary look and shook her head.

"You're going to try it, if it's the last thing you do."

"That's what troubles me," she muttered.

She backed across the room while he followed her, the cup in his hand. Followed her, until her back was up against the curved wall of the lodge. With one forearm on the wall behind her, he caged her in, his long hard body inches from hers. The cup nudged against her bottom lip—she resisted with tightly pressed lips.

Abruptly, there were no more inches between their bodies as Jarrk held her hard against the wall and his free hand took the nape of her neck, tipping her head while the lip of the cup edged between her lips.

Chiarra sniffed sharply. She would have gasped if she'd dared to open her mouth. She would have gasped at that first startling instant of contact except she knew it would earn her a mouthful of blue poison. As it was, her body gasped for her, stunned at the man's abrasive nearness, hard and strong at every touch point. Her nipples tightened at initial contact then screamed for more. Her lower body heard and cried out for connection. Her pubic mound canted toward him automatically and she smeared her body against the hard male length that pinned her to the wall.

Jarrk stopped with a curse. Chiarra's body ground against his as she struggled beneath him. The stubborn little human was getting him totally ruffed up. Her struggles inciting his dick to action. Her tense little body, a provocation to everything male stirring—and stirred up—in his loins. Ignoring his growing erection, he tried to get a finger in her mouth and almost spilled the cup. With one hand gripping her nape and the other holding the cup, he cast about for other options. Decisively, he put his head down to hers, put his lips at the corner of her mouth and shot the flat tip of his tongue between her lips.

Her mouth opened in surprise.

He dropped the cup in astonishment—unprepared for the ready heat of that warm, moist envelope.

He heard the cup hit the ground with a light thud. Felt the thud in his heart, in no way light. He groaned as he clutched her shoulders, pulled his tongue, his mouth from hers with great force of effort, and tried to remove his hands from her. They wouldn't quite come free, instead they moved down over her mounded breasts, damp and wet where the cup had spilled. He left his hands where they were, unwilling, unable to remove them.

"Now see what you've done," he said unevenly. "I've spilled."

"What," she breathed back, just as unevenly, "no friendly drop left for me?" She lowered her eyes in the direction of his groin but stopped when she found his hands cupping her breasts. "Your hands!"

His hands jerked an inch to hover above her breasts. Slowly, he made a fist and raised it to her mouth. He wasn't too surprised when his hackles rose for her. By now, everything *else* was up. Ruff. Cock. You name it.

He clenched his fist. Watched a single drop of blue trickle out across his fingers and gave her a look of warning. "You're going to get it one way or another," he told her. His lips were against her ear as he whispered. "One place or another. If you won't take it in your mouth, I imagine there's enough poison in my semen to do the trick."

He heard her suck in a breath and watched her tongue flick out to capture the thin line of blue liquor. She closed her eyes.

The poison, cool on her tongue, slid down her throat with a hint of intoxicating fire and she waited a moment to assess her body's reaction. Almost immediately, she was blindsided by a stunning vision that robbed her breath. A vision as beautiful and complete...as total orgasm.

Jarrk stood in a moonlit clearing, silver light on his shoulders as he turned toward her. There was a geyser pool behind him and the moonlight on the pool was a thousand silver leaves floating on the water's surface. He smiled at her as he pulled the string on his pants and let them slide down his legs.

She tilted her head back to rest on the leafy wall behind her. "Jarrk," she whispered.

He was smiling when she opened her eyes again.

"Okay, so I'll build up an immunity," she said reluctantly, dragging herself back to the present. "Do I have to worry about Grat or any of the other Gryffin males for that matter?"

He shook his head as the tension between them eased a fraction. "None of the other males, but Grat's — an asshole, if I've got the word right. Watch out for him."

Their eyes failed to disconnect and Chiarra felt that hint of fire continue down past her stomach and settle lower, where it had no business exploring, let alone settling. Jarrk's eyes glinted an instant, as if in understanding or in answer. With narrowed eyes, she gazed into his neon ones. Okay, so Jarrk's venom wasn't going to kill her but what other effects might it have on her?

An aphrodisiac?

Mightn't Jarrk's venom act as an aphrodisiac on her — excite her and compel her to couple with him? Perhaps he intended to drive her into a maddened frenzy of desire then refuse her.

Chiarra frowned, dissatisfied with that conclusion. Or not refuse her, she thought, reasonably.

And perhaps *that* was just wishful thinking.

She watched Jarrk's smile widen, probably at her dopey expression.

Tar, she thought warmly, he had a nice smile.

Too bad everything she did annoyed him, she thought, as she gazed at his stiff ruff. Too bad he was attached. Her eyes slid around the inside of the lodge. In fact, she'd never known a man with so many attachments.

Pushing off from the wall, Jarrk crossed the room to Akela's worktable. Chiarra watched him as he pulled a narrow flask beneath his hand, turned his hand sideways, and milked a stream of poison to drip from his knuckles into the flask. When the flask was full, he crossed the room to pick up his bow. "I'll hunt tonight," he informed Akela...rather brusquely, Chiarra thought.

Several female heads lifted to observe their male. "Look for me at dawn."

With a troubled expression, Akela watched Jarrk stoop through the door then turned her eyes, full of recrimination, on Chiarra.

Chapter Six

Finished with the chores Akela had assigned her, Chiarra wandered to the edge of the clearing where several young idlers gathered in the early evening. Her life with the Gryffin had been reduced to a comfortable routine. She rose at dawn with the rest of Jarrk's fold and joined them in their activities. She'd made herself an extra jerkin, rough but functional, and Shani had loaned her a pair of shorts.

When Grat stalked into the clearing, she shrank into the shadow of the trees, holding her breath. But the golden Gryffin crossed the open space and disappeared without noticing her.

One of the young Gryffins palmed a set of toned drums while another played a brass bowl. Chiarra stood and watched the wet stick circle the bowl at different levels, producing notes to accompany the song of a third young male. Tar and Breeza! Gryffins could sing! Swaying in time to the music, her head nodded and her foot tapped with a mind of its own.

Another male joined the circle along with several young females. Raising her eyes from the drummer's hands, she found the Gryffin smiling at her. She returned the smile politely, removed her eyes, and discovered the bowler smiling as well.

Fingers like steel talons sank into the soft skin inside her elbow. She gulped back a squeal as Jarrk yanked her from the clearing. "What do you think you're doing?" he hissed in her ear.

Several trees flashed by as Chiarra was propelled forward under Jarrk's rough direction. He stopped suddenly, slamming her back against a tree. Chiarra took a quick breath just before Jarrk's mouth opened. The next thing she felt was the pressure of his teeth, hard and possessive against her lips. Firm lips followed where his teeth had bruised. Chiarra caved beneath his onslaught.

Abruptly, he pulled back his lips, eyes angry on hers. "I took you into my fold! How dare you—"

But Chiarra's attention was on his mouth, as her lips reached for his. With a curse, he turned her to the tree and plunged his hand between her legs. His body held hers tight against the tree. Spreading his fingers, he dragged his forefinger along the line of her pussy and back through her crease. Her gasp of outrage was followed by a shudder of desire, an outrageous, unexpected response to his finger's inexorable incursion across intimate, yielding ground.

"If that's what you want, little human, you'll have to get it from me. As my female, you have *no right* to offer yourself to others." Again, Jarrk stroked his finger over the thin material of her shorts and through her warm crease as his lips moved against her ear. "Don't *you dare* make me a fool in front of my own clan." his breath was harsh with a ragged edge. "You're lucky Grat didn't see you. You're lucky Grat didn't take you and fuck you."

She gritted her teeth and put ice into her voice. "Get off me, you fucking animal."

With the recoil of a bowstring, he jumped backward. She only just registered his stunned expression, his raised ruff, before she ratcheted on her heel and stalked away. "I didn't offer myself to anyone, you jealous bastard."

"Jealous! Jealousy has nothing to do with it!" he shouted after her.

Once inside the lodge, she jerked off her rough top and borrowed shorts before reaching for her original jerkin.

Jarrk blasted into the lodge behind her. And stopped to stare at her breasts just as they disappeared beneath her short jerkin. "Where are you going?" he asked, with a strained voice as his eyes dropped to her naked lower body.

His females scattered and she turned to face the furious Gryffin.

"The forest," she told him, reaching for her wrap. "I'll take my chances with the dragons. Dragons are looking pretty good right now —"

"Dragons don't give you many chances."

"—compared to rape by a fucking rooster."

If he didn't look angry before, he did now. "Don't flatter yourself, woman," he growled, "I wouldn't have —"

"I was talking about Grat."

He stopped, stunned.

"You needn't look so disappointed," she mocked, and tied her wrap off at her side.

"Actually," he gritted, "Gryffin are more closely related to reptiles than birds —"

"Chicken. Lizard. Whatever."

"—but as long as you brought it up, which do you prefer and how do you like it?"

She threw him a glare.

"Because I like mine hot...and running with juices. How about you?" he challenged, "light meat or dark?"

She gaped at him. Then. "Dark," she answered, recovering quickly, "chopped fine in salad."

He winced at the imagery. "Dark meat—Gryffin, then." His ruff stiffened further as she watched. "And what will you do for meat in the forest? You don't have a bow. How will you hunt?"

"Unlike you, I'm not a complete carnivore," she grunted. "I can live on greens and roots. But if I get peckish for meat, I'll dig for voles." She brushed past him but he caught her upper arm in his hand.

She jerked her arm in his grasp without noticeable effect.

Her cool outer shell cracked then shattered. "Didn't see me?" she cried, brokenly. "I'm lucky Grat didn't see me? What's wrong with me?" Her eyes filled with angry tears and she looked down her body, searching for offense. "All I did was smile at a young man! I didn't realize that was a crime in your culture."

Jarrk caught the glint of angry tears and, for an instant, looked uncertain. But his ruff was still up. He leaned over her. "Don't feign innocence, Chiarra. It wasn't the smile, it was what accompanied the smile!"

"I don't know what you're talking about!"

"I'll show you what I'm talking about." Roughly, he took her chin between his finger and thumb. She clenched her jaw as he moved her head up and down several times. "Tar," she heard him whisper, just before his mouth covered hers again, briefly, harshly. His body was all-over hard on hers as he crushed her in his arms.

Again, she felt her body yield to his just before he recoiled from her.

"Jarrk!" She screamed, frustrated. "What did I do?"

He stalked across the room then turned to face her. "Do you really not know?" he gritted out with great care. His ruff was still raised and he still looked angry.

She felt a tear slide down her cheek.

"I'm sorry," he said fiercely, having evidently realized his mistake, which still made Chiarra none the wiser. He turned from her. His back was stiff but his shoulders dropped a bit. "Tar! I'm sorry, Chiarra."

She shrugged helplessly. "Now I don't know what you're sorry for," she said, wiping at her cheekbones.

"I'm an ass."

"No, you're a dickhead."

He dropped to sit on a stool. "I'm that, too."

"What did I do?"

He winced as he raised his eyes to her. "You were...nodding."

"Nodding?!"

"You were 'nodding up' the drummer and the bowler for that matter. It's an invitation to mate...if you're a Gryffin." He shook his head. "But you're not a Gryffin."

"An invitation to—"

He gave her a curt nod. "With whomever you're nodding at."

She gaped at him. "You should have told me," she whispered in horror. "Tar's Ugly Children! I must have looked like a fool! I was...nodding at everyone."

"No," he said painfully.

"Yes, I was!"

"No. You didn't look like a fool," he said soberly. "It was...very sexy." He shook his head. "But I'm afraid you sent every male home with a hard-on. Including me." He raised his eyes to her carefully, hopefully.

But she'd turned from him, mortified, her face in her hands. "Tar, I'm sorry, Jarrk. I've made you lose face—again. I'll...I'll try to be more careful."

"Will you?" he asked with a small smile.

She turned back to him, lifted her face from her hands and nodded.

Then stopped.

They smiled at each other.

"Once a female is accepted into a male's fold, she shouldn't be looking outside her fold for satisfaction," Jarrk explained. "Of course it happens but it implies the male can't satisfy his females." He shrugged. "Most Gryffin have no trouble mating several women—a night."

"Oh?" she said, her voice a bit weak, her knees in total sympathy with her voice. "Several being...how many, exactly?"

Jarrk shrugged. "Four or five, easily."

"He can raise it five separate times!"

Jarrk frowned at her as though he didn't understand. "Maybe I'm saying this wrong. Normally it takes four or five females to...subdue a male. Before he comes."

She stared at him with only an instant's disbelief, as she recalled his mating with Shani and Akela. "And...ah...how many...ah...females does it take...for *you* to..."

He held her eyes. "Generally more than eight," he answered with dissatisfaction.

She couldn't stop the smile. "You say that like it's a bad thing."

He cocked his head a little as his eyes narrowed. "And you're looking at me like it's a good thing."

She returned his gaze with something warmer than sympathy. And didn't mention how much she liked a challenge.

Rising to his feet, Jarrk lifted a wide leather pouch from a hook on the wall and strapped it around his waist. "I have to go. I'm joining some others to help young Gerak finish his lodge. His initiation is tonight." He smiled at the girl. "Try to stay out of trouble, will you?"

"I'll do my best."

"Jarrk," she said suddenly, stopping him at the door. "Your females. Why do they not...use other means to satisfy you?"

He stared at her. Here it was then. He stood face-to-face with every young Gryffin's fantasy of having a human female in his fold. "What do you mean?"

Her small laugh was a little impatient. "Why do they not use...their mouths — for instance?"

Jarrk swallowed in a dry throat. And that was the problem. "That doesn't sound as good as you might think. Our mouths aren't as moist..." his eyes were glued to her full lips, "as yours." He breathed the words out. "It would be abrasive."

Her full lips crimped into a little "O" and he couldn't help himself. He gave himself up to a short mental aside, visualized his hand beneath his dick, feeding his cock into that pretty little "O". His ruff was still up, his cock was still up, and his knuckles ached to stripe the woman before him.

He groaned at that last realization. When it came to sex—especially where this female was concerned—he really wasn't much more than an animal. His nails dug deep into his palms as he clenched his fists.

"Your mouths aren't very wet," she restated in revelation and calculated what else might not be exceptionally wet. "And that's why...that's why you were holding your own, at the geyser pool the other day."

He nodded and didn't tell her that was only part of the reason.

The other part of the reason was her.

And she was driving him crazy.

Chapter Seven

It was dusking when Jarrk's fold made their way to the clearing but two large fires illuminated the circle of trees. The mood was festive with an undercurrent of cheerful expectation. Members of Gerak's fold passed through the crowd, long platters on their shoulders heaped with pit-roasted offerings. Jarrk took a place at the circle's edge and knelt in the grass as his females joined him. Chiarra was surprised when he pulled her close to his right side.

"Tranth!"

A copper Gryffin raised his chin to acknowledge Jarrk's greeting then made his way across the clearing to drop down on Jarrk's left.

"You just get back?"

Tranth nodded, his interested eyes on Chiarra. "Wedding gifts." He leaned forward to include Chiarra in the conversation. "I think my brother's females will like the stones I found." He reached behind Chiarra's ear and produced a small dark emerald. "To go with your eyes." He opened her hand and closed her fist around the stone. "I'm Tranth," he said. "You're...?"

"My female," Jarrk filled in, a firm warning in his voice.

"Who's asking you?" Tranth laughed. He returned his eyes to Chiarra.

"My name is Chiarra."

"Chiarra. That's nice," Tranth decided. "She's nice," he told his friend, "even if she is tiny."

Jarrk grunted. "Only next to you."

The circle quickly filled in, the only negative aspect being Grat's arrival and installment to their immediate right. Chiarra watched Jarrk's mouth tighten and turn down at a hard angle. He said nothing, however.

There was a mountain of food and laughter. Loud conversation which Chiarra followed with interest in the midst of which the drums started up. This appeared to be the signal for more-to-follow. The crowd quieted with interested anticipation. When Chiarra lifted her head, she caught Grat staring at her.

"Ignore him," Jarrk instructed and pulled her closer.

A young Gryffin stepped into the circle. Tall and lithe, he was the most beautiful youth Chiarra had ever seen. Chiarra watched, entranced, as he sank his teeth into his bottom lip, his expression one of youthful vulnerability combined with boyish confidence. The bowls joined the drums in a swirl of music. Raising his hands above his head, the copper Gryffin twisted into a spin.

Chiarra's eyes widened and her breath caught as Gerak rotated his hips slowly into the turn. Watched those hips all the way through the turn as the Gryffin continued his mating dance. Elbows bent, hands above his head, the male's pelvis undulated in perfect rhythm with the music. The male's eyes were closed and his lips pouted, sulky in a hard mouth. Mesmerized by his dance, Chiarra couldn't drag her eyes from the youth's body.

Chiarra's mouth dried and her breasts sparked as the copper male slowed, nodding as he offered his hand to a young female.

Jarrk growled, as did many of the other males in attendance and then leaned to his left to share a word with Tranth.

"What?" Chiarra asked. "Why are the men growling?"

Jarrk leaned right and Chiarra sparked some more when his lips brushed her ear. "It's a polite challenge, for Teela's sake. Not that any male here is actually interested in the female. She's too young and inexperienced."

Chiarra watched as Gerak circled his chosen, crowding his body close against hers in the dance, nodding slowly as she returned his invitation, finally halting behind her and dragging his hands down the front of her body. Chiarra let out a breath she'd been holding and realized she was all sparks. The young female fell to her knees, pulled one of Gerak's hands to her mouth and ran her tongue along his knuckles. Turning her face, she put a kiss on his sporran. The youth gave her a look of surprise and Jarrk chuckled. "Cheeky lass," he murmured.

Chiarra looked a question at him from the side of her eye.

"Her behavior's forward for a first-picked," he explained. "The boy will choose three females tonight. As the first-picked, she's the least of his choices. He'll save his favorite for last."

Chiarra frowned as she shook her head. "That doesn't make sense."

"When a Gryffin mates, it's the last female that receives his seed," Jarrk pointed out.

Chiarra nodded slowly.

"Jani will be his last-pick. He's mad about her. She's already carrying his childing."

Now Gerak pulled a turquoise female out of the circle. Another round of growls followed as the youth started his dance around his second choice. The dancing stopped when a bronze Gryffin stepped into the circle.

The bronze male was only slightly older than Gerak. He rumbled a threat as he approached the youth.

Chiarra shot Jarrk a look of concern.

Jarrk smiled. "More posturing. It's an honor for the female to have a challenger. Sometimes a cousin or even a brother will challenge the initiate, for the female's sake." He pointed at the challenging Gryffin. "Chacun is Gerak's best friend."

As the two males circled each other, Gerak's ruff lifted and his fists bunched—his hackles pulled back to reveal his barbs. After completing a circle around Gerak, the challenger backed away from the youth. Chacun shot a grin at his friend before he resumed his place in the circle.

Gerak completed his dance with the female. Like the first, she too dropped to her knees and pulled Gerak's fist to her mouth, as she appeared to suck on his barbs. Chiarra watched the young female run a hand up Gerak's leg to stroke him beneath his sporran.

Chiarra started to melt beneath all the sparking activity.

Gerak left the two females on their knees between the two fires. Now his dance changed subtly. The steps were the same but there was more passion in his movements and his eyes were lit as he made his way toward an elegant female with a purple fan. She jumped up to meet him, her eyes lit like his. He stopped before her as the couple nodded at each other slowly.

At Chiarra's side, Jarrk growled politely.

"*Tar's Pit!*"

Chiarra flinched at Tranth's angry words. The music stopped and tension flared as heads turned and craned. Grat stepped into the circle.

"*Bastard,*" Tranth gritted.

"What's wrong?"

"This isn't a polite challenge," Jarrk growled. "He's going to fight the boy. Grat's going to take Jani from Gerak."

Chiarra shook her head, horrified for the young female, obviously in love with her Gerak. "Is there nothing you can do?"

"Not the way you mean," Tranth answered. "We can't fight Grat. Not without making Gerak lose face."

Grat turned slowly and put insolent eyes on Chiarra. Jarrk jumped to a crouch. "I'll kill the bastard," he grated.

Chiarra gave Tranth a look pleading for explanation, but Tranth's angry expression was fixed on Grat.

There was a rustle at her shoulder. Akela leaned forward to whisper in Chiarra's ear. "Grat would *probably* back down if another female were offered for his temporary use."

"*What!*" Chiarra turned her eyes slowly to meet with Akela's.

Akela nodded her head at Chiarra but her hand gripped Chiarra's wrist tightly. Her lips formed the word *"you"*.

Chapter Eight

Jarrk exploded to his feet, flinging his fists downward as his barbs shot into position. Tranth sprang up beside him. Grat stood at the focus of three angry males— Gerak, Jarrk and Tranth. Teeth clenching silence ensued and the fires crackled.

On the other side of the clearing, a female stood and moved swiftly toward Grat. Putting her body up against his, she smoothed her hands down his chest and looked an invitation up at him. Grat didn't see the sly look she slid at Tranth.

There were a few more seconds of Grat's insolence before he swept the female to the edge of the circle. As the music picked up, Jarrk lowered himself slowly back to the ground. Tranth stood staring into the fire a moment before he dropped to a crouch beside Jarrk.

Self-conscious, Chiarra dipped her head.

"You're going to owe Sheena for that," Jarrk pointed out pitilessly. "She saved the night. Saved the initiation. Saved your brother's whole life!"

Tranth nodded, still looking a little stunned. "I didn't even know she was interested."

Jarrk allowed himself a small chuckle. "They're all interested in you, Tranth."

Jani turned with Gerak as he danced, her hands all over him. Dropping to her knees before him, she pulled her lips over his knuckles then dragged her hands down his flanks. With Jani's head in front of her male's groin, it was a moment before Chiarra realized she had Gerak's pants off. He stepped out of them as Jani turned on hands and knees and offered Gerak her bottom.

Chiarra found herself staring at Gerak's stiff cock as the youth stepped away from Jani and placed himself behind Teela. Lowered himself to his knees. Pulled her short skirt up and out of his way.

"He's not going to actually…"

Jarrk laughed at Chiarra's expression. "It's just a ceremonial mounting," he told her as Gerak thrust into the young female.

Teela let out a long wailing moan and Chiarra returned her shocked expression to Jarrk.

"Well," he said apologetically, "it's supposed to be ceremonial. Gerak's an attractive male," he reasoned.

Tranth leaned into the conversation. "She's fast off the mark."

Jarrk nodded. "She's got a hair trigger."

Gerak pulled out of the female as she jerked beneath him and left her writhing into orgasm on her own.

"That's it?" Chiarra intoned. "That's it? That's amazing!"

Jarrk turned to look at her.

"I could never—humans just don't get there that fast," she explained.

Jarrk just stared at her.

Gerak was up against his second, pulling her onto his erection. Chiarra shook her head as she looked away, uncertain she wanted to share in Gerak's final mating— the mating with his beloved. She found Grat staring at her. Sheena was in his lap and Grat's big hands clutched the top of her thighs as the female jerked on him. Jerked on his dick, Chiarra realized. Grat was inside her. He had her on his cock!

Grat smiled narrowly at Chiarra.

She was on her feet and bolting before she realized it.

Crashing and stumbling through the forest, she didn't stop until she came up against Jarrk's geyser pool. The clearing was well lit, the moon nearly full and reflecting from the pool's surface. Chiarra wrapped her arms around herself and paced irritably.

"Are you alright?"

She turned to stare at the silvery male at the forest's edge.

Again, she saw him in her mind's eye as he turned toward her, smiling, his hands reaching for the strings on his pants.

No. She wasn't alright! She needed a man. Needed a hard, male presence thick inside her.

Now!

Preferably this male, she thought with a helpless melting.

The corner of Jarrk's mouth tweaked upward, in a knowing smile, as he put his back against a tree.

Damn him.

"Grat frightens me," she said, to sidetrack him.

The smile was replaced with a frown of concern. "Stay close to my females...when you're not with me. You'll be all right."

Chiarra nodded at him. Unable to pull her eyes from him.

"Is there nothing else? You seem tense." When she said nothing, he continued. "You need to find an outlet. Work off some of that stress," he suggested.

"Yeah. And I'm just betting you've got some input on an outlet."

He smiled slowly. "What do you mean?"

She tossed her head impatiently. "You know what I mean. I'm not a fool, Jarrk. I know what you've been doing to me."

He raised his eyebrows. He knew what he'd like to be doing to her.

"I know your poison is an aphrodisiac…when I drink it. To make me want you."

He covered his smile with a hand.

"You had no right!" she exploded. "You have no right to *force* this on me. I don't *want* you. I don't want to…to…*want you*," she said in a diminishing voice.

He nodded, head down, lips twisted into a serious expression. Slowly he raised his eyes to hers. "It isn't."

"*Wh-a-t?*"

"It isn't. It doesn't. Gryffin poison doesn't act as an aphrodisiac…on anyone."

"No? Wh…why. Why do your females lick…?"

"It's arousing for the male. It's an expression of love. Devotion. Submittal, if you like."

He watched her expression as she realized how much she'd revealed. She looked horrified. Then she looked angry. He caught her arm as she stormed past him. "Don't be angry with me, Chiarra," he teased. "I can't help it if you fantasize about me…constantly."

"*Constantly!* It isn't constant."

"Occasionally?" He pulled her up against him.

But she broke free. "It's the poison," she insisted. "After...after I taste it, I have these...visions. Visions of you!"

"Visions of me. And what am I doing in these visions?"

She looked at him painfully.

"Sounds like fantasizing to me."

"No!"

He sighed with mock regret as his laughing eyes slid sideways in a considering pose. "Okay," he said finally. "I have another theory. But you're not going to like it, either. In fact, you'll like this one even less than the last."

"What do you mean?"

"Occasionally, certain females experience hallucinations..." he started slowly.

"That's it! It's a hallucin—"

"...that foretell the future."

Her jaw dropped. "No," she whispered. "No. You're yanking my chain."

He shook his head slowly, pushed off from the tree, his ruff lifting as he took several threatening steps toward her. She backed away.

"I'm ready to see the future, Chiarra. How about you?"

She shook her head, eyes on his angry ruff. "No. It's not...I'm not seeing us..." She raised a finger as she continued backward. "If that's the future, it doesn't work for me."

His eyes got very hard. "What's the matter, Chiarra?" he growled. "Don't want to fuck with an animal — like me? Good luck stopping the future, little human. Good luck stopping me."

She shook her head again, took a step backward, teetered for an instant as she held a brief argument with gravity.

Gravity won.

She fell backward with a splash.

She gasped as she got her head out of the water.

Jarrk laughed as he offered her his hand. "Sorry. But you should have seen that coming."

"Yeah. Well, I might have *if I could see the future*!"

She took his hand and let him lever her out. Liked his big hand wrapped around hers. Liked his strength.

He pulled her against him for an instant then, without giving up her hand, dragged her back toward the village. "We'd better get back. I have a speech to make, if it's not too late."

"Shouldn't Tranth be the one making speeches for his brother?"

Jarrk nodded. "My speech precedes Tranth's toast."

"What about *your* family, Jarrk? *Your* brothers?"

She caught his wince, felt his hand tighten on hers. "A lot of Gryffin were lost…five years back. You remember…that winter. The cold."

She caught her breath at the look in his eyes.

"It was bad," he said simply.

"Have you no one left?"

"I have my own fold now," he pointed out gently. "But no. None of my home fold." He tipped his head, diffidently. "It could have been worse. Some lost more than I. Tranth."

"But Tranth has a brother, at least."

"Tranth was to have been initiated that spring. He lost his girls. All three of them. They were sisters."

Chiarra was silent as she watched him struggle to get the next words out. "He...they...all three of them were to have been his last-picked." Jarrk squinted at her. "Do you know what I mean?"

She nodded. "And he never found...anyone else?"

"He never found anyone."

She tightened her grip on his hand. "Tranth...looks different from the other males in your clan."

"His father was human. Like you."

"But, Tranth is so big."

"The Islanders are tall."

"Did he live here, on The Spit?"

"Tranth's father? No. He never knew his father. His mother was carrying him when she was taken into Cherak's fold."

"So tell me," Jarrk said as they made their way back to the clearing. "Was I any good...in these visions of yours?"

She shrugged.

Oh Tar, yes, she thought.

But.

"Not bad," she told him.

"Not bad?" He frowned. "Are you sure it was me?"

Chapter Nine

A rumbled growl froze Chiarra in place. Scanning her companions' faces, she confirmed what she suspected—they were all in serious trouble.

"We're dead," Akela said flatly.

"Spread out," Chiarra ordered quietly and wished she had a crossbow. She'd accompanied Jarrk's females to forage for eggs. Weeks of sharing tasks, sharing tears, sharing laughter—and sharing Jarrk—had closed the gap between Chiarra and the women in Jarrk's fold. Now she watched the women move apart and away from her. Thick trees and tall rock outcroppings moved between her and her companions. She didn't turn since she knew what she'd find. There was no confusing the rumble of a dragon with any other creature.

She held Akela's eye. But the women had no weapons other than their small knives. They were indeed dead. At least most of them. And she had to assume she'd be the first to go.

"Where's a male when you need one?" Akela intoned flatly. Her ruff was up and she stared at the hackles on her knuckles, raised but useless without poison barbs. Only the males were barbed.

Chiarra still hadn't moved, knowing that any movement on her part would draw the dragon's attack. "Does Gryffin poison kill them?"

Akela nodded carefully. "Unfortunately, there are no males within screaming distance. Generally, one male distracts the dragon while another puts his barbs in."

Chiarra reached into her pouch and pulled out the long narrow flask containing Jarrk's venom.

The two women stared at each other.

"The poison acts quickly," Akela told her, as Chiarra opened the bottle and dipped her blade into the thick blue liquid, "but you must move rapidly to escape the dragon. The venom is agonizing and he'll thrash himself to his death. I'll run right—my right—to distract him. Are you ready?"

Chiarra nodded, fractionally.

"NOW!"

Chiarra turned and threw herself at the huge scaly creature. She'd seen dragons before but never this close and never this big. It was a mountain! With claws longer than her hands! Its thick scales glinted green and gray, as its keen eyes shifted to the running figure. As the dragon lurched toward Akela, Chiarra lunged at his foreleg, ignoring the scorching breath that raked her back.

Terrified the blade would rebound on the dragon's armor, she took the time to angle the blade so it would slide beneath its scales. Tough flesh gave beneath slashing steel as she used both hands to shove the blade deep. The last thing she remembered was the dagger ripped from her hands—just after she was yanked into the air.

* * * * *

Tranth watched his friend's ruff stiffen. "Hey! Pay attention."

The two males were on the low branch of a tree, repairing a leak in the water delivery system.

Jarrk gave him a lopsided smile of apology.

"It's no mystery what you're thinking about. The question is: Who are you thinking about doing—what you're thinking about—with?"

Jarrk shot a reluctant grin at Tranth, pulled the split chutes together. "You wouldn't believe me if I told you."

Tranth applied the tarry resin to the break. "Oh, I don't know. I might. I've heard stories about human females." He laughed as Jarrk's head snapped up. "So how is she?"

Jarrk winced and shrugged with one shoulder.

"You haven't taken her yet?"

Jarrk frowned painfully. "Are they true?"

"The stories? Tar. I hope so. I'd like to think so. I'd like to think there's a woman that could wring me out, all by herself." Tranth smiled, his look distant. "I've heard that they're a long time coming. That they're tight. Always tight. They don't open and loosen the moment they come. According to Grat's females, he couldn't leave his little human alone. As long as he had her."

Jarrk's face was grim. "Don't remind me."

Tranth shook his head. "There wasn't anything you could do, Jarrk. There wasn't anything any of us could do. He never let her out of his lodge. We didn't know what was going on. And we didn't know he was going to kill her. The stupid bastard probably forgot she was human and striped her as he came."

Jarrk grunted. "He'll never harm another female."

Tranth nodded his agreement. "Chiarra's lucky you challenged for her — and won. She's got to be grateful. So, what are you waiting for? Permission? Get on with it, man!"

"She thinks...we're animals, Tranth. She thinks *I'm* an animal."

"When did you decide that?"

"When she called me a fucking animal."

"Really." Tranth frowned. "And what were you doing when she said that?"

Jarrk shrugged, reluctantly. "Pretty much acting like one."

"Well, then. I'd say — from the way she looks at you — she's into animals." Tranth grinned at his friend. "*Way* into animals. Take it from me, man. And take the girl."

Jarrk laughed. "This from a Gryffin with no female in his lodge."

Tranth looked like someone had slipped a knife under his heart.

"I'm sorry, Tranth. But you've grieved long enough," he said awkwardly. "Have you settled your account with Sheena?"

Tranth forced a smile. How could he tell his friend the only woman that attracted him — in the last five years — was in Jarrk's fold and was in love with Jarrk.

"You need to do that."

"That I must." Tranth stopped smiling as his eyes, focused beyond Jarrk, registered alarm.

Jarrk turned. Then vaulted to the ground and was on his feet running.

"Jarrk! It's not as bad as it looks," Akela was trying to tell him.

But Jarrk had the girl in his arms and was striding toward his lodge.

* * * * *

She woke once, but everything hurt, so she thought, *Tar's Pit*, and went back to sleep. The next time she surfaced, the pain had diminished to a dull, overall ache and she decided to open her eyes. It was dark but she could tell she was in Jarrk's lodge. She was curled up on a cool, unyielding surface that was somehow molded to fit her body. She snuggled her cheek into a soft bed of feathery silver.

"You're back," Jarrk murmured against her temple, and she would have jumped, except she estimated that would be a painful mistake. The mold that encased her moved slightly and she realized Jarrk held her. Closing her eyes, she nestled her head into his shoulder. "How do you feel?"

"Don't ask."

His chuckle was reassuring warmth. "It was a miracle you didn't break every bone in your body. As it was, all I could find were some bumps—very big bumps, mind you—some scrapes, as well as a long slash on your shin which we painted with linden."

"Hope I didn't bleed all over your coat," she murmured.

He shrugged. She winced. "Sorry," he said quickly, realizing his mistake.

"It's not a coat," he put to her mildly. "It's skin. Like yours, little human. And it washes up nice." He went on to catalogue her losses. "You got a bit singed. Lost your jerkin. A few inches of hair on the right side. Half your right eyebrow."

"How much hair?"

He stroked his hand through her hair and brought the ragged ends up to brush against his lips.

"It needed a trim," she allowed. "But half an eyebrow? How do I look?"

"Overall? Pretty good for having wrestled a dragon. I wouldn't kick you out of my pit."

She smiled a contented sigh. "Why is it so dark in here?"

"It generally gets dark, at night."

"Why aren't you hunting?"

"I took a few nights off."

"A few nights! How long have I been out?"

"Don't ask," he murmured.

There were several moments of silence and she was thinking she would just go back to sleep.

"Thank you for saving my women," he said quietly.

"I was only saving myself," she murmured, sleepy. "And Akela helped me do that."

He started to nod before he realized even that would hurt her. "Well in that case, I hate to criticize but you didn't do a very good job...of saving yourself. A quick stab and immediate retreat might have done the job. As it was, the dragon almost crushed you. You should know there's nothing more dangerous than a wounded animal," he lectured. "Shani and the others had to drag you out of the way — at great risk to themselves. And then there was all the trouble of getting the fire put out, carrying you back here and tending to your wounds. You should have heard them complaining."

"After I saved their lives?" she said, her voice full of hurt.

He looked down on her with neon eyes. "After you saved their lives," he said, softly, "and thank you."

Chapter Ten

She spent the next several days sleeping for the most part. She saw Jarrk every evening. He checked on her just before he disappeared to hunt for the night. He must have been pleased with her, Chiarra decided, because for the first time she could remember, his ruff wasn't up when he was in her presence. Well, not so often, anyway.

She continued to have the visions. She didn't mind all of them. Some of them she quite looked forward to.

Jarrk shoving her wrap up to her waist, reeling her in tight against his groin.

Jarrk lifting her, hands gripping her bottom, thumbs splayed beneath her cheeks and every one of his fingers, from both hands, sliding into her pussy.

Her hands tied above her head while Jarrk's hands swept over her body. Every inch of her body.

Others were not so pleasant.

Grat's hard fingers digging into her arms as he dragged her from the edge of the chasm.

Jarrk's words, "I'd have killed him, if I'd known about this."

As harbingers of the future, these last two visions seemed to lead to a chilling conclusion. But there was no reason to believe they were prophecies. As yet, she'd seen none of these visions fulfilled.

When she felt up to it one morning, she limped across the lodge to help Akela. The woman was preparing a marinade for the boar skin that lay stretched and scraped on the table.

Chiarra pulled up a stool and pitched in. And only stopped when she saw the phosphorescent tears on Akela's cheeks. "Akela," she started fearfully, thinking immediately of Jarrk. "What is it?"

Akela struggled with her response for several moments. All at once, the dam burst. "I don't know what he sees in you," she finally sobbed. "You're all lumps!"

"Sees in me! Who?" It took her a few moments to come to the obvious conclusion. "Jarrk? He can't stand me. He...his hackles — his ruff — is up whenever he's near me."

Akela stopped stirring and gave her a look of horrified pity. "You are so slow, Chiarra. He doesn't rise because he's angry! He rises for you because he wants you."

"Wants me! Wants me to what?" Chiarra stared at Akela. "No! I've seen him mating with you...and...and Shani. His ruff isn't up when he takes you."

"Don't remind me," she minced out between clenched teeth.

Chiarra frowned at the Gryffin, trying to understand.

"He doesn't want me — or Shani. He only took us into his fold out of kindness." Her eyes spilled more tears. "Have you never wondered why Jarrk has no childings? We can't bring him to sleep! Did you not notice that little fact — when you watched us?"

Chiarra shook her head, completely confused. "Bring him to sleep?"

"Bring him to sleep! The mating sleep."

"You...sleep after mating? But why? Why do you..."

"The males sleep. How can they not?" She stopped. "Don't humans?"

Chiarra shook her head then smiled with a reluctant nod. "Well, I mean, not necessarily. Not always."

"But it's exhausting. I mean, your heart rate doubles—" She looked at Chiarra then corrected herself. "Our heart rate doubles."

Chiarra nodded with sudden understanding. "It's exhausting for you."

"It's especially exhausting for the male. His arousal lasts much longer than the female's."

"He falls asleep afterward."

"I can't...we can't satisfy him. He wants you." Akela dropped the bowl on the table and covered her face. "Gali Nigita, I love him. I love him. We all love him and he wants only you."

Chiarra watched Akela's shoulders as they shuddered. It broke her heart to see Akela cry. Akela was so strong!

"That's why he disappears every night. Because he knows we'll ask him for what he can't give anymore. His desire for you is tearing our family apart and you...you don't even care about him."

Chiarra stood and slammed across the room.

"What do you have to be angry about?"

"I'm angry with myself. I...get...angry when I've made a mistake."

"Then you must be angry a lot."

The two women stared at each other then burst into laughter. "I'm sorry, Akela," Chiarra confessed with regret. "You've been so helpful and tried so hard to get along with me, even when I was difficult." Her arm went around the woman's shoulders. "Thank you for taking care of me. Tending to my injuries. This last week."

Akela shook her head. "It was Jarrk who tended you, Chiarra—I mean—we would have. But it was Jarrk."

The two women looked up as Jarrk ducked through the door and stopped. His usually serious eyes softened and Chiarra watched his ruff as it slowly began to lift. She groaned.

* * * * *

Chiarra slept late the next morning. It was long past dawn before enough light worked its way into the lodge to wake her. She found herself alone at the edge of the sleeping pit. The women, absent on some chore, hadn't been waking her since her injury.

It was a good day to leave, she thought, as she stared at the leafy roof. According to lodge gossip, the maelstrom winds had begun to abate two days ago. It was time to move on, out of the reach of the yellow uniforms. Chiarra frowned. Shani had questioned Jarrk yesterday at dinner about the winds. Jarrk's eyes had flicked to connect with her own.

He hadn't answered Shani.

She stretched on her back and thought of Jarrk, let the idea of Jarrk trickle in from every point of her body to pool at a point just below her belly button. Chiarra sighed. The more the pool filled, the emptier she felt. She rolled onto her knees and rummaged for her clothes.

And jumped when she heard her name.

At least she thought it was her name. But Jarrk lay asleep in the center of the pit, on his stomach, his handsome, rugged ass face up. That empty spot responded with a twinge, followed by a lurch, as her lips curled around a ragged bit of breath and she allowed her hungry eyes to feed on Jarrk's long, clean lines.

Gryffin males had nice bodies, without anything spare, saggy or sloppy about them. And this silver Gryffin in particular was all hard, compact male, she thought as her eyes slid down the length of Jarrk's legs. She stood and turned to pull on her wrap but dropped it when she heard her name again. When she turned back, Jarrk had rolled onto his back.

And *there* was a sight for sore eyes.

He was erect. Straight up erect. His rock didn't slouch lazily against his belly but rose purposefully, with promise, straight out of his groin. Splayed out in the center of the pit, Jarrk looked like a man with a *lot* of promise. Chiarra took a few tiny steps toward him, wondering just how asleep he was. She stopped, holding her breath, as he moaned. Did the man suffer nightmares? Falling to her knees beside him, she checked his face carefully then returned her eyes to his long, throbbing erection. Oh Tar, yes, she could actually see him pulsing. But, at this point, Jarrk's erection wasn't the only thing in the lodge that was throbbing.

Pure, female instinct took over. Chiarra's lusting body decided it was mating season and her legs shifted apart. Moist lips between her thighs parted as her legs opened for the man. Her cunt gulped with a surging, tidal wave of wet response. Pulsing warmth climbed her channel and was replaced by prickling heat as her vagina wept to hold the man, to lick the man, to suck the man to his finish.

Reaching out cautiously, she put a hand on Jarrk's forehead. When he didn't wake, she moved quickly—before she could change her mind—and closed her hand tightly around his shaft. His dick was taut and tight inside her hand as he filled his skin entirely. Her fingers met her thumb for an instant, until a strong surge thickened his erection and forced them to part. Mesmerized, she watched his cock as the pulses came harder and faster. At the same time, the fringed scales that surrounded his penis expanded in a ruffled display then settled again. Chiarra watched the scales lift with increasing frequency that matched the accelerating pulse throbbing inside her fist. Concerned, she laid her other hand on his chest and felt his heart galloping at a brutal pace. Something cool slid down her hand.

Tar! He was coming. Her eyes widened on the thick head of his cock, her hand beneath it, where a stream of iridescent silver crept over her fingers.

"Chiarra," he whispered again.

And Chiarra realized. He was coming for her.

Quickly, she straddled one of his legs and covered his cock with her mouth, pushing her lips down his shaft to take in as much as possible—just as he shot into her mouth. She swallowed and swallowed again as he kept coming—long past the legal limit of male ejaculation. With pure female stubbornness, she stayed with him through the last spurt, drank him off and pulled her tongue up his length as she leaned back, looking for his eyes.

They were open and on her.

He blinked several times—disoriented—as though he doubted his eyes. Then his lids dropped to close his neon gaze.

She swallowed and licked her lips. Tar and Breeza! She'd never tasted anything like that before! Like icy fire, it slid down her throat. Like strong spirit, she could feel it working its way through her system, filling her with prickling life, warm energy. It hit her solar plexus like a wakeup call and if she didn't want him before, she had to have him now.

The man was asleep. She regarded him tentatively. According to Akela, Jarrk wouldn't wake for at least twenty minutes. She bit her lip and cut a look at his erection, still semi-rigid and largely upright then cut a look at his sleeping face. She didn't have much time, if she was going to get away before he woke. Spreading her legs, she lowered hot, wet lips onto Jarrk's cool, hard thigh and accepted the rush of pleasure that accompanied the act. Slowly, she ground against his smooth flesh. Tar, she was hot for him.

With a barely contained whimper, she reached between her legs with both hands and pulled her lips apart to put her clitoris firm against the cool skin of his thigh and rubbed her hot clit against the cool touch of him, rubbed herself until his leg was slick with her moisture and she slipped against him easily, rubbed herself to within an inch of orgasm. Then she mounted him and fucked herself into a short, hard climax.

She threw her head back and strangled his name in her throat.

Bringing her head back down, she gazed sadly at her stiffened nipples and sighed. She dressed quickly and stopped a last time to look at him. "I'm sorry if I caused trouble in your home," she told the sleeping man.

Chapter Eleven

Chiarra stood alone, poised on the edge of the maelstrom, thoroughly unhappy and entirely determined. A long rope whipped in a circle over her head. At the end of the rope, was a forked antler to serve as a grappling hook. The hook shot across the maelstrom channel and almost gained the other side.

But not quite.

The winds kicked up. Grappling hook and rope were sucked into the channel as Chiarra, refusing to sacrifice her tool, lurched toward the chasm, a toy on the end of a string. She dug in her heels as she was tugged inexorably toward the bluff.

A strong arm circled her waist and jerked her backward. The rope was torn from her grip.

"I've heard human women orgasm for an eternity."

She dug in her heels and bolted.

He caught her quickly, his hands like grappling hooks at her waist. As they fell to their knees, she scrabbled away from him. She felt her wrap tear as he shoved it up to her waist. His hands fought to win her flanks and own her lower body. *Reeling her in tight against his groin,* he got his hands firmly positioned on her hips. She felt his cock, hard and cool, thrust between her cheeks.

With a cry of frustration, she twisted and clawed at the ground as his shaft ground between her lips and searched for entrance. Missing the mark, she felt him withdraw and slide through her folds again.

Jarrk cursed. "I know you want me," he growled. "I saw you with my cock in your mouth. I'm going to take you, Chiarra and I'd rather not hurt you."

Desire spiked in her cruelly and she stilled, aching for the punishing discipline of his rod.

He caught her hair high on her head, groping for the ruff she didn't have. Clutching her hair between his fingers, he pulled her head back. "Where in *Tar's Pit* did you think you were going?"

She gasped. "You *told* me I could leave, Jarrk. You *told* me."

She felt his finger run into her slit, probing for her opening. "That was before you branded my cock with your lips. Now I've a taste for the rest of you. You're my female, Chiarra. When I'm done with you, you're going to know you're my female." His finger stopped at her opening.

"That's it?" he panted with surprise. Sliding his finger inside her, he withdrew it suddenly. "You're wet!"

With a jerk, he was on his feet as he took a step backward. He pulled up the edge of his pants.

Chiarra got to her feet slowly and faced him, rubbing her arm.

"You're crying! Your body's crying." His expression was a combination of barely contained heat and tearing angst. "What am I doing wrong? Why is your body crying?"

She approached him slowly as though sucked into the maelstrom of his desire. She nodded at him and held his neon eyes with hers. "It's crying for you, Jarrk."

He gave her a look of disbelief. "I thought...you've...said nothing."

She shook her head. "I thought you were angry with me. Every time your ruff went up, I thought you were angry with me."

His hand went into his ruff. "Tar, no."

Her chest was against his by then and she reached for his lips. Almost as soon as their lips touched, he was crushing her in his arms. He opened her mouth with his and drove the thick chisel-tip of his tongue between her teeth. His tongue was smooth as it moved into her mouth. She heard him groan and felt his heart hammering at the door to her heart, felt his cock jump into the space between her legs. He pulled away suddenly. "Tar! Are you wet everywhere?" She tried to return her lips to his and he caught her head in his hands, angling her head harshly before he delivered his lips again to hers. "Tar help me," he whispered into her mouth as his fingers dug into her scalp and contained her head between hard hands that demanded complete submittal from mouth and tongue.

Not that she had plans to argue at that point.

He broke away from her — wild, thick lust surging in him fast, and hard enough to choke him. The kiss wasn't enough. Not nearly enough. He had to have more, more of her, all of her. And he had to have her now.

He looked down their bodies, pressed close together. "Is it true," he sucked at a breath. "Is it true, what I've heard about human nipples — that they raise like a Gryffin's ruff?"

As she pulled her body away from his, he caught the edge of her jerkin and hurried it over her head. Jarrk stared at her breasts in rapt wonder. "It's true," he whispered.

One of his hands traveled quickly from around her back, hesitating just an instant before he brushed a knuckle across the peach tip. He stared, amazed when it poked its head out a little further. With his fingers, he plucked at it carefully and was stunned when Chiarra closed her eyes and arched her breasts forward. Then both his hands were cupping the breasts he'd longed to claim, to hold, to cage in his hands. "Tar!" he rasped. "You have so much of everything." He watched her closed eyes as his hands slid into the curves of her waist then down to cup the swelling globes of her bottom.

Turning her suddenly, he felt between her legs and again found her opening. Reaching into his pants, and with his hand on his dick, he spread his legs and flexed his knees as he guided the tip of his cock through her crease. But the human was built differently than Gryffin females. And his penis was set further back than a human male's. "Help me, Chiarra," he breathed. "I don't want to hurt you."

She pulled away and turned to face him. Taking his hands, she drew them behind her and placed them beneath the curves of her bottom. "Lift me," she told him.

He did as he was told, not quite understanding her intent but very anxious to comply. She opened her legs for him and he moved quickly to support her thighs with his forearms.

"Help me find your tip."

He stilled an instant. "You do it like this? Face-to-face? But how does that work?"

She moaned. "Help me find your tip and I'll show you."

A few steps put her back against the smooth bark of a wide chestnut. Moving his hands beneath her, he pulled her cheeks apart and found her opening again, with *every one of his fingers, from both hands, sliding into her pussy.*

She was whimpering as he relinquished his hold on her cheeks and got his pants pushed out of the way. Palming his dick forward to meet her, he nudged his thick cock-head into her notch and, with a blasted breath of relief, pulled her down on him. Then stopped as they pulled away from each other, regarded each other with stunned shock.

"Tar! You're so hot and so...so wet. So incredibly wet."

She moaned. Jarrk's cool sex inside her hot cunt was as perfect as iced drinks on a summer day. She tried to kiss him.

"Not yet," he rasped.

And then she discovered how Shani and Akela, without moving, were able to orgasm on Jarrk. Without any action on his part, Jarrk's dick surged inside her in pulsing waves that increased in strength and frequency. His cock was manually massaging her cunt toward climax as it stretched her cruelly wide one instant to follow with the kindest relenting.

His heart rate was going through the roof, she noted, an instant before she was distracted by the persistent movement at the top of her cleft.

"Oh Jarrk," she whispered, "what are you doing to me?"

Both his hands still gripped the cheeks of her bottom; she knew it wasn't one of his fingers that intruded into her cleft. Staring at the small, fringed scales on his chest, she realized they lifted with each heartbeat. With sudden intuition, she looked down between their bodies to find the crescents that swept down into his groin committed to the same the action. Every fringed scale at chest and groin lifted and fell with his increased heart rate. The smooth curved tips stroked into her wet lips while Jarrk pulsed hard and fast inside her.

The persistent stroking continued, as the scales lifted higher and moved faster. Inevitably, several scales made real headway. Intruding between her lips, they fingered into every wet, pink rut and crevice that stretched between her vagina and her clitoris. Throwing back her head, she waited, perfectly still, as the sweet feathered touches approached then retreated from her sensitive trigger. She held onto herself, willing her sex to remain open until that touch reached her clitoris.

"Oh no," she whispered. "Oh no." Several scaled touches scraped across her clitoris in relentless sequence and her cunt quaked, then triggered.

Jarrk's erection gave a huge surge that stretched into her savagely then allowed her vagina to close on his dick. His cock jump-started her cunt into orgasm. At the same time, his blunt tip expanded hard against her cervix. Her eyes widened as she stared into his. "Jarrk," she screamed. "Jarrk! Hold me."

His eyes lit and he smiled ruthlessly just before she started to come on him. "Now," he whispered and lowered his smiling mouth to hers.

With her wet lips on his mouth and her hot, wet sex opening for his cock, Jarrk held himself motionless to appreciate every twinge of his coming release. Her cunt had a leveraged hold on him that racked his dick forward with unyielding pressure. The unfamiliar sensation yanked hard on his sex, resulting in brutal, excruciating pleasure. Jarrk stopped smiling as Chiarra's cunt shuddered along its length and played him tortuously close to the edge. The tip of his cock expanded in warning. His hands, filmed with his own weeping poison, moved to grip her hips, and he forced her down on his dick.

Then all hell broke loose.

Jarrk gasped as soft and wet hugged and sucked then opened again to let him surge to fill her even wider. He felt his blunt head thicken, stretch wide and full inside her, felt—with satisfaction—his tip hard against her cervix. Heard her scream as her body wrenched against his in a wild cataclysm the likes of which he'd *never* experienced. He fought to hold her on him, hold his shaft deep inside her climaxing cunt.

There was a roar in his ears and he realized it was his own voice. He cried out in triumphant defeat as her body racked his cock out to the point of absolution and her climax impelled his seed from the depths of his scrotum into violent ejaculation, as her cunt continued to suck on him for a complete eternity.

"Don't stop. Don't stop," he rasped harshly, as he continued to orgasm long past normal bounds of male ejaculation, or at least what Chiarra considered normal for human males.

His forehead was damp against hers when he finally finished. "Grat should have killed me," he whispered.

Chiarra watched his eyelids come down.

"*I'd have killed him, if I'd known about this.*" Without warning, he crumpled to his knees, taking the girl down with him. His eyes fought to remain open as his hard fingers clutched at her narrow flanks and he sank his nails into her. "Chiarra!" he groaned in sudden panic. "Don't leave."

Still coupled, Chiarra lay beside him, for the instant stunned. "*I'd have killed him, if I'd known about this.*" Her prophetic visions were being fulfilled—in no particular order—in a way she could never have anticipated or interpreted.

She could see the future. She just couldn't see what was coming.

Snuggling into Jarrk, Chiarra clenched her muscles to squeeze the slackened length that stretched inside her. But Jarrk was completely still. Her ear was against his chest and she listened to his heart's erratic drumming. The man was entirely asleep. Completely, helplessly, asleep. She shook his shoulder but this did nothing to disrupt his smooth, even breathing. "Jarrk?"

Uneasy, she cast her eyes around her.

Chapter Twelve

He knew, before he opened his eyes, she was gone. She should have been warm against his side. Empty dread coiled and tightened the length of his spine as he scrambled to his feet and started toward the chasm. Abruptly, he halted, staring at the ground. What he saw at his feet put cutting terror in his soul. Fear was an icy trickle the length of his backbone as he searched the ground, established the trend and direction of the huge spurred tracks.

Grat.

Turning on his spur, Jarrk hurtled into the forest.

The clearing was mobbed with his people, as some sort of council meeting appeared to be underway. Cursing the delay that forced his detour, Jarrk skirted the crowd's edge on his way to Grat's lodge.

"She's a murderer."

Jarrk stopped at the sound of the human accent, turned his eyes to the clearing then punched through the crowd and into the clearing.

He stepped into the circle.

Grat stood behind Chiarra, pinioning her arms at her back.

"Get your hands off my female," Jarrk commanded in a low snarl.

Grat turned to find the silver Gryffin, ridge up, fists bunched, barbs out in warning.

"Hey Jarrk. See you finally got your ridge up."

Jarrk struck without further warning. His open palm sent Chiarra flying as he cleared the path to Grat. His closed fist rammed hard into Grat's abdomen. As Grat doubled, Jarrk brought his knee up to crush his face at the same time both elbows cracked down on the back of his skull. Grat collapsed at his feet.

Spinning, he searched for Chiarra. He found her struggling in the grasp of two human men, at the edge of the crowd. He took a step toward her.

Tranth held him back with a thick arm.

"She's my female," Jarrk scraped out as he struggled against the gate of an arm that held him. "I'll kill the man who touches her."

The two men who held Chiarra took one look at Jarrk's face and released the girl with a forward shove and a step backward.

"Jarrk!" Tranth struggled to restrain his friend. "You can't fight all of them." Tranth got his large hands on Jarrk's shoulders. "The Gryffin Council has gathered to hear the humans' complaint against the girl. If she's guilty of criminal offense in her country, the council must turn her over to these *representatives of her government*." As Tranth emphasized the significance of these last words, he caught and held Jarrk's eyes. "You can't save her if you're dead or wounded," he hissed.

Jarrk stared angrily at his friend then at the humans behind him. His heart dropped. Two of the humans wore the uniform of the Yellow Guard, representatives of the Benign Dictator who, from all accounts, wasn't benign in the least.

Slipping his friend a parting look of caution, Tranth turned toward the uniforms. "You have proof of the girl's guilt?"

Casually, one of the uniforms waved a paper at Tranth. "Eleven witnesses are generally considered sufficient proof where I come from. The murder took place on a public street."

Jarrk shot Chiarra a stunned look.

Chiarra held his eyes, while Tranth took the paper and handed it to a Council Elder.

"It was self-defense," Jarrk insisted, without taking his eyes from his female.

The uniform laughed and shook his head. "It was broad daylight, in the middle of the street, with eleven witnesses. It was murder."

Jarrk looked at Chiarra. He didn't ask the question.

"I killed a man," she told him. "Crossbow," she explained. "It turned out he was an important man."

Something like pain or disappointment filled his expression. "Why?"

"He was kicking—"

"He was kicking an animal," the uniform interjected.

"To the death," she gritted between clenched teeth.

But Jarrk had already turned his back to her.

"I only meant to stop the man. His death was an accident."

Jarrk pushed his way out of the clearing.

* * * * *

The men hadn't ridden two hours before they stopped. But Chiarra wasn't surprised. She'd been expecting it, as often as the yellow uniforms glanced back at her. It had been a heart-cramping two hours, filled with the image of Jarrk.

Jarrk's face, full of stunned disappointment.

Jarrk's back, as he turned and strode from the clearing.

Just as her vision had predicted, Grat had come for her. *Dragged her from the edge of the chasm*, and back to the village for the hearing. Only she couldn't have known what the portent meant. Grat wasn't the real threat—the humans were.

The soldiers left her tied to her saddle as they broke down their mounts.

Immediately, one of the uniforms put the sentries out. All eight of them—before setting up tents or even starting a fire. "Fifty paces out," he ordered tersely and sent the men off in pairs. Several of them glowered their way into the trees. The uniform turned and raped her with his eyes, never raising them higher than her chest.

Chiarra shivered as her heart drummed a warning.

The second uniform cut a willow branch. It moaned as he whipped it into a stinging song. Pulling his knife, he began to strip the bark from it. He grinned at his friend. "String her up, Bork."

With a nod, Bork pulled a rope from his kit and, standing beneath a spreading oak, tossed a length into the air. The rope came down on the other side of a thick limb and he tugged on both ends to test it then put his whole weight on it. With a grunt of approval, he took one end to tie off around the tree's trunk. His eyes were on her legs as he yanked hard on the final knot.

Moving quickly toward her, he cut her legs free and, with a fist in the rope that held her wrists, dragged her from her horse.

She landed on her knees, hard.

Jerking her to her feet, the man turned her, grabbed all her hair in a knot and twisted it until tears pricked her eyes. With a fist in her hair, he shoved her toward the tree.

Kicking backward with her heel, Chiarra caught him hard on the shin. In the instant his hand loosened, she spun as she brought her locked fists around to connect with his chin.

He almost broke her neck when his hand ratcheted to lock its hold on her hair. He almost broke her neck again when he backhanded her across the face.

The world went black for several moments then was filled up with pointy sparks of light. By that time, she hung—twisting—at the rope's end. As the rope bit into her wrists, she struggled to rearrange her weight so the ties wouldn't cut so badly.

The man was breathing in jerks, his eyes dark and shiny, and hard as mean black stones. He stared at her crotch. "Hurry up with that switch, Slicer."

"Shut up and get her clothes off," Slicer returned.

There was a harsh tearing sound as a rough hand caught the front of her jerkin and yanked downward. She felt the remains of her jerkin slide down her back as Bork sliced at the ties on her wrap and tore the small skirt from her hips.

Stepping away, he watched her body as she twisted slowly.

Painfully, she lifted her head and watched him rub the front of his ties while his tongue licked out of his mouth.

"You going to be much longer?" Bork demanded. "I'm ready to drill a hole right out of these leggings."

She heard the switch sing through the air.

"Same deal as last time?" Slicer suggested.

Bork rubbed himself again, harder. "Yeah. You got something to mark her with?"

"Here." Two abrasive hands gripped her hips as Slicer turned her.

She felt Bork press something greasy against her right buttock.

"Not there! Higher. At the small of her back."

"I want it here." Bork clutched her ass selfishly.

"Put it higher. She'll scream more. Take my word on it."

"What! You're an expert now?"

The greasy touch moved higher and Chiarra groaned as the men marked an X at the small of her back.

"First to bring blood at the mark wins two gold," Slicer reminded his friend.

Chiarra shuddered.

"First scream gets the first fuck," Bork further clarified.

Chiarra looked at the two men. She didn't like either option.

"You got a coin?" Bork demanded.

"Heads or tails?"

"Tails."

"You always take tails," Slicer complained.

"I like tails." Bork leered at Chiarra's ass. "You always toss the coin.

"Shit," Bork cursed, staring at the ground.

"Never mind, Bork. I'll soften her up for you," Slicer offered, as Chiarra circled slowly to face the two men.

She tried to shake the cobwebs that clung to her brain, tried focus on the men, but they wavered a bit. She tried to think of some brave, defiant comeback. Realized — late — she should at least have spat at the bastards. She'd done that much for Jarrk.

Jarrk.

"Give her a bit of a spin for me, Bork. I like a moving target."

"Get on with it, man. I'm about to shoot in my leggings."

"Why don't you yank it off? You'll have plenty of time to get it up again while I'm fucking her."

"While *you're* fucking her? I'll be the one fucking her, Slicer. And you'll be the one yanking his dick. She's not going to scream at the first stroke!

"And then...it's my turn," Bork delivered with hopeful optimism.

"They always scream for me," Slicer said, pityingly. "You see, Bork, it's not how hard you hit, it's how you lay it on. Tell you what, Bork. One time deal only. You can fuck her in the ass while I violate the rest of her."

"Get on with it, then, you sadist!"

The world went by in a blur of stripes. Chiarra ground her teeth as her muscles tensed in terrified anticipation.

The world slowed a bit.

"Don't say a word." A gentle hand cupped one of her breasts as Jarrk took her weight on his chest. His hands raced over her body, *every inch of her body*, searching for injury before he reached up to cut her down. She collapsed into his arms. "Shhh. You're all right. You're alright, Chiarra. Don't cry, love."

Two yellow uniforms were sprawled awkwardly on the ground. A long, red knife dripped in Jarrk's hand.

"Can you stand for me, Chiarra? That's it, darling. There's a brave girl." Stooping, he pulled the Guards' weapons and dragged the blades through the dead men's clothing, staining the steel red. He closed the men's hands around their own hilts, arranged the bodies then grinned up at her from a crouch. "How's that look?"

Shaking her head, she wiped her eyes, feeling very gray and woozy. "Like they killed each other?"

He nodded.

"What about the others?"

He shook his head. "The sentries are widely spaced—I was able to slip between them. But we have to get moving. Are you up to it?"

She nodded, though she leaned a bit. She watched him grow before her as he rose to his feet, and she leaned into him, leaned into his strength. "I...didn't know...you were coming."

He pulled her away enough to stare his disbelief at her.

"I thought you were angry. That I'd killed—"

He put a finger on her lips. "If you killed a man, I imagine he deserved it," he said, as he scanned the edges of the clearing. "Did any of the others touch you?" he asked in a voice like gravel and ice.

She shook her head into his chest. "You stopped them before—"

"That's not what I asked. Did any of them *touch* you?"

Realizing his deadly intent, she raised her eyes to his, shook her head quickly.

He took her face in his shaking hands and kissed her with all the gentle restraint he could muster. When she clung to the kiss, he was forced to cut it short. Swiping her ruined clothing off the ground, he scooped her up and, with the silence of a shadow, blended into the forest.

Chapter Thirteen

Jarrk groaned as he felt Chiarra's hand wrap around his aching dick. She was more work than all his other eight females put together. And more arousing. And more tempting. It was frustrating. After finally finding the female who could satisfy him—all on her own—he didn't dare let her mount him, couldn't chance his own release. Couldn't risk sleep.

The Yellow Guards—and their murder—was only two days behind them. The next unit? Two hours? Two minutes? He couldn't be sure. He couldn't afford to be asleep for twenty minutes. Not that kind of sleep. The kind of sleep where you wouldn't wake if lightning struck you in the ass.

"Chiarra," he complained. "Don't make me want you." A second hand insinuated itself between his legs and groped at his balls. He removed the hand quickly. Held it to his lips as his eyes burned into hers. "It's not safe," he told her.

She pressed her body to his side and smudged herself against him. "Please Jarrk. I'll watch while you sleep."

"And that won't do a bit of good. If someone comes, you won't be able to wake me."

"But Jarrk."

"Don't argue." It was just as well he'd discovered alternate ways to satisfy her. Humans were so extraordinarily diverse! Sexually diverse. Pushing her onto her back into the cushioning grass, he moved a hand between her legs.

"I need more this time, Jarrk. I need you inside me."

His answer was a growl of pure male hunger.

The problem was, Chiarra found herself aroused almost to the point of madness, as several erotic visions assailed her in unrelenting sequence.

Jarrk pushing her up against the bars of an ancient, iron headboard, spreading her legs and pinning them wide.

Jarrk kneeling before her with jutting cock, pulling her onto his dick as he forged into her.

Jarrk behind her as he penetrated her to her limit.

Chiarra felt Jarrk's hand slide through her soft ridges of pussy, her sex already crying for him, wet for want of him. She pulled away bravely. "Not this time. Not without you."

He laid his forearm on the top of her chest and pinned her to the ground. His other hand moved back and forth between her legs to spread her lips. Struggling beneath the iron bar that was his arm, she bucked under his hand. The heel of his palm on her mound forced her back to the ground as her body strained against the hold he had on her. Ignoring this, he played his fingers into her slit. Two large fingers spread to bracket her clitoris then came together, capturing her clit as Jarrk vised it gently between his fingers.

She was slick when he started and streaming when he'd finished teasing her nub into erection. When she squirmed beneath him, he increased his hold at chest and rise. She made some very telling sounds as her breath sang into her lungs. She was on the verge, he decided. He wasn't that far off, himself. Blood surged up the length of his dick and expanded the blunt head of his cock. His ruff ached. His knuckles ached.

Pulling his hand out of her spread lips, he massaged her labia back over her clit. She was wet beneath his hand, her female essence running between his fingers as he stroked her into a slight calm. The heel of his hand still restrained her and she was soon squirming beneath it, this time struggling not for escape but for release. He smiled as he watched her face, full of desperate need, poised on the edge of the sexual trance.

"Jarrk." His name unraveled in her throat.

"What?" he teased, gruffly. "Decided you want some after all, Chiarra?"

She was still a moment before she nodded helplessly.

His hand stopped altogether and she moaned.

"Open for me, Chiarra."

"Jarrk?"

"Spread your legs for me," he whispered breathlessly, his eyes on the pussy that burned beneath his hand. "Spread your legs. Pull them wide for my hand."

She moved her legs apart on the ground.

He shook his head. "Wider, Chiarra."

He watched her spread her legs and groaned as his dick screamed to get at her. His finger slipped a fraction into her parting lips.

"Bring your knees up," he commanded. "All the way, Chiarra."

She brought her heels up almost to her bottom and spread her feet wide. His long finger dropped into her folds and she strained against the hard hand on her mound, the rough fingers in her slit. Gradually, he reduced the pressure and allowed her to push her sex up onto his hand.

"Rub yourself out on me," he rasped. "You're wet. Tar, you're so sweet, Chiarra. So sweet and sexy and so wet. I want to watch you jack yourself into my hand. You've got my fingers in your slit. They're yours, love."

He watched Chiarra rock into his hand, as all of her wet, rutted sex slid up and down on his finger. Watched her back as it left the ground and she took her weight at her feet and at her neck.

"That's it, Chiarra. Come into my hand."

She shook her head on the ground but continued ratcheting against his hand. "I want more," she panted.

"Keep going, darling. Keep going," he whispered. "Do it for me. Give me what I want and I'll give you what you need. Do it for me and I promise to fuck you with my fingers."

She stilled just an instant. "Put it in," she cried in sudden anguish. "Put it in! Put it in!" Moving quickly, he pushed between her legs with his elbows and rammed two fingers into her cunt.

Just in time to feel her cunt grab and hold, grab and hold. Just in time to watch her body rip into a series of convulsions, pretty enough to make a strong man discharge in hemorrhaging lust. Several contractions later, his hand was dripping as she sobbed in broken defeat and crushing completion. But Jarrk wasn't done with her.

"You deserve a kiss," Jarrk whispered, when she finally touched down again, her back and bottom on the ground once more.

She opened unfocused eyes.

Repositioning himself between her legs, he put his shoulders under her thighs, pulled her legs apart. With an iron hold on her lower body, he licked his tongue from her vulva to the top of her cleft before placing a small sucking kiss on her swollen clit.

Her moan was a frail wisp of agonized ecstasy. Pressing her legs wide, he sucked at her mercilessly until she came again.

Chapter Fourteen

He was beyond arguing. There'd been no sign of the Yellow Guard for two days. They'd been on the run for four, and he'd wanted her every minute of those long four days. The little stone croft looked like it had been locked down and left alone for some time. It seemed safe enough. He jimmied the simple lock with his knife and pushed the door open. The small room was clean and orderly without frill or adornment, a simple man's abode.

Chiarra's blood drummed. She recognized the bed — the old iron headboard. Recalled every evocative, erotic vision that went with it. She walked over to the bed and stroked the edge lovingly then turned to him as he bolted the door and leaned against it.

"It's hard," she told him.

He raised an eyebrow. "Yes, it is. But how did you know?"

She smiled at him with warm affection. "I was referring to the bed."

"You talk too much. Quit stalling and get your clothes off."

She looked down at the ragged bits of cloth he'd tied around her, the sorry remnants Bork had left her. "This hardly qualifies as clothing," she pointed out, as she worked at the knot between her breasts.

As her breasts were revealed, Jarrk tipped his head to the side and let out a pent-up breath. "Oh yeah, there they are. Bring them here to me."

She got up against him and, with her hands beneath her breasts, pushed her nipples up to him. His back curved as he stooped to suck one into his mouth. His dry lips took in the whole of her aureole as his slick tongue pulled at the hard knot of her nipple. A rumble of masculine pleasure vibrated against her nipple and set up an answering resonance at the deepest point in her vagina. She tipped her head back and let him suck, first one aching nipple then the other.

He pushed her away an inch and got both his hands around her breasts. "Don't tease me, female. These are nice, but I need more than these." He grasped one of her hands and rubbed it hard down the length of his cock. "I need somewhere to put this."

She shuddered as she sucked in a breath chilled with desire. "I...I think I can accommodate you," she said. "I can offer you a couple of choices," she pointed out weakly.

He smiled down at her evilly. "Only two?" he asked in a cruelly teasing tone. "Come on, Chiarra. You can do better than that." He pushed her away, took in her uncertain expression. "Use your imagination. After all I've done for you these last four days, and as long as I've waited? I, myself, can think of at least three different possibilities. And right now I'm thinking it will take all three to satisfy me."

"Jarrk?"

"I'll take your mouth first. And after you've had a taste of me, you'll be begging me to...put it in...everywhere else."

She closed her eyes and brought back the memory of his exciting taste, what it did to her body, then opened her eyes again. She would probably beg. "But you'll fall asleep...in the first place."

He shook his head. "All you get is a taste. I save the rest for the second place and...the end. Drop the wrap," he commanded.

She unknotted the wrap and let it fall.

"Get on the bed." He pushed his pants from his waist and stepped out of them as they fell. "I want your back up against the headboard."

He came at her quickly as she sat. Kneeling between her legs, he pulled her knees up with his hands and spread them with his legs, *pushing her up against the bars of the ancient, iron headboard, spreading her legs with his and pinning them wide.* Then his cock was against her lips and she opened her mouth for him.

But Jarrk wasn't prepared for the pleasure that accompanied lips hot and wet against his sex. Human lips. And he hadn't anticipated how good it would feel— the sucking action of that wet mouth, that rough tongue scraping at his dick. "Stop that you little minx, or you'll have it all in your mouth and nothing left for anywhere else. I'll be asleep before you're satisfied."

She hesitated and he took the opportunity to clamp her head between his hands, forcing her to be still as he shoved it into her as deeply as he dared. He groaned. He could hardly merit that while it took more than eight women of his own kind to satisfy him, this little human only had to waggle her tongue at him and he was ready to come all over himself.

His ruff stiffened painfully as he held her head. His hackles, aching for attention, pulled back on his knuckles as his barbs crept forward. Carefully, he angled the barbs away from her skin.

He felt his cock swell just before he blasted into her mouth. With steel determination, he held back the next surge. Pulling out of her, he watched her eyes close as she swallowed him down. Her eyes opened a moment later, unfocused, sultry and full of the want of him. Breath rushing, he reached for her hips and pulled into her, *pulled her onto his dick as he forged into her*. He threw back his head and closed his eyes. "Tar, woman," he rasped, "you feel so good."

He didn't know the half of it.

With hands clutching the iron bars behind her, she started to move on him and he gasped as her cunt slipped along his length. He gritted his teeth as he felt his release building at an accelerating pace he had *no* control over. "Chiarra," he said in a strained voice of agony. "Tar, Chiarra. I want to make this last. I need to make this last. I've waited too long for it." He felt her legs wrap around his hips and her heels as they drove into the small of his back, exhorting his cock to fill her more deeply.

Poison wept from his barbs as he gave up his grasp on her hips and, with his hands gripping hers on the headboard, braced himself as she drove her body up onto his. He thought he would come when her tight, hot cunt started to contract around his dick in orgasm. Her vagina grabbed at him in a series of sweet, clenching pulses and she garbled something out of her mouth that sounded very much like his name. Eyes lit, he bared his teeth and grimaced a smile down at her. She opened her eyes.

"Again?"

Her eyes widened at the word. And she nodded. He was still thick where he stretched inside her. His dick pulsed with hard male insistence and her body's female response couldn't refuse him.

"Again."

He pulled out of her and flipped her quickly. Taking her hands, he wrapped them around the bars of the headboard. With a rough jerk, he pulled her hips up so that she was on her knees. Hard hands pulled her legs wide then pushed her thighs toward her chest so that her bottom slanted toward him. He spread his legs outside hers and, with his hands at her hips and pulling her downward, shoved into her, *as he penetrated her to her limit.* She felt him pulsing hard and thick inside her, his dick surging into her with swelling frequency.

Pushing the flat of his thumb against the puckered little kiss of her ass, he spread his fingers out to clutch at her smooth skin. His broad thumb pressed against her crimp and he felt her tighten. He nudged his thumb against the gripping muscles and she shuddered along her whole length. He gave her more pressure and watched her back arch, felt her push back at him.

He watched his pubic scales lift to scrape into her crease. Unable to resist the temptation of Chiarra's smooth, curving bottom, Jarrk made a fist with his free hand and dragged his barbs carefully over the exposed silk of her rounded cheeks.

She started to come on him again and he realized he was never going to make it to Door Number Three. With her elbows on the bed, she pushed up to meet him, to take and absorb his full penetration. It was too much. With his thumb covering her kiss and his dick, brutal and hard against her limit, he blasted into her with the ferocity of a flamethrower. His head jerked back. "Chiarra," he roared with his eyes closed and his groin pressed tight to her bottom as he met and matched each of her gripping contractions with another rushing wave of ecstatic release.

Matched her then bested her—her body slackened beneath his in defeated completion as he continued to pour into her, each prolonged moment a gift of extended gratification.

His dick gave a final spurt of satisfaction and, sliding both hands to caress her hips gently, he stared at the point where their bodies connected. He loved that connection. Loved her warm wet socket, the tight crimp of her ass.

Loved her.

He loved *her*.

He gripped her hips as he fell back on his heels, pulling her with him. He wanted to keep that connection, was his final thought, before he fell into helpless sleep.

* * * * *

When he woke, it was morning, and she was kissing him. Her demanding lips required immediate attention. She must have gotten up and washed, he realized, as he pulled her cold little butt beneath him. He rolled on top of her and entered her. For a long time, he just kissed her while his erection built up a head. But when her legs moved apart, he settled in between them and decided to give her some of the action she seemed to crave as a human.

Gryffin females were relatively dry inside and any movement was abrasive for both parties, but with Chiarra...with Chiarra anything was possible. He pulled his mouth from her clinging lips and watched her head drop back to the bed, eyes closed, forehead wrinkled in a frown. He pulled his dick back an inch and she whimpered in protest. He nudged back into her and watched her lips curl as she sighed. He pulled his hips back and grinned at her pouting response. With his weight on one elbow, he put his other hand at the small of her back and pushed into her, hard. She murmured with agonized delight.

Something leapt within his loins and his hips responded with delicious instinct. His big hand spread behind her to keep her pussy cocked up into his groin as his hips drove into her with increasing regularity and growing response on her part.

Tar. This was the way to take a woman. Forcing yourself into her canal, fucking into her, as she opened for you, wet, soft, yielding. He thrust into her hard and deep. As she writhed beneath him, he kept her cunt tilted for maximum delivery. Each time he thrust against her limit, he held his bulging head hard against her, prolonging that moment of contact when his dick slammed up against her cervix. She started to buck at one of those touching moments and he held her tight against him as he gave her the full impact of his swelling cock-head. Then, with a contained roar that started in his chest, he came inside her.

Chapter Fifteen

Jarrk pulled his hood down over his eyes, put his back against the wall and slouched into the corner. He kept Chiarra at the center of his attention while he scanned the dark tavern for potential danger. As the girl slid their payment across the counter, he noted the taverner's interest in the small stone, saw the man's eyes flick toward him then across the room where four men shared a table.

It had been a hard day. A hard sequence of days. A small unit of Yellow Guard, led by an energetic young captain, pursued them relentlessly. Twice they'd had to abandon their camp to fly before the Guard's approach.

The stones Tranth had pushed on him had saved their lives several times over, kept them fed when there was no time to hunt, bought Chiarra new clothing, paid for rooms when they dared take one.

Jarrk watched Chiarra as she made her way back to their table. When she dropped onto the stool beside him, he returned his eyes to the table of four.

"I got dinner and a room. Ale's coming in a minute." Chiarra pushed an empty tankard at him.

"We won't need the room."

Her eyes cut to his and then followed his gaze across the smoky room. With a pitcher in his fist, the taverner was trying to fill four tankards that were already brimming. Chiarra flicked a frown at her lover.

The men traded words and the taverner turned in their direction. As the thin, greasy man filled Jarrk's tankard, the door scraped open but Jarrk kept his eyes on the table across the room. The taverner moved in front of Chiarra and Jarrk caught a glimpse of yellow in the corner of his eye. The taverner moved again. And revealed a yellow uniform. With a knife sliding toward Chiarra's throat.

"Move and she's dead," the captain warned. The young man's voice was louder than it needed to be, edged with nerves.

It was too late to draw steel.

"Don't touch me," Chiarra garbled as the man's arm went around her neck. "He'll kill you."

"Hands on the table. On the table *now!*" The captain cursed, his attention caught on the huge, hackled knuckles splayed on the table. "*Gryffin.*

"Get his steel. Watch his hands. Stay clear of his barbs." The captain issued a series of tense orders.

Jarrk moved his hands slowly away from his body, allowing one of the soldiers to snatch his knife away.

"Shall I kill him?" The soldier with the knife looked anxiously between the tall Gryffin and his captain.

"With what? That? He'll have his barbs in you before you can scratch him."

"What then? We can't just leave him. He'll follow us."

"We'll tie him and take him with us."

Or tie him and kill him, Jarrk thought.

"Right big fella? You'll let us tie you, won't you?" The captain jerked his blade hard under Chiarra's chin.

The heavy stool grated on the stone floor as Jarrk started up in anger. His eyes flashed with raging fury that centered on the man—that dared—put hands on his female. He drew in several hot, angry breaths before his shoulders sagged. As he dropped back onto the stool, his head sank and his forearms rested on his knees.

The young captain jerked his chin at one of his men and his sergeant approached the Gryffin with a short length of tough rope.

Jarrk's hands hung loose between his knees then moved lower to grasp the stool's legs. Suddenly, Jarrk was on his feet as the heavy stool came between his legs and smashed upward, crushing the soldier's face. The man crumpled, clearing the way to the young captain.

The last thing the captain saw were four blue barbs in a massive fist—just before they smashed away his life.

As he fell, Chiarra jerked the captain's blade from his slackening fingers and spun to join Jarrk but the conflict was done. With the stool in one fist and barbs out on the other, Jarrk had crushed his way through the remaining five soldiers.

Chiarra looked at the dead captain, his broken sergeant. "I told him not to touch me," she muttered, shaking her head. Her eyes caught those of the men across the room. Mouths agape, they stared at the pair. Four men scraped back in their stools in an automatic attempt to distance themselves from the violent Gryffin.

Jarrk's eyes swung to the taverner, a rage of challenge in his eyes. The greasy little rat of a man shrank to the far end of the counter. "You'll want that food to go," he suggested in a croak.

Jarrk gave him a dangerous nod.

* * * * *

That night Chiarra lay beside Jarrk, under the low-slung boughs of a giant conifer, shaking under the hand of that terrible trembling weakness which accompanies the worst nightmares. Only she hadn't been sleeping. And it wasn't a nightmare. She nudged up close to him, hungry for reassurance and connection, hoping to stop the tremors, desperate to regain all she'd lost in one unwelcome vision.

She'd lost something. Something important—precious—in a vision she knew, with cold certainty, she would one day witness.

She'd seen herself tied. Seen Jarrk with a purse in his hand. "Take her," he told the yellow uniforms.

She trembled against Jarrk as she clung to him. Trying to bring back everything that the vision had cost her. But something had been lost.

Trust.

Love.

Chapter Sixteen

Jarrk turned concerned eyes on his female. Throwing off his cloak, he glanced around the dingy little room they'd rented then stooped to build a fire in the small grate.

The incessant running was taking a hard toll. She was barely eating. Her once delicate curves had all but disappeared—she looked so small and fragile. Tar's Pit! Every time he thought they were clear of the Yellow Guard, the damn uniforms showed up again. They made a conspicuous pair—the tall silver Gryffin and his little human. The reward offered for their capture was enormous. They might escape the Yellow Guard, but they were never going to escape that reward.

"Who in Tar's Name did you kill?"

She shrugged and mumbled an answer. Something about the Benign Dictator.

"The Benign Dictator's brother?"

"No," she said sorrowfully. "If I'd killed her brother I'd have probably been given a medal. I killed her lover."

"Oh."

"I didn't know who the man was. And I didn't mean to kill him."

He sighed. "I know. You were just trying to stop him. But next time you see a man beating his horse, try not to get involved, will you?"

"It wasn't a horse," she said quietly.

So quietly that he didn't hear her and was left to wonder why she looked so sad.

"I think—"

"—we should split up," he finished impatiently. "I know, Chiarra! We've had this discussion."

"We might escape notice if we were on our own. We could meet up again on The Spit."

"And if you never showed up?" His eyes narrowed as he stared at the ground. "I would never know...how you died." He raised his eyes to her. "I would only know you'd died alone and I'd done nothing to stop your death."

"If we don't split up, we'll both die—certainly." He watched her lower lip tremble. "I don't want to watch you die, Jarrk. If we split up, we *might* both live."

"I won't leave you," he said quietly as he stood. "We'll head north."

"North! You wouldn't survive the winters."

"You'll just have to keep me warm." He smiled at her. "I'll keep you busy. We'll be all right." He looked away when she didn't smile then threw himself on the small, hard bed—left her staring into the fire. "And you're sure you see nothing of our future?"

She shivered.

"Think, Chiarra."

Her voice was dull. "I can't see the future, Jarrk."

He was only silent a moment. "I don't believe that."

She exploded. "I can't *see* the future. *I can't.* I...*sometimes* get *useless*, meaningless visions that foretell nothing!"

He sat up and frowned at her. "Tell me about the visions."

Silence.

"Are we together? Do you see us together?"

She squeezed her eyes shut.

She saw Jarrk. There were yellow uniforms behind him, a wall of green beyond that. "Take her," he said, and stepped aside. One of the uniforms put a purse in his hand.

"Are we together?"

Her eyebrows drew together to make a sad little arch and she nodded.

"We'll swing by The Spit on the way north," he announced. "I need to make arrangements for my fold. Let them know I won't be coming back."

She shook her head slowly, the leafy background of a vision bothering her. "It'll be dangerous. They'll be expecting us to turn up there—the Yellow Guard. If they're anywhere out there—waiting—that's where they'll be."

"We'll be careful. Slip in at night. Go to Tranth." He didn't see her shake her head again. Her voice was small when she finally spoke. "What?"

"Make love to me," she repeated as she stared into the fire.

He took her carefully, gently. As she lay beneath him, his hand stroked down over the skin stretched tight over her pelvic wing and he was reminded just how much she'd lost. He didn't move on her, knowing his surge alone would bring her to climax. Her eyes were closed and he watched a tear swell at the corner of one eye. Then another.

He pulled out of her.

She turned her head to hide her tears. "Make love to me, Jarrk."

"So you can leave me when I sleep?"

She didn't answer.

"You're my female," he said. "I won't let you leave me."

"Make lo—"

Standing quickly, he disconnected the strap from his quiver, returned to the bed and had her wrists wrapped before she could react. He stretched her wrists above her head and tied her to the headboard.

"Jarrk!"

He covered her mouth with his hand then replaced his hand with his lips. "I won't let you leave me," he said into her lips. "You're my female. Don't you get it?!" He got between her legs and kneed them apart. "I've taken you so many times, your blood runs with mine. I own you, Chiarra. I've put too much into you to let you leave me now. You're my female," he said as he thrust into her. "To do with as I please. To take when, and where I please." His knuckles burned as his hackles pulled back and his barbs thrust forward. Blue poison welled at their tips and he ached with an instinctive, primal need to drag them across her flesh, to mark her as his own.

Tar! Was this how Grat's human died? And was he no better than Grat? He clenched his fists beside her head and put *all* his weight on them. She turned her head and—Sweet Tar Below—sucked hard on his barbs as she pulled her mouth over his knuckles. His vision blackened at the sheer erotic pleasure evoked by the presence of her lips. Falling on one elbow, he brought his other fist to her mouth. He gasped as she sucked off the aching excess then smiled down at her as he dragged his barbs lightly around the swell of her breast. The barbs caught at her skin and four blue lines followed his hand up around the side of her breast.

A whimper wrenched from deep within the girl as she arched and lifted from the bed. Like bands of steel, his arms went under her and crushed her in a pure male desire to bind her to him. His hips took her hard.

His heart took it harder.

Chapter Seventeen

Tranth jumped to meet them as they stepped inside his lodge. "Tar, man. What are you doing here? The Yellow Guard..."

"I know. We saw them." Jarrk flashed a grin at his friend. "But they didn't see us."

"You can't..."

Jarrk gave him a warning look and Tranth bit back his words when he saw the limp girl Jarrk supported in one arm

Later Jarrk sat with his friend, staring at the sleeping girl as they talked quietly. "I might have turned back when I saw the Guard but the girl could go no farther. Besides, there's nowhere else to go—believe me, we've been there—everywhere except north."

Tranth shook his head. "You won't be able to go too far north."

But Jarrk wasn't listening. His eyes were on the sleeping girl.

"You killed those two yellow bastards?"

Light glinted on the hard surface of Jarrk's eyes.

"Any others?"

"One other." Jarrk shook his head. "Chiarra tried to warn the man."

Tranth nodded his understanding. "So are the stories true? About human females?"

Jarrk's hard expression softened slightly. "Tar, Tranth. You can't imagine—what it's like. To have that little bit of female thrashing on the end of your cock—"

"*Thrashing?*"

"She's so hot and so tight and so…wet. All over. Her mouth, her cunt, her—"

"I'm getting the picture," Tranth interrupted with a laugh, "as well as getting hard."

Jarrk shook his head. "She's so small. And so strong." His eyes narrowed on his friend with keen emotion. "There is *nothing* so beautiful as fucking Chiarra." Jarrk turned his eyes to the sleeping girl. "She's exhausted," he said softly.

"Sleeping like the dead," his friend affirmed.

Jarrk blinked as he stared as his friend.

"Does Akela know you're here?"

"What?"

"Akela."

Jarrk gathered his thoughts. "No. I need you to take her a message for me. But first, bring me something I can use to tie Chiarra's wrists."

Tranth gave his friend a look of surprise.

"She's been trying to leave me. To protect me. Who would have guessed humans could be so noble?" His smile was more than a little proud. "Do you have something I can use as a stake?"

Tranth put a short knife in his hand and, while Jarrk pounded the steel into the ground, he gave Tranth his instructions for Akela. After Tranth had left, he dragged Chiarra's loose pants off, wrapped her wrists and knotted her off at the steel's hilt.

* * * * *

She woke to the realization that something was wrong. Jarrk's body was wrapped around hers, his hand inside her jerkin and tucked around her breast like he owned it. Dawn light filtered into the lodge in a thin green wash. Sounds outside filtered in and almost suffocated her. "Jarrk!"

His eyes blinked open as he stared at her, listening. She watched his eyes fill with fear. He gave her jerkin a tug downward to cover her breasts. In one smooth motion, he was on his feet and moving to the curtain of vines at the door. Moving his head back and forth, he peered through the vines, sifting the images as he put together a picture of what lay outside.

"Jarrk!"

"It's the Yellow Guard." He pulled on his pants and reached for his knife.

"Jarrk!"

"Be quiet, Chiarra," he commanded.

"Jarrk! Untie me."

"Be still."

Sounds of command from without became louder.

"Jarrk! They'll kill you."

He shook his head as he headed for the light at the door. "Remember what I told you, Chiarra? When the dragon almost killed you? An animal is at its most dangerous when wounded."

He ducked out the door.

"No," Chiarra screamed.

Chiarra twisted against her bonds, raging tears of frustration, fear and dread as she fought to her knees. *An animal is at its most dangerous when wounded!*

He was going to sacrifice his life for her! Knowing he couldn't survive but thinking he could take them all with him. Take them with an animal's wounded rage. But Jarrk wasn't an animal.

She found her own tears wet on Tranth's blanket and stared at the dark stains. Outside there was a fearful silence, ominous and dead. She held her breath, stared at the door and strained her senses, trying to understand the message in the silence.

Eventually the light blotted at the door. Jarrk stepped through.

Three uniforms followed.

Jarrk's eyes were on the floor as he stepped aside for the uniforms. *"Take her," he said.*

The captain sneered at the sight of the woman, naked from the waist down, bound and staked to the ground. "Tar and Breeza," he said with disgust. "She's been letting him fuck her. She's been letting the animal tie her and fuck her." The captain's eyes scraped over her body like an unsharpened knife.

But Chiarra's eyes sought Jarrk's.

Jarrk watched the ground carefully.

"Look at that! She expects the animal to help her!"

"Jarrk?"

Jarrk took a breath. "I've negotiated for your life, Chiarra."

"Wh...what?"

"You'll be permitted to live."

She shook her head in disbelief.

"It will be prison. But I've assured each of these men that if anything happens to you, I'll hunt them down singly and kill each one of them."

She stared at him as her mind raced to understand.

"It's better than death, Chiarra."

She watched as *one of the uniforms put a purse in his hand*. And that hurt. She couldn't help it hurting, no matter how she looked at it.

Their eyes connected as the captain cut her free and pushed her at the door.

Jarrk whirled on the uniform, angry. "Let her dress," he hissed.

Fingers numb, feelings numb, Chiarra fumbled her pants on.

Jarrk backed through the door ahead of her.

The bright light stung as she stepped through, her wrist went up to shield her eyes.

The clearing in front of Tranth's lodge was packed with curious Gryffin. She frowned at them. Frowned at Tranth's concerned expression, Akela's downcast eyes, Grat's cold look of satisfaction.

Then at Jarrk.

"Don't look at me that way, Chiarra." He put himself in front of her, blocking her. "Chiarra. Please. You might as well put a knife in my heart." She saw the glint in his eye as he pulled her head down onto his chest. She saw the glint of his knife.

"You sold me," she said, in whispered disbelief. She took the knife.

Chapter Eighteen

There was blood everywhere. Jarrk's blood. She didn't recall stabbing him. There had been a struggle — just after she pulled Jarrk's blade. The uniforms pulled her away from him.

In the next second, she watched Jarrk as he reeled away a step, opened his bloodied hands to stare at them. Full of shocked disbelief, his eyes swung to her.

His fist shot out and the back of his hand caught her hard above her jaw; her head snapped around and she crumpled in the arms of her captors. All in the space of a second.

Jarrk gasped as the men let her slide to the ground. Blue poison welled from two red slashes near her ear.

The uniform choked back a sudden snort of laughter as he watched, with morbid interest, the blue line of poison snake down Chiarra's jawline toward her chin. "Well," he said, staring at the girl, "it wasn't the execution we'd planned but it was very effective, nonetheless. I suppose I should thank you for saving us the trouble—"

"No!" Jarrk shook his head, unmindful of the blood streaming down his chest. Akela was at his side but he shook her off. "She was to have lived!"

The uniform turned to his friend. "I told you he'd believe us." He shook his head at Jarrk, his face full of scornful pity. "Stupid animal."

But Jarrk had fallen to his knees and dragged the girl into his arms. His shoulders curled as he buried his face in her neck. "No," he whispered. "No. Chiarra. I didn't mean...I didn't mean to..."

The yellow uniform brayed his hard amusement. "Sweet Breeza," he choked. "Look at him. He loves her!"

"That poison will finish a dragon in ten seconds," his companion drawled. "She's screwed."

The first uniform's eyes lit with mean fire. "How many Gryffins does it take to screw a human woman?"

His companion just laughed.

"I guess it's true what they say about animal intelligence," the first snorted, "there isn't any."

Jarrk lifted his head with slow dawning realization. "What kind of animal was it?" he asked with sudden, quiet menace.

The uniforms didn't appear to understand his question.

"What kind of animal?" he repeated, as Chiarra slid from his arms and he stood to face his tormenters. "What kind of animal was Chiarra trying to save, when she killed that man with her crossbow?"

The uniform stopped laughing long enough to give the Gryffin a haughty sneer. "An animal not dissimilar to yourself." He cocked his head arrogantly. "The Gryffin was smaller, younger —"

Jarrk's hackles rose on his bunched knuckles.

Four crossbows lifted to train on the silver Gryffin.

Jarrk glared at the uniform with helpless fury. Powerless to do otherwise, he watched as a shadow loomed behind the man and a golden arm came across the man's neck, jerked tightly. Grat sank his barbs into the human's life vein.

A crossbow bolt crashed into Grat's skull and the clearing exploded into violence.

It was all Jarrk could do to stop his people from killing all the humans.

It was vital that some of them live.

Chapter Nineteen

Jarrk sagged to his knees beside the small form slumped on the ground. He regarded the little human tenderly.

"Stop that," he said.

He pulled Chiarra into his arms and nuzzled his face into her neck.

"Stop laughing," he scolded.

Chiarra snuffed at a giggle. "How many Gryffins *does* it take to screw a human woman?"

"You tell me," he advised her, his tone threatening.

Her fingers lifted to trail over the jutting curves of his mouth. "In this case, one will do nicely, thank you."

"How's your head?"

"Ringing! Did you have to hit me so hard?"

He winced as he scooped her up and stood. "Sorry," he grunted, "but I had to convince the Yellow Guard you were dead, so they could take the news of your death home with them."

"Take it from me, you were very convincing." She rubbed her jaw. "You know, you had me going there for awhile."

"That *was* the plan." His expression sobered. "Grat died. Died well—in the end. Did you see any of it?"

"A bit. You're very sexy when you're angry."

He grinned down at her. "You think so?"

She nodded—several times—then continued to nod at him.

He laughed. "I'm glad you think so, because as it turns out, I'm feeling a little more than sexy at the moment." He headed into the trees. "Glad you built up a resistance?"

"To your poison, yes. Now, if I could just build up a resistance to you…" she sighed as she stared at his chest. "Your women love you, Jarrk."

He frowned then swept the regret from his eyes. "I can't help that, Chiarra. And I can't help the fact that I don't love them. I haven't mated any of them in months, other than Shani and Akela. Shani's waiting for a younger Gryffin to come of age. I took her in to spare her from Grat's pit. The rest of them can move into other folds as they find males they're happy with."

"And Akela?"

"Akela's a problem," he muttered.

"I think we should keep her."

He smiled and shook his head.

He carried her through the door of the lodge and was relieved when Akela shooed his females out the door then followed them. Laying Chiarra on her side in the center of the pit, he snuggled up close behind her, pulling her wrap open. "Tar, you look good for a dead woman."

She stretched into him. "Mmmm," she murmured, "I don't feel dead."

"Yeah? Tell that to the Yellow Guard. The human Chiarra is dead." He pulled her knee up to her chest and dragged his hand slowly down the inside of her thigh, stroked his hand—tantalizingly—alongside her sex and through her crease before returning to fill his hand with the warm, sexy lips that pouted into his palm—pulsed into his palm. Leaning over her upper body, he watched his hand as each of his four fingers nudged their way into her warm, wet pussy. She gasped when one of those fingers slid into her cunt and another pressed tight against the puckered little kiss beyond her vagina. Two fingers teased at the nub of her clitoris, teased at her slowly, until the finger in her cunt was coated with her wet heat. Dragging his wet fingers up through her channeled folds then down into her crease, he placed two fingers at each of her openings.

"You can forget about your past life as a human, Chiarra. You're my female now," he rumbled against her ear. "You're going to love being my female. And you're going to love what comes next."

She gasped as he entered her with all four fingers. "I've got a feeling I'm what comes next," she moaned, "But Jarrk..."

"Mmmm?"

"Will you do that thing...with your barbs...for me? As I come?"

Jarrk groaned as his dick thickened unreasonably. "You want me to stripe you?"

"Just a little. If it wouldn't be too much to ask. I'll never ask for anything again. Consider it my last request."

"I'll consider your last request, Chiarra...if you'll agree to be my last-picked. The very last, for the rest of my life."

Epilogue

Akela took a final look at Jarrk's lodge. Hitching her satchel on her shoulder, she headed for the clearing. There, she stopped only long enough to select one of the crossbows left behind by the humans. Slinging it up onto her shoulder, she continued east through the forest. She ignored the crushing vise that clamped around her heart.

If it hadn't been for Jarrk, she told herself, she'd have struck out years ago.

It was only a little lie. She was long overdue for an adventure. And that was the truth.

A shadow separated itself from the edge of the clearing — a tall shadow with coppery highlights — and followed.

* * * * *

"That's what I like about you, Chiarra."

"What's that Jarrk?" she said, digging for the compliment.

"Everything, my love."

Jarrk stood in a moonlit clearing, silver light on his shoulders as he turned toward her. The moonlight on the pool was silver leaves, floating on the water's surface. He smiled at her as he pulled the string on his pants and let them slide down his legs.

"Of all my visions, I think this is my favorite."

"You saw this coming, then."

She nodded.

He grunted. "As if it would take a visionary to predict my hard-on. And what else do you see in our future?"

"*Our* future?"

"Our future," he said firmly. "You may be able to see things I can't see, my little human, but I know things you don't know." He gave her a supercilious smile. "You see, Chiarra, only certain females have hallucinations when they take a male's venom. Only one female that tastes of mine can see the future. The female that is meant to be mine. The female to whom I give my heart, my soul. The female that returns that gift with the same."

She gave him a stunned look of wonder.

"To paraphrase, darling...it was basically love at first sight...and the feeling was mutual." He grabbed her and kissed her. "So what do you see next?"

She squealed as his hands tightened around her waist. "What do you think?" she threw back at him.

He closed his eyes and she used the opportunity to run her fingers into his ruff. He rumbled his appreciation. "I see two beautiful daughters with their mother's long dark hair," he intoned with dramatic mummery.

She laughed. "Look again, Jarrk, because those are your sons."

"Hmph," he grunted and opened his eyes. "In that case, they need haircuts."

Redeeming Davik
Kingdom of Khal

Chapter One

"Look what the spoils-of-war goddess left us." Warrik pushed a woman into the room. "I'll be back later to share in her rape. Don't start without me," he added cheerfully and disappeared.

Prince Davik of Southern Khal glanced up from his maps, did a double take, and stopped to stare.

A woman stood just inside the door; a woman who bore further examination. She was exquisite; almost as tall as he, and he was a good six feet. Her skin was warm caramel on a hot day. Her long hair lifted from her forehead and rolled down past her shoulders in thick, black waves that were tipped with a tapered three inches of white. Westerman blood, he decided, and wondered about her night vision as his eyes traveled to hers. Dark doe-eyes gave her a vulnerable appearance while her quiet, solemn expression insisted she would be brave despite that vulnerability. The tilt of her chin and her generous, full lips managed to convey the idea she had not lived her life without daring.

Davik tipped his head and continued his appraisal. The nose might be considered prominent on another woman, but on her anything less would have been swamped by those wide liquid eyes and full lips.

Difficult as it was, he pulled his eyes from her face to travel down her body. In a world where nothing stayed clean for long, her tightly laced bodice was inordinately white. Her rustling skirt of silk was vivid blue. Under the hem of her skirt, the toe of one doeskin boot could be seen. Unconsciously, he ran a hand through his hair; it wasn't long, but he'd been meaning to have it cut. Now he wished he'd gotten around to it. As he pushed his straw colored hair behind his ears, the Prince's fingers furrowed his mane to reveal rich gold beneath the straw.

Her dark eyes were wide as her full lips parted. "I'll not be forced."

He leaned back in his chair and gave her a small smile. "You don't appear to have a choice."

"I do," she said quickly. "I can submit, willingly."

An interesting stance, he thought; one, which should fit well into his own plans. He covered his next smile with his hand. "Warrik will be disappointed. But yes, that might work." He pushed the papers around on the table, found a length of cord, and stood.

Her face was pale. "No! I give my word, I'll submit."

"That's fine," he said, "but you'll have to be bound anyway. You *are* from the rebel camp, and I'm a cautious man by nature."

Her face grew paler with each of his approaching steps, and she backed away from him until she came up against the wall. She shot a panicked look around the room, then at him.

That look of appeal almost halted him.

He watched her take a breath of resignation; then she clasped her hands together and held them before her. He wrapped the cord once around her wrists before she fainted clean away. Catching her in his arms, he looked down on her with surprise. How could such a fragile creature survive in his world?

Then he noticed her wrists, and there was no question as to the manner in which she had survived. Old scars, the harsh product of years in chains, ravaged her narrow wrists like a siege line. With growing suspicion, his eyes fell to the bottom of her skirt. He lifted the hem with his foot to see if her ankles bore similar markings, but her doeskin boots hid them. Shifting her onto one arm, he unlaced her bodice and opened it. For a moment he neglected his purpose, distracted by the lush curve of her breasts, her tiny waist, and hard flat stomach, then he slipped his hand around to her back and winced. His fingers traced the harsh pattern of scars crossing her back.

Cradling her in his arms, he backed into his chair and sat. With his fingers he pushed her dark hair from her chest, greatly improving his view. Quietly, he watched her breasts rise and fall as color slowly returned to her face. Curious about the rest of her, his eyes cut to the hem of her skirt then back to the luscious breasts. He was particularly interested in the height of her boots.

Most women wore sandals or clogs. She must have had the boots specially made. He wondered if they stopped at mid-calf or if they rose to just below her knees. Past her knees?

Unable to resist the temptation, but without removing his eyes from her chest, he tugged the blue silk up to the top of her knees, took a quick look at the high boots on her long calves, and nodded. He gave the blue silk a final tug then released it. Having crested her knees, the silk slid conveniently into her lap, revealing most of her slender thighs. As though he hadn't planned this very outcome, his eyes lurched to her legs, vacillated between the choice of upper and lower body, then stuck on her thighs. He cocked his head as he gave her legs a thorough appraisal, returned his eyes to her breasts, then shook his head, unable to decide which of the two views he most preferred.

She awoke with a small jump. When she opened her eyes, they went from his face to her open bodice then to the skirt hiked high on her legs. "Has it started, then?" she asked in a quiet voice, not looking at him.

"Your rape?" He shook his head. "Your rape has been postponed," he said. She looked up at him with wide eyes and he felt something rearrange itself in the vicinity of his heart. "Until you're feeling up to it," he said with a smile.

Chapter Two

It was dusk before Warrik shouldered his way through the door and threw himself into a chair. Davik had already started his meal, his drawings and maps pushed aside to make room for the food. Warrik glanced around the room and found the girl.

"What do you think?" He grinned at his brother as he shrugged his cape from his shoulders.

"The gods are good," Davik returned with a smile.

"She's not bound." He raised an enquiring eyebrow. When his brother shrugged, he turned to the girl. "Davik is normally a suspicious man," he explained.

"Normally cautious," Davik corrected him.

"Normally, he's abnormally cautious. Normally, you'd be bound." The big man tossed his tawny hair behind his back.

"Normally, you don't complain."

"Why should I? I like bondage," Warrik grinned and winked at the girl.

"This will make a diverting change for The Heir," Davik told the girl.

"Have you fed her?"

"I thought you'd want to." Davik pointed at his brother's belt. "Get rid of your steel first."

Warrik pulled off his belt and threw his weapons across the room, away from the girl. "Come here, darling."

Hesitantly, the girl stood and cautiously approached the big soldier. He swept her onto his knee.

"Here's the drill, sweetheart. I'll feed you. That way your hands will be clean...when it's time to remove my clothing."

Reaching for a greasy joint, Warrik tore at the meat with his teeth, rescued a small piece from his mouth, and held it before her lips. When she opened her mouth, he fed it to her. Leaning back in his chair, Warrik smiled as he watched her chew self-consciously. He popped another piece in her mouth, then set his teeth into the joint with serious intent. "Bread?" he offered her in the middle of a bite. She reached across the table, but he stopped her. "No, I'll get it." He broke a small loaf in half and watched her open her mouth to chew off a bite. With a contented sigh he put the remaining bread in his own mouth, chewing mechanically as he gazed at her face. He shifted in his chair.

"Where did she come from?" Davik asked.

"The city. She'd dropped into a dry gulch and was almost to the sentry line before she was discovered. Jaym and Mavrik caught her." He looked at her hair. "Do you suppose she has the Westerman's night vision?"

"Apparently not."

Warrik raised his eyebrows in question.

"Otherwise she'd have attempted her escape at night."

Warrik nodded his understanding. "She didn't have any messages on her, nor any weapons. Just a small knife and five gold."

"No food?"

Warrik rolled his eyes. "This is a siege," he pointed out.

"Water?"

That seemed to stop the big blond. He considered the girl thoughtfully.

"She could have been trying to get an oral message out."

Warrik nodded; his blue eyes laughed. "Well if she was, she didn't." He smiled into the girl's eyes. "Do you have anything you want to share with me, darling? Anything oral? Anything at all? Ah, come on darling. Offer me something. Even if it's only lip service." He turned to his brother. "She doesn't look like a spy to me," he pronounced with decisive optimism. "Most like, she was just hungry. Look at the poor girl. She doesn't make more than a handful." His eyes slipped down to her breasts. "Well, maybe two handfuls."

"And she was dressed like that? She hoped to escape notice in those clothes?"

Warrik frowned at the girl's blue skirt then glanced at his brother impatiently. "You're just being suspicious."

"Cautious," Davik corrected him. "She hasn't offered any explanation," he pointed out. Davik turned his blue-green eyes on the girl. She stared back at him quietly.

A laugh burst from Warrik's chest. "And evidently isn't going to! How goes it inside the walls, darling? How much longer can the Northern Rebels hold out?" The girl regarded him quietly. "My spies tell me the Rebels grow tired of that Pretender, Kartin."

Davik snorted. "She's not going to tell you anything."

"Of course she's not. She's too loyal." Warrik regarded her face with pride. "I like loyalty in a woman," he murmured. His expression was one of open adulation as he shifted in his chair uncomfortably. "Hadi's Saints! These breeks are getting tight. Already! Would you mind, darling?" His laughing eyes went to the laces at the front of his breeks.

Submissively, her hands went to his ties. She fumbled a long time.

Davik rolled his eyes. "Did he double-knot them again?"

Suddenly she looked up at Davik. Then slowly — uncertainly — at his brother.

Warrik threw back his head and laughed. "I like to be untied. Take your time darling." He looked at his brother. "Is there any fruit?" Davik rose and went to the door where he spoke to one of the guards. "If you're so suspicious, why isn't she tied?"

"She promised to submit," Davik said, leaning against the wall beside the door.

"Without a struggle?" Davik nodded. "Damn! I like a bit of a struggle." Warrik grinned at his brother.

"*He's kidding*," Davik interposed when he saw the girl's expression.

"I'm kidding," Warrik echoed. "There won't be any struggle. I'm going to sneak it in when you're not looking."

Davik returned to the table with a small basket of apples. "Good luck sneaking up on her with that battering ram you keep between your legs."

Half an apple disappeared between Warrik's teeth and he held the remainder to the girl's mouth while she continued her struggle with his ties. "If you don't hurry up sweetheart, I'm going to storm the gates and bust out of there all by myself."

"The Heir grows impatient," Davik laughed and caught the girl's eye.

"The Heir grows, sure enough," Warrik countered suggestively.

Warrik nudged the fruit against her lips and she opened her mouth, her eyes still slanting onto Davik. He watched a shining ribbon of juice unfurl from the corner of her mouth and curl down toward her chin, watched as Warrik reached up and caught the golden drop on the end of a thick finger, then moved the finger to her mouth. Her lips parted for his finger as she cast her eyes demurely down, her long eyelashes dark on her dusky cheeks. Her lips closed around Warrik's finger. Slowly, she raised her eyes to connect with Davik's.

He lost a breath or perhaps two.

Actually, he lost count before the spell was broken.

His cock stirred and straightened. As he moved his legs apart, the action drew her eyes downward. Her eyes, fixed on his groin, affected an amazing result on his sex, the like of which he'd never experienced. Her eyes brushed up along the length of his ties with an interest he could almost feel; his steel pulsed with ready life.

A final tug and Warrik's ties were loose. He shifted the girl on his lap then presented her with his greasy fingers. The big man sighed happily as she sucked on each of his digits. Running a shining thumb over her bottom lip, Warrik watched her lips part beneath his thumb. "Straighten me out," he said softly.

She hesitated only an instant, then her hands slipped into his breeks. The big man's eyes closed, his expression that of minor ecstasy. "The plot thickens." His lips curled and his eyes opened a fraction, enough to watch her hand move to stroke out his swelling length. Slowly, he raised his eyes to her face. "Help me off with my jerkin." His voice was a husky slur. Davik watched her loosen the strings at his chest then pull the jerkin over his head. "Now this." Warrik indicated her tightly laced bodice.

Obediently, she loosened her own ties and opened the bodice.

The air thickened appreciably as Davik heard Warrik's breath hiss in through his teeth. Davik watched his brother's hand reach into the bodice to expose then curve around a perfect round breast. "Take it off," Warrik said softly, without moving his hand.

Reaching up with her hands, she pushed the bodice off her shoulders and shrugged it down her arms. This was accomplished without inhibition, with wide-eyed compliance that lacked shyness. As though—he thought—as though it were her job. Not so much willingly, as with soldierly resignation. Davik watched the bodice slip to the ground, and frowned. Had she done this before? And perhaps been paid for it?

He flinched as her back angled toward him, and looked to catch his brother's eye. But Warrik's eyes had slid over the girl's upper body then lower, to her skirt, where his gaze rested between her legs with unabashed greed. "Your skirt." His voice was hoarse.

She reached behind her for the ties and Davik bit back a gasp as her breasts lifted and jutted forward. His eyes flicked to his brother, whose hot gaze was riveted on her breasts. Davik shifted in his chair to improve his perspective. When her ties were loose, Warrik lifted the girl by her waist and put her on her feet. The skirt slipped down her legs, and the two men watched her body as it was revealed.

Davik tried to swallow without much success. His eyes ran down her long body from her swollen breasts, past the tiny waist, the curving hips and the long, long legs. She was wearing shorts. Pink silk shorts; a very expensive shade of pink. And soft doeskin boots that laced up almost to her knees. He watched her thumbs slip into the top of the shorts.

Warrik reached out for her hand. He tried to say no, but could only shake his head. "Leave the shorts for now," he finally croaked. "Hadi's Saints. All of this. All in one place." He ran his hands down her sides, lingering on the shining pink silk. Opening his knees, he pulled her between his legs as his hands went behind her and caressed her silk-covered bottom as though he would be content to do nothing more for the rest of his life. He smiled at the pink shorts then reached for her shin and pulled it up to rest her foot on his chair then, with a deep groan of pleasure, slid his hand under the back of her thigh and between her legs.

Davik watched as Warrik's big hand came up over her rise then returned between her legs several times. Then his fingers splayed out behind her to squeeze a curving cheek and came up under her thigh again. Now both hands smoothed the front of her shorts over her stomach and continued around her hips to her bottom again. Sliding off the chair, Warrik dropped to his knees, leaned back on his heels and pulled her to him, settling his cheek against the sleek pink shorts that stretched over her stomach. He caught his brother's eye and delivered him a look of consummate joy.

With his big thumbs beneath the jut of her pelvic wings, he held her away from him and lifted his eyes to her face. "Off," he said.

The two men watched the pink slide down her legs. Warrik groaned again as he rocked to his feet and back into the chair. "Come here darling," he whispered. He turned her as she joined him on the chair, putting her back against his chest. Taking both her hands in his, he guided them behind his neck and left them there. One of his hands spread over her breasts while the other stretched out across her stomach. Restlessly, his hands moved over her, hardly knowing where to go, where to stop. Davik watched his brother's large hands slide down her thighs toward her knees. He pulled her knees to the outside of his thighs, slid his hands past her knees to her ankles and caught her ankles around the back of his calves. Then he opened his legs. His hands returned to push her thighs further to the outside of his; he then spread his knees even wider.

Davik realized he was gritting his teeth in a clenched jaw. With aching jaw and throbbing cock, his hungry gaze consumed the girl's long caramel limbs as Warrik stretched her on his body. She was warm and dark against the background of his brother's fair coloring, his buff colored breeks. Her calves, doeskin-clad, were twined around The Heir's dark leather boots. Scarcely able to draw a breath, Davik watched her brown nipples quietly rise and fall. She wasn't going to be ready for his brother, he realized as he noted her quiet breathing. He felt sorry for the girl, considering the sheer magnitude of what would happen next; the magnitude of The Heir's massive dick. He felt sorrier for himself, as his problem was the reverse of hers. As though to torture himself, his eyes fell to her cleft, a gleaming pink streak set in a thatch of curling black hair, like a long marquis gem in black filigree.

"Let's have your hands," Warrik said, as he pulled her hands from behind his neck. With his hands over hers, he guided them between her legs. Warrik's large hand dropped in front of Davik's view as he rocked one of the girl's hands over her rise, while he pressed the other flat against her inner thigh. "Relax, sweetheart. Put your head on my shoulder. That's it. Show me what you want, darling. Guide my hand, sweetheart. Don't be shy."

Davik almost smiled. Warrik's foreplay was improving, he began to think, then changed his mind when, moments later, Warrik had her stretched out again, pulling her arms behind his neck. With a chokehold on his excitement, Warrik reached behind the girl's back to clear access to his cock. Then he lifted the girl by the hips and eased into her.

There was a good deal of starting and stopping and Davik's eyes returned to watch the girl's face, her eyes clenched tight, lips caught between her teeth. "Come on darling, let me in," Warrik crooned into her ear. He made a face at his brother. "She's tight," he explained, "and dry. What's the matter, darling? Don't you want me?" She opened her eyes a fraction and he followed her half-closed eyes to Davik's face. "She wants you!" he exclaimed.

Davik looked up sharply, but her eyes were lowered. Again, he experienced a sensation surrounding his sex akin to but somehow better than warm and wet physical contact.

"She does. She wants you!"

Chapter Three

"Don't act so surprised," he tried to say lightly, but his breathing was interfering with the nonchalance he was attempting to convey.

Warrik pulled out of her. "I don't want to hurt the girl, Davik."

The girl opened her eyes and looked at him hopefully. Inside Davik's jerkin, every hair on his chest lifted with tingling sensation. Still he hesitated an instant before he stood, caught in her dark gaze. They were blue, he realized. Earlier he had thought her eyes were black, but there were the darkest, deepest blue he had ever seen. So dark you could hardly see the boundary between pupil and iris.

Davik knelt between his brother's knees as Warrik's big hands cupped her breasts and pushed them to Davik's mouth. He took one of her brown nipples between his lips, placed his palms against the inside of her thighs and stroked outward toward her knees, then returned to repeat the long caressing sweep. His dry lips prodded her nipple to attention; he then turned his rough cheek and brushed it against the inside of her breast. He licked his lips and started kissing his way to her second nipple, reached out his tongue to warn her of his approach, breathed warmly on her wet nipple, then took it in his mouth. He felt, rather than heard her sigh. Catching the small, hard bud between his top teeth and bottom lip he flicked her out of his mouth, sucked her back in hard, pushed her away with his flattened tongue and let her go. "Open her for me," he rasped.

Warrik spread her legs wide with his.

Longingly, Davik's eyes rested between her legs. Sinking onto his shins, he closed his eyes and touched his lips to the top of her open cleft.

"What can I do to help?" his brother interrupted.

Davik brought his brother's hands underneath the girl's legs, placing Warrik's thick fingers carefully close to her cleft. He felt the girl's small jerk. "That's too rough. Go gently. Just run your fingers into her hair, tease her open a little."

He was panting, he realized.

He brushed his lips lightly below her belly then returned his lips to her warm, open sex. Wetting his tongue, he slid it up along her slot, feeling his way through the roughly delicate ruts that led to her clitoris. Tasted her simple clean warmth, heard her suck in a breath. Smiled with relief, ached with regret. Applied his lips and tongue softly, rhythmically against her clitoris. Drew away to watch her flat belly rise as she began to pant, returned her several kisses with slight suction, withdrew again and heard her murmur, watched her opening contract in a needy gulp—hungry for a man's presence—took his tongue to that opening, ran it around the outside then delved inside. Felt her shiver and quake around his tongue. Tongued his way back to her clitoris and kissed her until she moaned with every touch, a low needy sound that fueled his own mounting need. He closed his eyes and rested his forehead on her rise, panting, waiting for her response. She arched and cried out.

She wanted more.

He caught a glimpse of mounded breasts straining upward as her body bowed in Warrik's arms then his eyes returned to the long slit of her sex, now nicely filled out and pouting at him provocatively. His hand rubbed the agony that ached swollen and granite-hard inside his breeks. With both hands he loosened the ties constricting his erection while he returned his tongue to feather across her clitoris. She stretched into his mouth, and he groaned through the constriction in his chest.

"Mithra," he heard his brother whisper. "Look at her. Isn't she something?"

He pulled away from her, wiping his mouth on his sleeve as he gazed up the long stretch of her arching body. Her head had rolled back onto Warrik's shoulder, her black hair poured over his brother's chest. Her breathing was deep and hurried. Her arms stretched back as her hands clutched at his brother's thick hair.

She was close, he knew. She was making her own moisture now, lots of it. Her slit gleamed slick and wet. He was tempted to apply his tongue one more time, to give her a long slow stroke and lick her right over the edge, then pull back and watch her in her arrival. But Warrik was waiting — patiently, so far.

Warrik's keen, smoking gaze traveled down the girl's body to his brother's face, where it halted, startled and surprised at Davik's expression. "You first," he said, his voice strained. Warrik reached for the cape draped over the back of his chair.

Hope seeped into Davik's expression as he came up on his knees and blindly fumbled his cock out into his hand. His brother handed him the tightly rolled cape. The cape beneath his knees raised him the few inches he needed—desperately needed—to put his hood at her notch, wet and waiting. He touched his hooded tip to her clitoris and she jumped and shivered as excitement raced along her length, tightening every muscle. His brother forced her legs wide as Davik pushed into her with desperate eagerness.

"Easy," his brother reminded him.

Davik squeezed his eyes shut and fought for breath before he started. His hands clutched her hips harshly, but he stroked her carefully, watching her face. She licked her lips and moaned, then gasped when he gave her more of him. Her eyes opened a fraction, and fixed on his face with longing. He gave her his full length and watched her writhe and arch, cry out. Then his hands tightened on her flanks and he pounded into her, desperate to reach her core and crash against it as hard and as often as possible before his release rushed through his steel. He heard her guttural, wrenching sob, felt her hands behind him, pulling him into her. His cock spasmed inside her sweet warm depths and pleasure shot like a drug though every vein in his body as his hips slowed and ratcheted down in their final pumping action.

"No!" Her cry was a helpless wail as The Heir jerked her off of his brother and thrust her onto his own thick steel. Davik's heart was still hammering. The girl's eyes blinked spasmodically as they frantically sought his.

"Ah Mithra. That's sweet," Warrik rasped. "She's still coming."

Warrik closed his eyes and was still for two instants as Davik watched the girl's face; watched a tear appear at the corner of one eye. "Oh no," he whispered. "It's alright. It's alright sweetheart." With a hand to cradle the side of her face, he took her lips and kissed her. Warrik was moving her on him now, but Davik managed to maintain the connection. Desperately, she stretched her neck to reach him. He opened his eyes long enough to catch the pain in her expression, and closed them again quickly. With infinite gentleness he slid his hand down her belly and fingered her open, all the while maintaining the kiss. With two fingers just inside her slot he massaged her lightly with increasing speed until she stiffened and convulsed. Now both his hands returned to hold her face as he kept his eyes shut and his lips on hers, ignoring his brother's explosive curse of pleasure invoking both Mithra and Donar's names.

Of course, the gods had heard it all before.

Afterward, Warrik wanted to take her to the river and start all over. "You'll drain yourself," Davik said, thinking quickly. "And wear her out at the same time. I'll take her." He hurried her into her clothes and got her through the door before Warrik could protest.

Leaving the inn, they headed down the trail that led to the river. As in most cities, Veronix had grown outside the city walls, especially around the gates and along the road approaching the city. The Southern army had commandeered most of these buildings for their use during the siege. Standing two longbow-shots from the city walls, the Princes had made the small inn their headquarters.

Cerces tears drifted across the sky, specks of light on a slate backdrop, as he took her hand and led her through the camp and down to the river. He nodded two of his men away then undressed her, gave her a soft rag and watched her wade into the sleek dark water. The surface of the still black river was like gleaming marble shot with golden star flecks and she melded into the marble surface like a goddess sculpted from bronze and onyx. He watched her perfect curving form as she washed, drinking in the sight of her, watching her hands as they smoothed over her breasts or down her legs. It was a quiet night. The water barely rippled as it slipped smoothly around her thighs in a long, lingering caress.

She turned her scarred back to him and the smooth picture of insouciance eddied and rippled. Anger tightened within him and torqued his mood without warning. It was like viewing a vandalized work of art, like the marble statuary at Pentre Mawr—originally, each sculpture a perfect god—today, every one minus an appendage and every one a cripple. Undressing her had given him the opportunity to confirm his suspicions about her ankles. Unlacing her boots, he'd slid a hand down to her foot and felt the thick ridge of scar tissue she wore on both ankles.

"Come," she said. The word interrupted his musings. He almost missed her invitation as the single syllable joined the river and floated downstream. But he didn't need to be asked twice; he peeled his clothes off quickly and waded out to her.

The water was kind and cool and caressed his legs with the same care given the girl. She dipped the rag and squeezed it above his shoulder, dipped again and did the same on the opposite side, then started rubbing him briskly from the shoulders down. By the time she reached his sex, the rag had warmed on his body. He was grateful. He had, by now, built up quite a decent erection he was a bit proud of and didn't want to see it discouraged by a little cold water. He looked down his body and watched his shaft as his desire took substance and form — solid form.

Very businesslike, she rounded his soft parts and swiped the length of his steel. Ready for business, his cock responded. His erection lost a little momentum as she moved behind him and worked on his back, but when she arrived at his buttocks, it picked up again as her hand slowed. Then both her hands were on his backside and palming him, her fingers tracing the crease where his buttocks met the top of his legs. He watched the rag float downstream and felt her hands come around his flanks. She was against him by then, her body warm against his back, melting into his. Her lips touched the base of his neck, stroking a nerve, pulling a wire somehow connected to his cock, which responded with an immediate 'heads up'. Her hands slid over his abdomen and he held his breath, waiting for her touch with aching anticipation. Then her hands were on him. One hand fingered his testes, while the other hand wrapped around the steel of his erection. Fascinated, he watched her hand on him as she pumped him slowly. Pleasure circulated through his loins as he expanded into her hand. He could take this, he thought as his eyelids came down to cover his eyes. He could take a lot of this, for the rest of his life. Then her thumb was pressing against his tip as her closed fist whisked his length rapidly. "Come," she whispered. Her voice was low and sultry, and with that encouragement, he exploded into her hand. His chin came down and he watched his cock lurch between her fingers as his seed hit the water and moved away in a silver swirl.

He turned to her, laughing and feeling a little breathless. "Where did you learn to do that?" he asked, not sure he wanted to know. For all he knew, she did this for a living.

"In prison," she replied.

Chapter Four

The smile left his face as he was left completely stunned. Why did that hurt? And why did he feel like he could kill a man?

She shook her head. "It's not as bad as you think. The guards weren't allowed to touch me."

That would be unusual, he thought. In any prison.

"But one of the guards liked to jerk himself while he watched me. I watched him back."

It should have sounded hard, that statement, but her words were weighted with guilt—as though the fault was hers—and his heart went out to her. Her accent was slightly foreign, with a mild slurring cadence that softened every syllable, yet lingered to sharpen every word that contained the letter 't'. "I'm sorry," he whispered and drew her into his arms.

She gave him a startled look, uncomfortable with his sympathy. "I'd never seen a man before, but—" there was a hint of laughter in her eyes "—he didn't appear to have much to work with. Not nearly as much as you." She paused for a moment's reflection. "And he'd be lost next to your brother."

Davik laughed. "All men are lost next to my brother. Warrik didn't hurt you, did he?"

She shook her head quickly. "Thank you," she said. "For helping me. It was..." Words seemed to fail her.

He raised her chin. "You couldn't have done it without me?" He gave her a small smile followed by a small kiss. Or at least it was meant to be a small kiss, but neither of them could leave it alone and kept returning to it, just when it appeared to be finished. This time when she washed him, he didn't mind the cool water on his well-used cock. Her hand was in his as they climbed the slope back to the inn. Having just been hand pumped, he should have felt a little juvenile, and perhaps he did—but not in a bad way. Rather, he felt like a boy with his first girl. He stopped her just outside the inn, pulling her into him, and put a final kiss on her lips. Davik pushed the door open and they went in to join Warrik.

In the dawn, Davik woke on the mat next to his brother and rolled in his direction. Warrik's naked body was wrapped possessively around the girl, his eyes closed in sleep, but her dark eyes were open and sought his. He smiled at her as she carefully disengaged a hand from his brother and stretched it out toward him. He met her halfway and curled a finger around one of hers.

When Warrik woke, he lifted the girl and placed her on her knees between his legs, then drew his own knees up on either side of her. His massive cock lolled at rest against his thigh. "It's all yours darling," he said, scooting back to recline against a trunk and stuffing pillows behind his back. "See if you can stir things up." He smiled, pleased with his own wit. "Stir until thickened. Use your imagination, darling." When she hesitated, he prompted her. "Or your sweet, sexy mouth." He punched some more pillows behind his neck so he could watch her and smiled lazily at his brother.

Davik felt his stomach tighten. He didn't feel at all like eating, but he pulled on his breeks and headed for the door to order the guard change and arrange firstmeal.

"Where are you going?" his brother challenged him.

It was an effort to turn and face Warrik. An effort he didn't understand. "I'll only be an instant," he offered in surly tones then pushed through the door. Outside the inn, he scraped a hand through his hair and motioned one of his captains over.

* * * * *

With a contented sigh, Warrik stretched like a big cat and watched the mass of black hair in his lap, felt her lips on him. His dick responded to her hesitant tongue with pleased surprise and growing volume. A sound of deep, male satisfaction rumbled in his chest. "Lip service," he murmured. "Just what I had in mind." His eyes traveled down her body; her legs were tucked beneath her, her weight on her shins. "Ah, no, sweetheart. On your knees." His eyes went to the door. "On your knees for Davik. Quickly now, before he gets back."

She raised the back of her body with her knees.

"That's better," he said approvingly. "Move your knees apart a bit more. That's it, darling."

* * * * *

Davik came though the door and groaned when he saw her body waiting for him. Stumbling backward, he dropped into a chair. Warrik shot his brother a grin, then his eyes widened when the girl's mouth closed around his cock.

Davik felt like he was trying to breathe in a vacuum; he simply could not get a breath. The sight of her sex cocked, primed and canted into position was a dream-come-true—or at least almost. For a strange, sudden instant Davik wished he could be alone with her—or have her to himself—he wasn't sure which. It was a novel idea. He and Warrik had been sharing women since…well, they'd always shared.

He watched the girl's head in his brother's lap while Warrik gently gathered her hair away from her face and collected it in a bunch above her head, holding it like a spray of darkly contrasting flowers. "You don't have to be that gentle," he was telling her.

"Mount her, Davik," Warrik said, then watched his brother hesitate. "Mount her. She wants you. Don't you sweetheart?" he murmured. "Do it for her. A little nudge is just what she needs to give her confidence."

Davik gave his brother an accusing stare.

He grinned slowly, "If you won't do it for her, do it for me. A little nudge from behind and she'll be swallowing my cock whole." He gave a little gasp. "Never mind," he groaned. "Ah, Mithra, girl. I didn't mean to criticize. No-no-no sweetheart. Not your teeth."

Davik didn't want to—well he did want to—but either way, he couldn't help himself. He was out of the chair and moving toward the invitation she presented on her knees. He dropped to his knees behind her, his knees on either side of her calves. Reverently, he palmed the back of her thighs smoothing his hands up over the curves of her behind, pulled her cheeks apart and settled his growing erection into her groove. He felt her warmth envelope him right through his breeks, felt his steel stretch and grow into her crease as his hands slid to the front of her thighs. Pulling her into him tightly, he rocked against her, rubbing his length into the saddle between her cheeks.

It felt too good to stop there.

He shot a look at his brother, who still held the girl's hair in his big fist. Warrik watched her head with eyes half-closed. "That's it darling," he murmured. "Right there. Give me your tongue right there."

Davik pulled his body away enough to slip his hand between her legs, carefully stroking her with a light touch. He didn't want to surprise her and he certainly didn't want to set her teeth on edge; not with The Heir's entire future so close to those teeth. When he was sure she was comfortable with the presence of his hand, he dropped a tentative finger into her slot to test her, ran it over her clitoris and down to her opening, easing his finger inside. He was surprised when she gave his finger a wet welcome; he'd hardly started on her. She was ready. Ready for a man. Wanted a man—thrusting on her.

It was enough for him. His restraint was beginning to shatter as his panicked hand fumbled to open his breeks and pull his cock into play. He wanted to forge into her and fill her with his thick hot steel, feel her fire banked hot and tight around him. Instead, with his steel in his hand, he slipped between her legs, not inside her. The thick tip slid up and along her slit, spitting in its excitement, his ejaculate easing the way. He heard her murmur and smiled, knowing her sigh was for him. He withdrew slowly and with a hand holding his tip tight against her, thrust his cock-head along her rut again. She gasped.

Warrik groaned. "Don't stop now sweetheart," he begged the distracted girl. "Ah please, just a little more. Just a little." Davik slowed his action so the girl could concentrate on The Heir again. Which she apparently did, judging from the look on Warrik's face, but at the same time she was bringing her rounded derriere tightly into his lap. Questingly. Beseeching his input. Begging him to reassert himself.

He inserted himself.

Penetrating her all the way to her limit.

She cried out, causing Warrik to just about go mad. With his knees still bent, he threw himself forward and curled his long torso over her. Davik watched his brother's tawny mop mix with the dark cascade he still held in his fist. With the black and white bouquet against his lips, Warrik came into her mouth; his head bowed over hers.

At the same time, she was stretching her bottom to meet and absorb Davik's every thrust. He moved his hand to her rise, covered it with his hand, firmly settled the heel and length of his thumb above her rise while his fingers curled between her legs, and rubbed the top of her crotch, the tempo of his hand matching the action of his thrusting hips. When he heard her whimpering sob and felt her start into her arrival, he drove in deep and held — rock hard against her core — while her sheath swallowed around him in a convulsive gulp, reopened and swallowed again. And again. He whimpered himself; then his hands snatched at her hips and he pistoned against her backside, ramming his steel to the hilt four more times before he jettisoned inside her in a scalding rush.

Chapter Five

Davik put down his pen about noonday, realizing he had accomplished little in the hours since dawn. Outside, at a distance, he could hear Warrik's booming voice as he drilled the men. Normally, he would be there also, but he had stayed behind—ostensibly to write up his weekly requisition. Ostensibly, he hadn't accomplished a damn thing. He was keenly aware of the girl's presence. When her silk skirt rustled, he used the excuse to look up at her.

He'd have used any excuse.

She was a distraction, he thought as he watched her beside the window, gazing out into the street. A small frown creased her forehead.

"What's your name?" he asked, suddenly wanting very much to know. Her eyes left the window and she returned him a quiet look. "I want to know what to scream out in the middle of my release." He grinned. "My name's Davik," he reminded her. "Should you ever need it."

She gave him a very small smile. "I know."

"What's your heritage?"

"Why do you care?" she challenged him quietly.

He returned her challenge with a teasing smile. "I don't believe a man can be in love with a woman he hardly knows."

She ignored this bit of flattery. "My heritage is the same as yours."

"You don't look like a Khal. Not even a North Country Khal."

"Mixed blood," she replied. "Khallic, Westerman, Yute, Agryppan."

"Westerman," he said. "That would explain the hair and eyes. And can you see in the dark?"

"Better than you, I would guess."

"But Westerman are fair-skinned. White." His eyes skimmed her brown limbs, but he was seeing—courtesy of his vivid memory—the scars on her back. "Did you deserve those stripes on your back?"

He watched her shoulders rise in a shrug. "Probably."

"Were they given you in prison?"

She nodded. "For stealing."

"Food?" he ventured, wanting to martyr her.

"Diamonds," she returned.

He whistled. "Where were you imprisoned?"

She was a long time answering, watching the hem of her skirt. "Taranis," she said finally and raised her eyes to his. "Your father's prison."

The space between his eyebrows closed in a grimace. He'd have that question back, he thought, and made a face of regret. "My father's a stern man. A hard man," he said flatly. "I'm sorry you got caught, then."

"No more than I," she stated. "I was fourteen."

Davik blinked before staring into the middle distance. "You're...you're not...you're the girl who robbed Fastig." He refocused on her in wonder. "His wife's diamond set..." his voice trailed away.

She returned him a look without expression. "You've a good memory."

"That was...a life sentence," he said slowly.

She nodded. "I lost five years of my life...and the young man who helped me escape."

Davik shook his head at the ground. "It's hard to imagine you—a reckless thief. You seem so—subdued."

"I was a wild kid." Her eyes held his. "Five years cured me of that."

Ouch, he thought. His eyes returned to his papers on the table. That was well done, he thought cynically. He'd gained a lot of ground—and dug a hole in it big enough to bury his whole damn family. She probably hated them. Fourteen! And five years—her entire adolescence lost in a rash act of youth. "Things will be different...one day," he said. "When Warrik takes the throne." It sounded lame, he knew, and he looked for a cynical response from her; instead she smiled. It was a warm, fond smile and that bothered him as much as anything else, because he knew that smile was for his brother.

"How long have you and Warrik been...sharing women?"

He put his hands behind his head and leaned back in his chair. "A long time. A long time," he repeated. "The first time? I couldn't bear to hear the poor girl whimper. Not that she didn't want Warrik," he explained quickly. "She'd followed him to his rooms. Only Warrik is so big, and she was so young. 'Course back then, we were young too."

"How did you know what to do?"

"I'd read. A lot."

"What did you read?!" she exclaimed, her voice a warm chuckle.

"Everything. Everything I could get my hands on. My father has an extensive library." He looked at her and grinned. "Lots of diagrams," he teased. "Stuff from the orient." He winked significantly then shrugged. "Literature. Poetry. I can recite all thirty-two verses of Morghan on the gates. Maps. Science. The latest advances in Arithmetic's."

"History of war? Decisive battles?"

He gave her a pleased smile. "Especially the more recent stuff. Chay; Morghan's general. 'How to Decimate the Enemy in One Easy Lesson'. The things she accomplished with the Maghmarin brothers! Peer, Poul, Petr. The raids they pulled off! I could wish I'd been there." Davik warmed to his topic. "It's rumored she had Slurian blood. If true, it might account for some of her success."

"Slurian descent isn't something anyone would admit to, is it?"

Davik shook his head. "Certainly not back then. Perhaps not even now. The word 'slur' has become synonymous with the worst kind of insult.

"Slurians were feared and envied by men of other races; for this reason they were attacked and slaughtered. Wiped out. They were accused of controlling men's minds. In reality, they could only sense others' feelings. Unable to talk or produce any sound, the people of the Dark Isles communicated amongst themselves without speech." Davik gave an impatient look of dissatisfaction. "There was additional reason for men to envy them; as lovers they were supposedly unmatched. It was said they could physically touch with their minds; touch in an entirely intimate sense."

"And that fact led to another excuse to hate the Slurians. Because after forcing you to mate—supposedly against your will—and bewitching you with unparalleled sex, you could never leave them and live." Davik snorted with cynicism.

"It was believed that after mating with a Slurian you couldn't live without him—or her. I mean you couldn't live! That, if separated, you would die, and horribly. Of course, that wasn't true either. Slurians could mate without problem with those of other races. They were only bound after mating with those of their own race."

"At any rate, Chay may have had some paranormal abilities—like sensing her opponents' intentions—but I don't think that was the only reason for her success in battle."

The girl nodded. "Element of Surprise. Chay's opponents constantly underestimated her and, as a result, were caught off guard. But then Chay had a weapon most others wouldn't willingly use. She'd risk her life...just to get her own way," she said. "At least up until her first child was born, anyway."

Davik stared his surprise at her. But the girl continued.

"In addition, she could sacrifice one man's life to save three, come to the decision quickly under extreme conditions, and never look back with regret. I'm not sure I could do that," she said quietly.

Davik closed his mouth when he realized his jaw was hanging. "You've read Chay? You've read Vauchn's memoirs?"

She looked at the ground without answering. "Did you know she had total visual recall?"

Intrigued, he nodded his head slowly.

"Handy skill," she said. "Almost as useful as true intelligence." She continued. "You and your brother make an effective combination—of skill and intelligence. He has the strength and skill. You have the brains."

"On and off the battlefield," Davik agreed amiably, then cast a glance over his shoulder and shot her a warning look. "But don't tell Warrik I said so. He'd beat the shit out of me!"

He watched her laugh and something warm shot through his system like an infusion of strong spirit. It was her first laugh.

"Warrik is so big," he returned to the subject at hand. "Of course you know that. But the real problem is he refuses to kiss anyone—anywhere. Most women have trouble getting started without a little…romance. Of course, with Warrik, a woman needs a great deal of romance."

"That's where you come in."

"That's where I come in—and, hopefully, that's when the woman comes."

"Does he not like kissing, then?"

"He thinks germs are spread through mouth contact. He doesn't even kiss Mother. Although, I don't kiss Mother either, come to think on it." He made a face. "She's a bit of a tyrant."

She smiled at him.

"Does it…bother you? Being shared?"

She seemed surprised he had asked. She frowned. "Not as much as I thought it would."

"What's your name?" he asked again. When she didn't answer, he found himself standing beside her, not quite aware of how he'd gotten there. He turned her to face him and lifted her chin. "It's only a name. Is it so much to give?"

Her dark eyes were screened as she avoided his gaze. "Petra," she said with obvious reluctance.

"Petra." He accepted the name with pleasure, then cocked his head. "Doesn't that mean rock, in the original tongue? Hard name for such a delicate creature."

"Hard name," she agreed, and he thought her expression troubled. "It's a family name. I'm named for one of my father's uncles. He had no children of his own." She gave him a worried look. "And I am not so delicate."

"No?" He ran the back of his fingers down the curve of her cheek, then his thumb over her lower lip. With his other hand at the nape of her neck, he raised her lips to his.

"Getting started without me?"

Davik jumped as though someone had slammed a door on his fingers — or some other extremity.

Warrik strode through the door and laughed at his brother's startled expression, threw himself in a chair, and started yanking off his boots. "Missed you at practice today," he teased his brother.

With a sheepish smile, Davik dropped his hands to his sides and crossed the room to join his brother. "I'll ride the lines with you this afternoon," he offered.

"How about you ride the lines without me, and I'll take over for you here?"

The two men grinned at each other. Shaking his head, Davik grabbed the heel of his brother's proffered boot. "How about we give the girl the afternoon off," he suggested as he pulled on the boot. "She'll get enough of us tonight."

Chapter Six

After grabbing a bite, and filling their water skins, the two men left to ride the sentry lines; it was late afternoon when they returned. "Roasted duck!" Warrik was pleased and surprised when he entered the inn. He looked at his brother.

"I sent some men upstream to hunt. I thought it would be a nice change."

Warrik crinkled a smile in the girl's direction and nodded knowingly, then grabbed her and placed her on his knee before he tucked in to the meal.

Davik didn't use the girl's name during the meal. He loved his brother — but — if The Heir would know her name, he could find it out himself. Surreptitiously, he watched the girl on his brother's knee and wondered how she had spent the afternoon, concerned that she might be bored. He should have offered her his books, he realized. Apparently she read, how else could she have known so much about Morghan's general? And that was a surprise — the fact that she could read. Most people couldn't — there was no shame in it — it wasn't like there were enough books in the world to make reading worthwhile. Considering what he knew about her past — being a thief and having spent five years in prison — it would be all the stranger if she could read. He would have to learn more about her, he decided, so he could arrange for her to be entertained, engaged, or at least occupied.

His eyes fell to the fine silk skirt she wore, the clean white bodice. Though plain, her doeskin boots were particularly nice work. She had carried five gold, a respectable sum. Evidently, she was a woman of means, or was wedded to or belonged to a man of means. He found he didn't like those last two ideas so he cast them aside, arguing that a wealthy man would have given her jewelry, and she wore none.

A woman of means then. The unwed daughter of a wealthy merchant. Yes, this was an idea he could work with, although she was a bit old to be unwed. Still. Men died. All the time, in fact. A young widow perhaps.

At any rate, a woman of means. Women of this sort usually spent their spare time weaving, sewing, knitting, embroidering. And yet her hands were rough, he realized, backtracking through his memory. He had taken her hand as he led her to the river last night. Rough for a woman's hands at any rate, as though she worked for a living.

And she was not so delicate, she had insisted. He was forced to revise his picture.

He didn't like the revision.

A well paid working woman. He blinked back an image of the girl shrugging off her bodice as though it were her job. A concubine? A prostitute? His eyes cut to the woman on his brother's lap. How much would a man pay for a woman like that? Mentally, he made some assumptions, tallied up some numbers then doubled the sum to include his brother's tab. At the rate they were going, they'd empty the treasury at Taranis long before they were done with her.

But she was fleeing the city. Her clothing would suggest she had left the city in a hurry, as would the fact that she apparently hadn't had time to collect food or water. Either that or she hadn't planned on going far. Perhaps she was—

His brother was wiping his hands on a rag, he realized, and he watched The Heir push back his chair. "Coming Davik?" he asked. Grabbing the girl's wrist, he went through the door.

Warrik headed through the camp toward the river, dragging the girl behind him. Davik followed, dragging his feet.

The girl turned her head as they passed an open shelter where a couple was on their knees, rutting in the shadows. Warrik watched her face with amusement. "Take it inside, Jak," he threw toward the shelter. He laughed at the reproachful look the girl shot him. "What! Can I help what wedded people do? You'd think they'd get tired of each other after ten years. It's Melani's fault, really. She deliberately provokes him. Deliberately!"

By the time Davik reached the river, Warrik had the girl stripped and pinned against the smooth cliff face, his hard body holding hers against the stone at his elevation. His forearms supported her open thighs while his hands clutched the round cheeks of her bottom. Davik watched Warrik's muscles ripple in his naked flanks, watched his cock slide out of her an inch, gleaming with her moisture. With eager hunger, Warrik forged back into her. Davik felt his stomach clench in a cold fist.

What was wrong with him? He wanted to turn and leave but the girl's clenched jaw and closed eyes forestalled him as Warrik banged her hard against the stone. "You'll break her back against that rock," Davik said irritably.

Warrik didn't cease in his motion. "Don't criticize unless you're willing to help," he panted.

Davik stared at them a moment longer. Then he walked over and leaned back on the rock wall beside them. "Give her to me."

Warrik lifted her into Davik's arms, never missing a stroke. Supporting the length of her thighs with his forearms, Davik had to bend his knees a bit to bring the girl to his brother's ramming elevation. Releasing his grip on the girl, Warrik planted his hands on the rock either side of his brother's head. Davik's hands were near the back of her knees as Warrik flexed his knees to thrust into her. Increasing the tempo and force, Warrik hammered the girl into Davik, and Davik back against the rock, the power of Warrik's thrusts punching him into the cliff. Like a winded warhorse, the big blonde's breath blasted from his chest; his eyes were shut, his teeth in his lower lip. Davik inched the girl's knees up with each thrust until they were tucked into his brother's armpits. Her head dropped back onto his neck and he felt her body attempt to arch within the tight confines of two hard male bodies. He pressed his lips against her ear, then followed with the tip of his tongue.

"Are you ready darling?" he breathed into her ear. "Are you ready? Say when Petra. Say when and we'll make it perfect." She murmured into his neck. "Say when, Petra," he reminded her. He watched her take a few more thrusts.

She whimpered and her head began to toss. "No," she moaned, her voice thick and honey-sweet. "No-no-no-no…"

"Now Warrik." Holding the girl tightly, he leaned forward, bringing her weight down brutally on The Heir's massive steel, watched the pair strain together a long instant, and felt her shudder, her body a captured wave in his arms.

"Davik." She whispered his name into his neck, a faint prayer of thanks. He should have smiled, but he felt like crying. He squeezed his eyes shut and hid his face in her hair.

His eyes opened when Warrik rumbled his exhausted laughter against her temple. Pulling her out of Davik's arms, he crushed the girl in a hug, and laughed at his brother. "How can you do that without getting hard?" he asked.

"I can't," Davik responded sullenly.

"Hang on. I'll wash her for you." He carried her down to the river, threw her in, and dove in behind her.

Resentfully, Davik watched them resurface together. If he had any pride, he'd leave.

Evidently he didn't have any.

He did, however, have an extremely irate dick that would give him no end of grief should he walk away at this point.

He watched the pair slosh out of the river together. With a hand on the girl's bottom, Warrik pushed the girl toward his brother then turned into the setting sun and stood, eyes closed, reveling in the late golden rays that slanted over his huge frame. Like a god, Davik thought. His brother was like a god. How could a man compete with that! He had never tried before. Never wanted to before.

The girl stood uncertainly on the bit of sandy bank, looking from one man to the other. Naked and splendid, she had to be Warrik's counterpart, his perfect match in the near-immortal department. Where he was polished ivory, she was burnished bronze. Where he was glowing gold, she was glistening jet shot with white quartz. She matched his sparkling aquamarine with opaque lapis. And where he was the exuberant day, she was the sultry night. They were made for each other, Davik realized with a pang. And he was out of his league.

Warrik strode across the sand, pulled on his breeks and threw his wet hair behind his back. "Need help getting started, Davik?" He wore a teasing smile as he tugged his ties closed. "Petra?" He said her name slowly and, at the same time, shot his brother an accusing grin. He swept up his jerkin and weapons and backed away from them as he pointed at the girl. "Don't fall in love with him," he ordered, then turned and jogged up the slope.

Davik watched his brother's back. Warrik wasn't the musclehead some people took him for.

She gave him a warm smile as she twisted her hair over one shoulder. He tried to return the smile, but it wouldn't come forth. He watched her as she wrapped her arms around herself, which only served to lift her breasts into full prominence and the center of attention—the center of his attention, at any rate. As he stood with his back against the cliff, she regarded him submissively— waiting for him to command her, he realized. The idea annoyed him.

"Are you wed?" he asked abruptly. "Do you have a husband?" he added impatiently when she didn't answer.

She shook her head slowly.

"A lover?" Damn. His voice sawed in the middle of the question.

"Other than you?"

His stiff expression softened as his cock stiffened in inverse proportion.

"I don't want you to submit, Petra." Andarta! Where had that come from? It must have sounded strange to her. It sounded strange to him. His voice sawed unnaturally.

She gave him her curious attention.

He shook his head. "Oh, I would have you make love to me, yes. But I want you to do it willingly."

She lowered her eyes. "Isn't that what I've been doing? Submitting willingly?"

He nodded. He deserved that. "Now I want you to make love to me willingly, without submittal. Would you, were you given the choice?"

She raised her eyes and he'd hoped she'd smile, but her expression was haunted. That was the only word to describe it, he thought. That look tugged his heart right out of his chest. He closed the distance between them in three steps. "I'm sorry," he said into her lips. "It's too much too soon." He started a kiss that only meant to ask forgiveness. He was relieved when she apparently forgave him—for a very long time—and willingly as far as he could tell, in a kiss that lasted from there right through to completion. Neat trick. She was underneath him on the sand when his cock coughed and spewed his silver stream inside her tight channel. Covering her mouth with his, swallowing her cries, he held onto the kiss as she lurched beneath him, held onto the kiss until her body quieted and her lips resumed the kiss with tenderness and yielding gratitude.

Chapter Seven

"Sieging is a dull business."

"They can't last much longer."

"Sieging is a dull business," Warrik repeated, determined to have his say. "Maybe that's why...all I can think about is sex." He turned to his brother. "Does she have the same effect on you?"

Davik stared at his brother. They'd left camp early and taken a mounted unit to meet the pay wagon reported en route by their scouts. The dawn was gray and cool and wreathed in wispy fog.

"When I'm fucking her I feel like..."

Davik waited politely about two instants. "A Prince? A King?" he suggested snidely.

"Don't mock me, brother, or I'll cut you off when I come into my inheritance."

Davik grunted. "I don't need your money, Warrik."

The Heir shook his head. "I wasn't talking about money."

"Oh." Davik made a face. "I don't suppose you're talking about my head, either."

With a hard grin, Warrik shook his head again. "...and when she comes on me! When her body ripples and her tight slot clamps along my dick...it feels like my soul is being sucked right out through my cock." Warrik halted, pleased with this imagery. "What is it about the girl?"

"She's quiet," Davik said dryly.

"That's it!" Warrik snapped his fingers. "Good quality in a woman." He grinned at his brother and went on. "I want her at least four times a day, and several times at night," he admitted. "I'd take her that often, too if you'd let me."

"You'd hurt her."

"I'd hurt her," Warrik agreed. "I'd probably hurt myself. She's so—willing."

"She's just keeping her word," Davik grumbled. "She agreed to submit because she didn't want to be bound—or raped."

"We weren't going to rape her," Warrik protested.

"She didn't know that."

Warrik looked surprised.

Their horses vied for position and Davik reined his mount back. "We took her captive. She had no choice! She has none now."

"I thought it was conjugal. Conjugal sex," his brother affirmed with bewilderment. "Or is that what you do to verbs?"

"Conjugate is what you do to verbs. Conjugal is what you do to your wife."

Warrik was silent a while. "One of us should wed her," he said, finally. "So I can conjugate without guilt."

The idea of wedding took Davik unawares. "Which—one of us?"

"You," he said decisively and grinned.

Davik made a great show of considering this. "If I wed her, I might not want to share her anymore," he pointed out.

Warrik gave this his shocked consideration. "What? You mean, like not at the same time? We'd take turns?"

"No. I mean, like you go find your own wife and leave us alone." Davik grinned as his gelding moved forward a few impatient steps.

"You're kidding Davik. You're kidding, right?" Warrik urged his horse to join his brother's.

* * * * *

The girl *was* quiet, he realized. Why should he find that interesting? Probably just the mystery, he thought. That haunting face. That haunted expression that made her seem so vulnerable. Why should vulnerability engage his interest so strongly? What was it that haunted her? Stupid question. Her years in prison, no doubt. And yet she talked about those years calmly, without rancor.

"Ride the lines today," Davik suggested abruptly. "That will keep your mind off her for most of the day."

Warrik nodded glumly. "And keep me from pumping myself dry between her legs. Mother will be furious if I pump all my silver into her slot and don't have enough left to produce an heir. You coming?"

Davik shook his head, his eyes already turned in the direction of camp. What was it that haunted her? Was there something she was bent to do, some purpose that was interrupted when they'd taken her captive? Or was she in some kind of danger?

* * * * *

Davik burst through the inn door before the day had got properly started. "Let's get out of here," he said. He threw a small pair of doeskin breeks in her direction then went outside to pick out a mare for her.

They raced through the lines without halting; he let her take the lead, confident his mount could catch hers if the need arose. Urging the mare into a stretching gallop, she streaked toward the foothills. He followed her up an open wooded slope, out across a meadow, finally dropping into a winding valley that led to a minor mountain thrusting into the sky like a rebellious fist. She slid off her mount and threw the reins around a branch. Without waiting for him, she started up a narrow fault that split the giant rock. The breeks were a good idea, he thought as he watched her derriere rising above him. When she disappeared from view, he hauled himself up the last few feet to burst upward into a complete, perfect, panoramic view of Northern Khal. Breathless from the climb, he turned in awed silence as she grinned at him.

"You've been here before."

She nodded.

And she'd spent a great deal of time in the saddle, too, he thought. Her eyes shone, as her face was turned northeast to the mountains. "You're a quiet woman," he started.

She nodded. "Habit. Five years of silence will do that to a girl."

Ouch and Damn, he thought. He fell into that one. Someone ought to kick him from here to Hadi's Gates. And yet, she had spoken without bitterness. She turned and he followed her to a small bit of meadow spread like a green blanket on a gentle slope. "Where were you heading when my men stopped you?"

"Leaving the City. I didn't get far."

"They didn't…harm you — "

"No, of course not," she said quickly.

He smiled at this stout endorsement of his soldiers. She dropped onto the grass and he threw himself down beside her. "Where were you going?"

"I have a grandmother in Thrall."

"Any other family?"

"One brother still living. My parents died when I was ten. They had a farm in Northern Khal. Near the coast."

He rolled from his stomach to his back and put his hands behind his head. Drawing words out of her was like trying to pluck tears from the heavens. "That's good. That must have been all of ten words. Go on."

"Go on?"

He smiled up at her. "Go on, as in keep talking. I like the sound of your voice.

"You promised to submit," he reminded her when she wasn't forthcoming. "Do you sing, play an instrument? Can you read, write. What do you read? What is your favorite song? If you can string a dozen words together, we'll call it a conversation."

She gave him a stinging smile. "I can sing," she answered, "although I doubt many people would enjoy it if I did. I play the lyre and the pipes fairly well, I suppose. My favorite song is an old Slurian melody. A sort of a love song."

"The one about the pyramids?" The stinging smile warmed a great deal. "I read it somewhere, but I've never heard it sung."

"It needs a lyre," she said. "If you can find me one, I'll attempt it for you. I like to read," she continued, "when I have time."

When she had time, he wondered. What did that mean? "Poetry," he guessed, disingenuously. "Romance?"

She shook her head. "History. I've read everything written about Conan, the Warrior King."

Everything written, he mused. And only a farmer's daughter—who had spent five years in prison. When had she read?

"How of you, Davik? You have other brothers?"

"Davik? Not Prince Davik or My Prince or even My Lord."

She smiled. "It's a little late to stand on ceremony. But if you wish, I can call you My Prince. Of course you won't know to which Prince I'm referring in the middle of my—"

He laughed. "So you do possess a sense of humor."

"It's a bit rusty," she admitted.

"A bit! It's so rusty it's practically seized." She smiled at him reproachfully. "We'll give it some oil and get in running again," he said, patting her knee. "Yes, to answer your question, I have three other brothers, all younger than Warrik and I, as well as two older sisters."

"Your sisters are older?"

"Father's a bit of a chauvinist. Insists on one of his *sons* inheriting the throne—unlike Morghan, who gave his daughter, Tien, the throne even though her brother was older."

"Halthar didn't wish to rule."

Davik nodded, impressed with her grasp of history.

Morghan was the Skraeling half-breed from overseas who befriended the Prince of Amdahl and inherited his throne when the Prince died. He earned the alliance of Agryppa when he helped drive the marauding Thralls from that country. Following the Thralls across the Middle Sea, he subdued that unruly country and brought it under his dominion. Wedding the Agryppan Queen, the two monarchs introduced self-rule to their combined countries of Amdahl, Agryppa and Thrall.

Morghan was a giant. Both in stature and in deed. Garrik smiled. And that was before Chay — his general — came on the scene.

Chay, a young soldier in Morghan's army caught his eye when she — through a series of unusual circumstances — inadvertently and unintentionally freed the slaves of Cymra, forcing the Cymran Prince to grant the slaves citizenship. Morghan and his wife, Tahrra, were tickled with this development; they'd had a long-running disagreement with Prince Gryfudd. The young soldier was working her way up through the ranks when the Maydayn blight swept across Skythia, threatening Thrall and the civilized world.

Morghan thwarted the massive Maydayn invasion when he promoted the girl and gave his new captain her head. Crossing the intraversible Labyrinth, Chay dove behind enemy lines with the Maghmarin brothers, causing complete and utter chaos. At the peak of this chaos, Morghan attacked the Maydayn army and drove them back into Skythia and beyond. Chay was eventually promoted to general and the continent enjoyed a long peace.

Davik shook his head. History had overlooked Chay—somewhat—because she was largely a peacetime general; historians had missed the fact that Morghan's general was *the reason* there was peace.

Late in life, Morghan left his throne to his daughter and sailed overseas with his wife. Tien had already proven herself—if you could call it that—when she went alone into Skythia to rescue her lover. Looking for an army to aid her in this purpose, she freed the slave miners at Black Flats. The last man up on the lift was Wyeth; the man she sought. Together they fought their way back home, forging a growing army out of the slaves they released en route. Skythia was eventually brought under Tien's rule and joined the Kingdoms of Amdahl, Agryppa, and Thrall, today referred to as Greater Thrall or Thrall And Etc.

The Old Queen still ruled. Her children, like her brother, showed little interest in ascension. Tien's brother had spent most of his youth on the Middle Sea with Morghan's admiral, Venatir. He, in turn, had served as Tien's admiral until his death. But Prince Halthar's reluctance to rule was a little known fact.

"How of you? Would you rule?"

The girl's question brought Davik back to the present. He shook his head. "Warrik will rule."

"But you will advise him."

He wasn't pleased with the direction the conversation was tacking. "Only when he wants advice. I've no wish to be King. I love my brother," he said brusquely. "Why did you leave the city?" he asked abruptly.

Like a douse of freezing water, his question seemed to suck the air out of her. She lowered her wide eyes, but not before they registered the horror of something previously forgotten, and just remembered.

"What is it?" he asked with alarm. "Petra? What is it?" She lurched to her feet and he followed her, scooping her into his arms as her fists fought him away. He forced his lips on hers, forced her to accept his kisses as though that could make her accept his care and protection.

Hadi's Saints!

A glimpse of brown wool out-of-place on gray stone had him holding his breath. The man must have followed them up the gap. Without bothering to conceal himself, the bowman was on one knee, about sixty paces distant, his bow drawn on the girl's back.

Chapter Eight

Adrenalin surged into arms and legs, pricking him to action as he dragged the girl out of the line of fire and threw himself on her. They hit the ground as the arrow hissed into the space they had just vacated. With recoiling reflexes, he was up and sprinting toward the bowman, too angry to be sensible. But with enough sense to realize it would be a close thing. Behind him, the girl screamed, ordering him to stop. His steel was out and in his hand as the arrow was nocked. The bowstring was drawn back. Then his steel was in the man's neck, hewing a wound large enough to end his life.

He wasn't satisfied with that.

The steel swung; a splashing red trail marked the path of his blade as it slashed and hacked at the man already dead. He gave the bloody remnants a final kick then swung around to locate the girl and assure himself she was unharmed, still cursing what was left of the pronking dead bastard on the ground. Having followed Davik, she stood not three paces from him, her face pale, her wide eyes full of dread as she stared at what had recently been a whole man. She took a few faltering steps backward. Davik moved quickly to pull her face into his chest.

"Andarta and Mithra's Bastard Children Together! Are you alright?" Although pale, the girl did not tremble. He turned her away from the body and looked over her shoulder at the man. "North Country man," he muttered. "A friend of yours?"

She started in his arms but did not answer. What in Hadi's Name did that mean?

Was this what haunted her? Was this what she feared? This man? "An angry lover?" he said jokingly, then swiftly lost his patience when the girl ignored his question. "Who then?"

She gave him a solemn, almost angry look. "He's a Northern Soldier. His name was Andrig." She pushed off from him and climbed back toward the gap.

"Are you going to tell me about it?" he called after her.

"No," she answered.

Swiftly, he moved to follow her.

Smoothly, she descended the gap, familiar with every hand and foothold while he ricocheted down behind her. She had her foot in the saddle loop when he caught up to her. Topped up with unspent rage and adrenalin, he dragged her from the horse and forced her to face him, then promptly forgot his purpose as her fists knotted into the front of his jerkin and jerked his lips onto hers.

Evidently the girl had some unspent passion of her own.

He loosed her with a shove and took two steps backward. He was too angry to take a woman. That is, too angry to take a woman without hurting her. She gave him a look not the least subdued, and he caught a glimpse of the wild kid she had once been, before her five years in prison—the girl she kept buried—and wished he'd known that girl. With two steps she closed the gap between them.

This time submittal was not an issue, unless it was his own. His anger was transmuted to awe in a body-chemistry reaction that produced measurable heat and an accompanying phase change in his solidifying cock. Her mouth twisted onto his as she energetically initiated their lovemaking, at which time he decided the breeks were not such a great idea after all. In fact, they presented such an awkward obstacle, he arrived at the conclusion that it was no wonder women were slow to undress men.

Not that breeks didn't work for men; they did. A man could perform adequately upon loosening a few ties. But a woman's prize was buried deeper; and it wasn't enough just to bare the prize—he tried that. The breeks had to come all the way down and off so her legs could be spread wide. And, oh Mithra, he wanted her legs spreading for him.

They had to come off.

The episode involving the bowman was shoved into a remote corner of his mind while he dealt with the very urgent problem of getting her breeks off and his cock out and settled between her legs. And of course, once that was settled, his problem became even more urgent as her legs spread to mount him and her body rocked to meet his in a long rippling wave. There is something distracting about a woman astride your loins, bending your steel to near snapping, he thought sublimely. Something that reduces all problems to one. He watched the woman on him as she rose on his cock and plunged back down along his length, watched as she took him in want. Watched with growing excitement as she got exactly what she wanted. Spine arched, head back and tossing, hair whipping about her face, she drove herself onto him. Ah, but a man could only take so much. His pleasure was expressed without words, sound wrenched from his lips in short hard bursts as his cock spat then surged into the suctioning void deep between her legs.

Afterward, when urgency had abated and they lay together settled and sated, he tangled his fingers into her hair. "Mithra, what did I do to deserve that?" he queried with a laugh. "Tell me, and I'll be sure to do it again."

He hadn't expected an answer and strained to pick up her muffled response. "I thought you would die," she said into his chest. "For two instants, I thought you would die."

She had never volunteered so much.

"It was a close thing," he admitted with pleasure. "I gained a fraction of an instant when the man hesitated. I don't think I was his first choice of target." He paused so she could add any speculation she might have, then continued when she offered none. "But he should have taken me out, if only to stop me."

Discussion of the bowman brought him back to earth with a jolt. If there were any other bowmen still around! Andarta! Startled into acute awareness, his senses raced. Nearby, the mare stamped impatiently. Aspen leaves rustled as they twisted in the breeze, masking the sound of potential approach. Rolling away from the horses, he dumped the girl off him, scanning the area as he rose from a crouch. Their two mounts remained standing where they had been left. A third horse stood off a ways, grazing; the bowman's mount, he had to assume.

Reassured they were alone, his eyes returned to the girl on the ground. Looking disheveled and used, she was lurching to her feet. She met his intent, assessing gaze with a return to wide-eyed vulnerability. Within her expression was a trace of hurt, he realized; she had mistaken his action for indifference.

He caught her to him quickly and pressed her up against him. He wanted to hold her now, while she was still naked and sex-damp, feel her every warm, strong curve against his skin, let her know it wasn't indifference that put her so abruptly on the ground. She pulled away from him and turned. He watched her back.

"Should I expect any more of your countrymen lurking about?" he asked, his question meant to be an explanation for his behavior.

She hung her head. "I don't think so."

He watched her as she pulled the tight breeks up her legs and tied the laces. Perhaps it was over then—whatever it was that troubled the girl—perhaps it was resolved with the bowman's death.

Upon their return to the inn, he opened a trunk of books for her and left her picking through them. He stepped outside and asked for his brother, then rode to find him.

* * * * *

"I sent Menlas and Jaym to bury the Northman."

"You shouldn't have killed him. I've a few questions I'd like to put to him."

"It was him or me."

"Oh! Well. Good choice then." Warrik gave his brother a sideways smile.

Davik grimaced. "I lost my head," he admitted grudgingly. "I was furious that someone would draw on her."

"Are you sure she was the target and not yourself?"

That stopped him. He stared at his brother while he reviewed his memory. "The arrow was drawn on her back when I pulled her aside. The bowman could have been waiting to loose on me. But then—he hesitated when I was between them." Davik shook his head. "You should have seen her face when she saw him! She knew him. Knew him by name. She went as white as milk." Davik thought a moment then continued. "But she was relieved I wasn't killed."

"You're sure," Warrik teased his brother.

"I'm positive."

Warrik nodded. "That puts you one up on me. Let's head back. I can't wait to get positive with her myself."

"Actually, I'm two up on you." Davik muttered behind his back.

The Heir turned slowly. "Really?" He frowned at his brother. "You know, we should spend more time together." Warrik's big destroyer jumped as Warrik spurred it forward. Davik's mount responded with a following lurch, but he reined the horse back. The tall gelding stepped out an intolerant circle as he watched Warrik fly toward camp.

He couldn't do it again, he realized. Could never do it again. Not with his brother—not with her.

He didn't want to share her anymore.

Holding the gelding to a constrained, unhappy walk, Davik followed his brother. Upon reaching the inn, he handed his reins to one of his men, glanced at the inn door, then turned to join his army in the kitchen tent.

Chapter Nine

The girl looked up from her book when the door slammed behind Warrik. For several moments, she watched the door. Finally, she turned her attention to The Heir. He'd thrown himself in a chair beside the table and was pulling off his gloves. When he asked for help with his boots, she wrestled with them while he shed his jerkin. One of his men delivered a platter of cold meat, bread, and mustard oil. And, with his usual enthusiasm, Warrik tore into the meal. When the man returned with a jug of ale, Warrik asked her to pour for him. His eyes cut to the door and he frowned for an instant then smiled as his eyes returned to the girl. He pulled her between himself and the table, reaching around her to feed himself. "Why don't you undress while we're waiting for Davik?" he suggested.

Slowly, she removed her clothing while The Heir ate. He stopped her several times, asking her to turn, or stretch her arms behind her head. Once he pulled her close between his legs so that her heavy breasts bumped soft against his face and he sucked in the warmth of her through his nose and into his lungs. When she was naked except for her boots, he stood to run a hand from her pelvic wing up to cup one of her breasts. Abruptly, he turned her around to face the table, pushing the food and papers to one side. "Put your elbows on the table," he commanded her with forced patience. "That's it." With his feet, he pushed her feet apart on the floor, then resumed his seat behind her. Having forgotten his meal, he viewed her in silent appreciation then cocked his head to one side. "Could you...darling..." He struggled with a breath. "Would you move your legs apart. Just a little more?" His breath released in a rush when she complied. "Ah, Mithra. You're a beautiful sight, Petra." His voice was getting thick, rough. "Turn around for me now, darling." As she straightened and turned, he lifted her and sat her on the edge of the table. Warrik's breath was working hard to get out of his chest as he swept the table clear with an arm that put papers and food on the floor together, his appetite now dwarfed by a deeper, more pressing hunger that rose between his legs. "Lie back, darling. Ah, Mithra and Donar, yes, like that." He reached for her ankles and put her feet up close to her bottom then pulled them apart. "That's it. Just like that." He backed into his chair, then pulled the chair closer to the table. Palming the front of his breeks, he groaned. Without realizing it, his hands went to his ties and he unlaced his breeks. "It looks like we're going to have to do this without Davik, sweetheart. You're going to have to help me Petra. Open your knees and show me just a little bit more. Just a little. That's it."

"Mithra," he cursed in a whisper as he stood. With sudden, rough impatience, he pushed her knees wide. Taking her hands, he pulled them down to the dark thatch between her legs. "Open your slot," he rasped. "Show me what to do. Where to touch you."

* * * * *

It was dark, the night half gone, when Davik opened the inn door and stepped inside. There was only a small lamp lit but it threw enough light for him to see his brother standing at the table edge, coupled with the girl, his cock rammed tight between her legs, his big hands clamped on her hips as she lay on her back, stretched across the table. The small gold light gleamed on his brother's exposed flanks, the hard muscles of his buttocks. Crossing the room quickly, Davik reached for a pillow and pushed it beneath the girl's head without meeting her eyes; he then stooped to rescue his maps and papers.

"Where have you been?" Warrik complained. "The girl could use your help."

For a moment Davik crouched motionless, back to the table, papers in his arms; then he dropped his scrolls as he stood and turned to the table. Lowering himself into a chair he put an arm over the girl and ran his hand into the hair at her temple. She averted her eyes, teeth in her bottom lip. With his hand, he turned her face and made her look at him. He gave her a warm smile. "Do you want help Petra?"

Her eyes were wide, her gaze beseeching.

She was so sweet. Even with The Heir slamming into her, she was sweet. Gone was the wildling, who had mounted him earlier in the day, exchanged for this vulnerable waif, sprawled naked and exposed on the table. He slid his hand down to cup the swell of her breast and placed his thumb against the quiet nub at its center. Starting a kiss, he felt her nub harden and grow, reacting to his kiss alone. He loved her nipples. They were small and dainty on modest brown aureoles placed at the tips of the fullest, proudest breasts he'd ever gotten his hands around. Gently, he rubbed the nub between his thumb and forefinger as he continued the kiss. With his eyes closed...he could believe they were alone together.

"I want her to come on me, Davik."

Warrik's words returned him to reality with a harsh jolt.

"I want the full fuck. I want her thrashing and moaning and screaming my name."

Davik winced. His brother could be so coarse. He shot a quick look at the girl, but her eyes were determinedly closed. Dark shadows hovered beneath her full lashes. "I'll see what I can do," he grated with cynical tone and real annoyance. Damn! He'd planned to avoid this. "Why didn't you do this earlier?"

"I did. But. It didn't work for her."

"You did — . When?"

"A few hours ago. We waited for you to join us…"

Davik cursed. "She must be tender. Slow down, will you? You'll have her thrashing and moaning and screaming your name, alright — followed by curses." He gave her a final small kiss, then stood. Her body stretched out before him on the table, a feast he would normally lap up slowly. But tonight, he just wanted to get it over with. He frowned at the bruises beneath her pelvic wings where Warrik's thumbs had gouged her; his brother was too rough.

He should have been here. Recrimination was followed swiftly by frustration. He frowned at her legs, hanging off the table's edge. "Pick up her feet and put them on the table. No! Don't hold her ankles. They're…sensitive." He lowered his lips to her ear. "We'll make this quick, Petra," he whispered. "Come as soon as you can." Leaving one hand behind to fondle her nipple, he moved the other to the top of her cleft and pulled her open. His wet tongue slipped into her slot. Access wasn't very good, with Warrik ratcheting so near, but with his mouth sideways against her cleft, he alternately suckled, paused, then dabbed his tongue against the nub of her clitoris.

Warrik sucked in a breath. "That's better," he rasped. "That's slick." A deep guttural rumble rolled in his chest. "She's creaming on me."

Again Davik touched his tongue to her nub. And again. He heard her breath catch in her throat. He laid the side of his tongue along her slot and stroked. Her body shivered beneath his arm.

Pulling his hand from her breast, he slipped both hands gently between her legs, along the insides of her thighs, and flattened her folded legs against the table. Returning his lips to the top of her cleft, he kissed her hard. Responding with a throaty cry of anguished pleasure, she jumped into his mouth. Close enough. Sliding his arms under her legs, he curled them around her folded legs and pinned her open. He gave his brother a nod and her strong young body bucked beneath his arms while Warrik hammered her full throttle. There was thrashing and moaning and a great deal of noise, most of it on Warrik's part.

When Warrik pulled out, Davik scooped her up and cradled her in his arms as he dropped into the chair. Panting and pleased, Warrik pushed off from the table. "Your turn," he announced and moved to take the girl from his brother.

Davik shook his head quickly. Unconsciously, his hold on the girl tightened.

"I'm willing, Davik."

Warmth joined the surprise in his smile as he looked into her eyes. "I know you are," he said softly. "I know you're tired too, and I'm guessing you're sore as well." Not much of a guess; she'd been taken three times since noonday. He smoothed a thumb over her bruised flank while his eyes strayed to the food on the floor. "Have you eaten?"

"I wasn't hungry," she said quickly.

Too honest to lie, too noble to complain, he thought with irritation. He glared at his brother.

Warrik responded slowly, with guilty revelation. "I'm sorry girl. I didn't give you much of a chance, did I?"

"Her name's Petra," he grated through clenched teeth.

"I know that!" Warrik remonstrated, at a loss to understand his brother's ire.

"Is that all she is to you," Davik ground out, his anger accelerating. "Just a girl?"

"Brothers." Petra's smooth warm voice was a soothing balm. "Don't argue." She shifted in Davik's arms. "Take me to the river, Davik."

He struggled to subdue his anger, then threw it off with a lurch. He took in the girl's heavy eyelids and hesitated. He'd like to, knowing what she probably had in mind. He'd take anything, right now, to relieve the aching pressure throbbing along his length. "It's late. You're tired," he repeated. "Leave it until dawn."

"Take me to the river," she ordered quietly.

He told her to be quick and watched her from the bank, refusing to enter the water himself. He was irritated she'd forced him this far; she'd force him no further. As she lowered herself into the water, he watched her disappear beneath the smooth black surface. He was getting edgy before she finally resurfaced downstream. She disappeared again and he held his breath to see if he could match her for lung capacity, but found himself sucking for air just before she broke the surface. Almost immediately she went under again and he watched a point downstream where he expected her to surface.

Then, suddenly, it had been too long. Next thing he knew, he was splashing into the river, fully clothed, boots and all. He threw himself at the place he had last seen her, grappling at the bottom stones, kicking himself along, groping for her in the empty, obsidian water. She rose beside him, grasped his soaked jerkin in her fists, threw herself on top of him, and fixed her mouth on his. Flailing beneath her, he was swept a few paces further downstream before he came to a dredging halt and dragged her to her feet. "Don't *ever* do that again!" he gasped. "*Don't you ever* disappear like that."

Ignoring him, she returned her lips to his.

He pulled away and backed up a step. "Not tonight," he said, a sharp edge on each of his words.

She dropped to her knees and dragged his sopping breeks down with her. He was cold and wet and, as a result, not at all in the mood—until she sucked him into her mouth. Her palms dragged the length of his flanks then moved behind him and pulled his lower body tight against her mouth. He warmed up almost immediately. Groaning, he ran his hands into her wet hair. "Be quick, then Petra," he told her for the third time that night.

Chapter Ten

Somehow in the night, she'd worked herself out of The Heir's arms. No small task. Dawn found her long body snuggled against Davik's, her arms around his waist, her cheek against his chest. He shifted onto his side, stroking her hair. As she stirred into wakefulness, her hand wandered down his naked flank.

Then Warrik was awake. Warrik's big hand was suddenly between them as he gave the girl's breasts a cursory pass then quickly traveled between her legs. He was on his side, with his front against her back. He pulled her legs apart, put her knee high on his thigh, pulled her ankle behind his back and entered her.

Davik felt like winter water had been thrown on him.

But Warrik wasn't done stealing his girl. He rolled onto his back, taking the girl with him, though a part of her clung to his brother. He pushed her upright so she sat astride his loins and, with his hands on her ankles, coaxed her legs to fold underneath her, at his sides. When he had her where he wanted her, she was straddling him.

Warrik watched her back with half-closed eyes as he stretched into her. "Good dawning, darling," he rumbled.

Davik stared at them in frustrated disbelief.

She caught his gaze and looked quickly away.

Davik spared his brother a few seconds of his resentment, then reached for his clothes. The girl's eyes were still lowered. He watched her cheeks color as she moved obediently to satisfy The Heir, her expression part hurt and part guilt.

Mithra. Why should she feel guilty; this wasn't her fault. She didn't want to do this. They'd forced her into this. Taken her captive and made her their slave. They should have given her the choice. Should give her the choice now.

She didn't want Warrik. Didn't want him at all. God that he was—and The Heir to Khal—she didn't want him. She preferred…the lesser son. The revelation was accompanied with relief as well as shame. Guilt pricked him for his part in her sexual coercion.

Swamped with regret, he moved swiftly to her side. "Hey," he said softly, kneeling beside her and running his fingers into the hair above her ear. Her hand wrapped around his wrist and her face turned into his hand, but she didn't look at him. He tried to lower his face to hers, but it was awkward. He had to straddle his brother's legs to get to her. Catching her bottom lip with his finger, he nudged her lips up to meet his.

It was one of those kisses that starts out as minor earthwork; not meant to result in major earth moving. A little dozing, a little scraping, he'd not planned to re-contour her mouth completely. But, Mithra, the earth moved. Her lips were crushed and scraped and pushed up onto her teeth then dragged into his mouth. When he finally pulled away from her they were on their knees, his hands in her hair—fingers spread—manipulating her skull with both hands.

Breathlessly, they stared at each other a silent, longing moment, momentarily unaware of their surroundings.

"Don't mind me," Warrik was saying with amused indulgence.

The girl's eyes widened an instant before she lowered herself back onto The Heir's shaft.

Davik straightened on his knees, glancing down at his own steel with startled recognition. Shaking his head, he started to move away but the girl's arms wrapped around him, pulling him against her body as she slid vertically on his brother. By convenient chance, his cock was positioned to take maximum advantage of her deep, generous cleavage. When she eventually released his legs, he had decided he wasn't going anywhere after all. Lust spurted along his steel, tall and thick, pleasantly at first, then with growing insistence. He gazed down on her head fondly. With her hands cupping her heavy breasts, she pushed them up to crowd his sex. The slick silk of her skin seemed to touch him everywhere, or at least everywhere that mattered. He slid between her breasts as she moved on his brother.

This could almost work, he thought as he gave himself over to sensory appreciation that started and ended in the hot center of his sex. Allowing sensuality to burgeon, he watched his cock's response. This could almost work, he thought again. And then it almost did work, as he felt moist lips against his hood, swelling dark and needy between her breasts. At the same time, her hand rounded his testes. It was almost all over. He gritted his teeth as he stared down at her, only vaguely aware that neither her lips nor hands were anywhere near his sex. "Mithra," he breathed, blinking hard to hold back his arrival.

"Mithra!" Warrik exploded through clenched teeth at the same time. The girl's movement stopped as Warrik clutched at her hips and forced her down hard onto his steel. With strained expression and jutting cock, Davik waited in a red haze of blurred need, just about mad to take his own release. Her eyes were locked on his. She hadn't arrived with Warrik, he realized. He was glad.

But mostly he wanted to ream into her.

As Warrik's erection died inside her, the big man moved to sit behind her, supporting her head against his chest. Years of experience worked to smoothly slide the girl into position for his brother. Grasping her ankles, Warrik brought them all the way to her bottom. "Relax darling," he whispered. "Open your legs for Davik." Swiftly he moved her feet to the outside of his legs then ran his hands up to her knees, pulling her legs open.

With rigid arms supporting his weight either side of the girl, Davik rose on her and slammed into her. By now he had forgotten how this had all started, forgotten how Warrik had robbed him, stolen the girl from his arms. He was hardly even aware of his brother's presence or that his presence was an issue; he'd forgotten everything except the need to release inside her. Forgetting even to be gentle, he drove into her in pure frenzy.

Something wasn't right, he realized in the middle of that frenzy; her body, the sounds she was making. He stopped in mid-stroke though his angry cock chastised him with throbbing vigor. Checking her face, he cursed; he'd seen that look of panic before. "Warrik!" he croaked. "Her ankles. Release her ankles!" As if in response, she exploded beneath him, her body fighting to throw itself against his tip while at the same time threatening to thrash itself right off of his erection. Her violent contortions battered his steel cruelly—at gale force—and he could do nothing but ride the wave of her body, balanced on the edge of arrival. He balanced and teetered then went off the deep end as she sucked his release right out from under him. For a final long moment he was hard, strong and thick inside her, then his release charged through his cock in an angry torrent and raged into her.

Chapter Eleven

"Slavery's all well and good," Davik was saying, "for slaves." Warrik shot him a look of amusement as he directed two of the supply wagons down slope toward the bulk of his army. "But she's not a slave."

"Of course she is. She's our slave. Spoils of war; perfectly legal." Warrik grinned at his younger brother.

"She's one of our countrymen! Do you intend to enslave all the Northern Rebels when we take Veronix?"

"Only the women. All of them, if they're anything like her."

"She reads and writes and plays the lyre. She speaks"—he held up his fingers as he counted off—"Khallic, Agryppan, Thrallish, Yute, Rhyssian."

"Thrallish doesn't count as a language! They have—what—a vocabulary of twenty words!" Warrik shrugged at his brother's stubborn expression. "So she's a well-educated slave."

"She's read Chay!" The significance of this evidence was lost on The Heir. "Vauchn's memoirs were lost after his death. They've only recently come to light."

"And?"

"There can be only ten copies in the entire world, and she has read one of them."

Warrik shook his head. "Most like, she's heard the ballads, like everyone else."

"No! She knows details she could only learn from reading the memoirs. What does she call you?" Davik burst out in exasperation.

"What do you mean?"

"What does she call you? Sir? My Lord? Prince Warrik?" Warrik pointed the last wagon toward the inn while he thought about this. The two men turned their horses and followed. "Because she calls me Davik. Just plain Davik. She says she's a farmer's daughter yet she calls you—The Heir to Khal—by your name, as though she were your peer."

"Well—we are on intimate terms."

Davik continued as though he hadn't heard. "I'm telling you, Warrik, she's something more than a farmer's daughter. We should give her her freedom," he grumbled. "Now." Before it's too late, he thought. Before...what? Before she hated them for enslaving her.

"Fine," Warrik agreed shrewdly. "But get me her forwarding before she leaves."

Davik stared at his brother, his expression alarmed.

Warrik laughed. "What! You were going to free her, but not let her leave? How are you defining freedom, Davik?"

"I thought..."

"That if she were free, she would choose to stay with you?" Warrik shrugged. "She might; it's a bit of a gamble though. She might skin-it out of here. She might choose me instead. I *am* The Heir, after all, and she might be ambitious." Warrik smiled kindly at his younger brother. "And Davik," he said announced glibly, "I love you...like a brother. But I'm not giving her up. At least, not this early."

Warrik called to a soldier by name as he swung off his destroyer and pointed at the wagon. The man hurried to unload it. A young recruit took the Princes' reins. The Heir sauntered toward the inn, an arm around Davik's shoulders. "I think we should offer to wed her first; then free her only if she accepts." The Heir opened the door for his younger brother, and followed him into the inn. Catching the girl up in a hug, he pulled her to join him on a chair. Warrik spread a big hand over her stomach and squeezed her to him. "Can you bear children?" he asked abruptly.

She looked puzzled and offended. "Why do you ask?"

"Duh! Because I'm The Heir. Which means *I* must have heirs."

Davik took in the girl's stricken expression. "Mithra, Warrik, don't scare the child."

Warrik grinned at her pale face. "Don't you like children, sweetheart? It's not as if I *want* to wed you," he said consolingly. "I want Davik to wed you but...he refuses to share his wife. Maybe you can talk some sense into him. He won't listen to me."

Davik watched the girl's face. She had decided the men were teasing her.

"Are Princes allowed to wed common s-slaves?"

"No. Only uncommon ones. I think she falls into that category, don't you Davik?" Davik nodded distractedly. "Besides, I know a good genealogist. He'd find nobility in my horse if I asked him to."

Davik frowned at his brother, not certain his brother was teasing—about wedding, at any rate. "I don't know how you'll convince Mother The Heir should wed a

North Country girl. She has her heart set on a wedding alliance with Thrall."

"And you can't wed a woman you've only known three days," the girl pointed out.

"She's right you know," Davik put in quickly.

Warrik sighed. "You're probably right." Then he grinned. "I'll ask again tomorrow."

"Come on, then," Davik was saying as he stood.

"What?" Warrik complained with a pained expression.

"We're supposed to join the men for lastmeal."

"They'll never miss us."

"Good for morale," Davik said shortly, tightening his sword belt. "And we need to shake up our schedule a bit. Don't want to fall into routine. It's dangerous. Come on, a few ales and we'll be back."

"Save something for me," Warrik winked at the girl as he bumped her off his knee.

* * * * *

It was past dusk when Davik returned to the inn. He'd left Warrik in the middle of a song, but expected him to follow soon. He would write Taranis, he'd decided, and find out what could be recalled about the girl who had robbed Fastig and spent five years there in prison. First thing tomorrow, he thought.

He stepped through the door and experienced a panicked moment of searing loss. The girl was gone. Immediately he rationalized. There were no guards at the door. Most like, they had escorted the girl somewhere. To the river, or for a walk even. Still, he felt uneasy. It was late for a walk.

The door broke open and the girl was propelled into the inn, shoved from behind. Two of his men followed her in. "She tried to escape," one of them reported angrily.

Chapter Twelve

Davik took in the girl's disheveled condition. Her arms and legs were scratched and dirty, her hair in a wild tangle. Her skirt had been torn off above her knees; the blue silk was full of snags and burrs. "Her dress?" he addressed his guards coldly.

The two men stared at each other in dismay.

"I ripped it off short so I could run," she said, swift to defend the men.

"You're dismissed," he told the two guards, never removing his gaze from the girl. "Ask my captain to post six men outside henceforth; two at the door, one at each corner of the building." The door closed behind the men. His eyes remained fixed on the girl, as he tried to understand. His heart thudded dully in his chest; he leaned back on the table for support. Conflicting arguments vied within him; 'I-should-have-freed-her' warred with 'how-could-she-run-away?' How could she leave him, actually. How could she leave him; that's what bothered him.

She stood quietly before him.

"Petra. The only reason you're not bound is because you promised to submit."

"I've submitted. Now let me go, Davik." She delivered this like a command. "I can't do this any more."

He felt breathless, stunned, as though he had just witnessed some unexpected tragedy. Unexpected! Any idiot could have seen this coming. They should have freed her. Or let her choose. Or even asked first, if she wanted to be drilled dawn, noon, and night—by the two biggest dicks in Khal. The two biggest dicks—literally as well as figuratively. He and his brother had treated her as though she was nothing more than a good pronk.

She was more. Mithra knew she was more. But this was no time to be defensive. He'd been a soldier long enough to know that a strong offence was the best defense.

She held his eyes with hers. "You must let me go, Davik. I'll come back," she offered. "Only let me go now."

"You'll come back?" Why should she! "How can I trust you when you've just tried to steal away without—? I don't understand, Petra," he stated sternly. "Explain it to me."

"I can't explain. But my presence here endangers you."

He grasped at the chance to divert the blame somewhere other than himself. "Does this have something to do with the bowman? The man who tried to kill you? Do you...belong to someone of importance? Are you afraid someone is coming for you? Is someone threatening you Petra? Is it Kartin?" She looked at the ground and shook her head. "Whatever it is, Petra. I won't let anyone hurt you." She groaned and turned from him. "Even if I failed to protect you, Warrik would crush the man who threatened you."

"It's not me, Davik."

He shook his head uncomprehendingly. "Then who, what? Tell me, Petra. I can't help if you won't share your problem with me." He waited several moments for her input. "You can trust me, Petra," he said softly.

"I *do* trust you, Davik," she said to the ground, then raised her eyes. "Can you trust me?"

"Enough to let you go? Even if I could, Warrik would never allow it," he said, knowing he was making excuses, treading water, buying time, while he tried to figure out how to stop this, how to make all this work. "You can't run away from this. You're going to have to find some other solution, Petra."

Disappointment flashed in her eyes and he felt like shit. He wasn't giving her much. He wasn't giving her anything! But, with her eyes fixed on the ground, she nodded.

"Give me your hands, Petra."

She raised her eyes, saw the cord in his hand, and started. "No!" This time her eyes held absolute terror. "No, Davik. Not *now*!"

"I'll untie you tomorrow, after I've discussed this with Warrik, and have more sentries posted." He set his jaw, approached her with determination, and grasped her wrists.

She fainted again.

Davik had only just finished tying off the knots at her ankles when Warrik pushed into the inn. "Bondage," he grinned. "I like it." Then he saw her white face, her closed eyes. "What! What are you doing man!" He knelt to untie her.

"She tried to escape, Warrik."

Warrik stopped and blinked at him in surprise. "Why would she do that?"

"I don't know," he said savagely. "Maybe she doesn't like being a slave. Maybe she doesn't like submittal—to us—to both of us—at the same time."

"She appeared to like it." Warrik checked her bonds and assured himself they weren't tight.

"Maybe—she was faking it. Until she could escape."

Warrik shook his head. "You know she wasn't faking it. At least, not with you. Look, she's coming back." Warrik caught her up in his arms and kissed her. Full on the lips. He kissed her, Davik thought with dismay.

She looked at her wrists, ankles, and groaned. "I've made a mess of things, Warrik." She buried her face in his neck.

"We can fix this, darling. Whatever it is, we can fix it. Only promise not to run away."

"I promise," she said swiftly. "Only untie me, Warrik."

"I'll give you your ankles tonight, sweetheart, and your wrists tomorrow." Then he touched his lips to hers again and grinned at his brother.

"I thought you didn't like kissing," Davik grumbled.

"I've bought in," he told his brother. "My conversion's complete. And as you might expect, there's nothing worse than a recent convert."

She clung to Warrik that night, buried her face in his chest, and did not look at his younger brother. It seared a hole in Davik's heart. Confused, crushed beneath guilt he considered well earned, Davik couldn't know if her behavior was in response to the cords knotting her wrists, or if she only craved the protection of his brother's massive thews. Either way, it hurt his soul. He couldn't watch Warrik make love to her.

He left the inn and kicked his way through the camp, wishing he could kick himself. At this point, he had only himself to blame. He could have freed her. Could have told her how he felt about her. Told her he didn't want to share her. Could have told Warrik. Could have done something!

He could have — *at the very least* — had the decency to walk out this dawn, when his brother started in on her. What must she think of him! He'd known she hadn't wanted Warrik, and he'd done nothing. Worse than nothing. He'd waited for his brother to finish with her — waited with jutting cock — for his turn to mount her. Then he'd fucked her right after his brother, like she was some sort of...

He'd gotten in line like a slavering cur waiting his turn to mount a bitch in heat.

He slammed around on his heel in frustration. He was worse than an animal. Animals at least fought for the female. Most of them. Deer. Elk. Even a pronking goat would fight. It would serve him right if she chose the stag with the biggest rack.

Dragging back to the inn after midnight, Davik frowned when he found his brother up and sitting before a crop of empty jars. The Heir seldom drank to get drunk; it was too big a job. Davik sat down across from the big man and helped him drain the last jar. His eyes went to the girl, asleep on the mats, her hands tucked beneath her cheek, her bound wrists against her neck.

Warrik was silently moody.

"What?" Davik prodded him.

Warrik shook his head. "Nothing," he said reluctantly. "Ah. Nothing." He looked at his brother and gave him a slim smile. "She...ah...doesn't come for me." He looked away. "Unless you're holding her."

He should have felt some sympathy for his brother. He should have, but he didn't. Any potential for sympathy was swept away in a rush of relief and gratitude. "It's...it's only you're so big," he managed to croak and hoped he sounded a little contrite.

Warrik nodded then shook his head. "It's not like you're so much smaller." He smiled with melancholy. "I think she likes you, Davik."

With hope thus renewed, Davik took a breath he felt he'd been holding several days. "We need to talk, Warrik," he said intently. "About Petra."

"You're right. We need to talk." Warrik gave his brother a somber smile "But not tonight, Davik. I'm feeling a little defeated tonight." Pushing himself out of his chair, Warrik staggered over to the sleeping mats and threw himself down beside the sleeping captive.

Chapter Thirteen

The girl stirred against him early in the dawn, bringing his restless sleep to an end. Rolling toward her, Davik smiled crookedly. "Have you been awake long?" he whispered.

"I've been waiting for you to wake," she said in a quiet rush. "Make love to me, Davik. Now. While Warrik sleeps." The thought alone made his cock jump. Rolling half his body onto her, he put his knee between her legs. She stretched her bound wrists over her head to get them out of the way. He slid his thumb over the high ridge of her pelvic wing then ran his hand up her side to her nipple and fingered it lightly. "I was afraid you wouldn't forgive me. For tying you."

Tears were suddenly in her eyes. "I am afraid, too," she whispered.

His heart ached. How did she do it? It was the vulnerability thing again. He rolled off her and reached for his steel, slid it between her wrists and tossed the blade aside. Sliding his hand up her neck to her ear, he lowered his chest against hers and helplessly surrendered his lips. She returned his kisses with hunger, or was it desperation? "Wait. Petra, wait."

She struggled beneath him, her eyes wild and distracted.

He gave her a pained smile. "If you're going to leave, you'd best do it now, before The Heir wakes."

She didn't understand, right off. And then she did. Her eyes filled with anguish as she shook her head. "No," she whispered. "The Gods are not so cruel."

But he knew better, or would soon enough. The Gods were cruel, all right, although they didn't lack a sense of humor, a damned cynical sense of humor.

Her hands knotted in his hair and she pulled his face to hers. Voraciously, her lips swallowed his kisses whole. Her mouth opened aggressively and her tongue fought its way into his mouth.

Relief flooded through him like strong drink. She wasn't leaving.

Her arms went behind his neck. Her body! Her body undulated beneath his in a powerful wave that wouldn't quit. She was rushing him! He moved off her so he could slide his hand between her legs. She was rushing herself, his hand discovered. He broke away from her voracious mouth to lick his fingers and return them between her legs. He pulled his wet fingers through her slot. But the girl had her own agenda. She struggled to roll on top of him. Wonderingly, he helped her over. Immediately, she opened her legs for his shaft and brought it inside her, her elbows on the mat beside his neck. Having attained this position, she rested her forehead on his and quit her exertions, panting against his mouth. He let her rest, barely moving his hips in small oscillations, just to keep her place, should she wish to take up where she had left off.

With a shuddering breath, she angled her head and kissed him with her wide full lips. And this kiss was a world apart from the hunger and desperation she had exhibited earlier. It was a long, slow, tender kiss with as much love in it as he had ever felt and, in the middle of it, she began to move on him slowly.

Sounds of struggle from without the inn finally reached him. Warrik was on his feet and pulling on his breeks, reaching for his sword belt. Davik swept the girl off him, rolled onto his knees, and pushed her behind him to shield her—and felt a knife at his throat.

He watched his brother freeze, staring at a point beyond Davik's left ear. At the girl, he realized.

"Don't—move," she shouted at Warrik. "If you do, your brother will die. If you step outside, *you'll* die, Warrik. Don't move. Let me—"

She had appeared so fragile. So vulnerable. But that fragile girl had taken the steel he'd used to free her and now held it tight against his throat. With a roar of angry betrayal, he ignored the blade's threat and tore himself from the girl's grasp. The steel slipped across his neck in a cold line followed by warm blood and sharp stinging.

"No!" he heard her scream, as Warrik went through the door. He kicked her away as he tried to follow his brother. She launched herself at him. He stumbled through the door and tripped, tangled in the slender arms that confounded his steps, and crashed on the ground outside the inn. Then her body was crawling over his before he shrugged her off, got to his knees, and saw his brother dead on the ground beside him.

It stopped him a bit.

It shouldn't have. A disciplined soldier shouldn't have lost those three seconds staring into his brother's sightless eyes. By then, several men wrestled with him. He kept trying to shake them off long enough to see his brother, to be sure. Were there really so many cruel shafts buried in his chest? His world blurred around the edges. Sound dulled. And—like an idiot—he slowly registered the number of enemy soldiers present in his camp. Long severe lines of them, standing with arrows drawn. The line of soldiers who trained their bows on him stood motionless, but throughout the camp his men were waging a battle of retreat, unable to rescue him without endangering his life. A tall, lean man with violent red hair was taking orders from a woman wrapped in a cape. His woman.

"You fucking whore!" Davik catapulted to his feet and hurled himself at her. The wrestlers pulled him up short before he could kill the harlot.

The tall redhead moved himself in front of the girl and watched as his men subdued the angry Prince. Wincing at the look of snarling hatred on the young man's face, the redhead turned and smiled apologetically at his captain.

Her face was grim. "Ambitious," she said in a pale voice.

The redhead raised an eyebrow slashed with a jagged tattoo.

"He left out ambitious. Ambitious, fucking whore. Give him a shovel," she said limply, "and his clothes. Let him bury his brother."

Chapter Fourteen

The army of Southern Khal remained outside the walls of Veronix, then slowly withdrew after receiving orders from Taranis. Locked in a small gray room, the Prince enjoyed two nights of the Pretender's hospitality. The room was windowless, bare, with cold stone walls. With his back to the stone, he sat on the floor and stared across the room. The Rebels would hold him hostage and sue for cessation of hostilities. It would be a long time — if ever — before they could afford to free him. Upon Warrik's death, he became the current heir to the Khallic throne and nothing would change that — except his own death. Kartin would want very much to keep him alive and keep him hostage.

Food and drink was delivered; he wasn't hungry. It was a while before he realized he was thirsty, and even then he stared at the jug a long time before he moved toward it. On the third day he was moved.

* * * * *

"It is vital he be kept alive and healthy," Petra had argued with Kartin. "If he dies, Hadi's Storm will rain down on us from Southern Khal."

Prince Kartin's eyes shifted around the hall. He hated to be seen as giving in. 'Keep your enemies as near as your friends' had been his father's advice. He wondered how the old man had known the difference. But then, his father had been immensely popular. With only a remote claim to royal blood, he had welded together the independent tribes long enough to rip the Northern Mountains from Stavrig's grasp, as Stavrig fought his own battle to hold onto the throne he had stolen from his brother's son. Now, a generation later, his Southern throne secure, Stavrig had sent his sons and his army to march on Veronix, determined to bring the Northern mountains back into the Kingdom of Khal.

Prince Kartin didn't enjoy his father's popularity. Not by a longbow shot. Ten years on the Northern throne had only been long enough to erode any popularity and goodwill he had inherited on the death of his father. He wasn't his father's son. Neither in looks, charm, sense, or mannerism. And, at over thirty—and having failed to interest a Khallic Princess in his suit—he was still unwed and without an heir. As long as the respectably legitimate Southern Princes were available, every noble lass was keeping her options open, hoping for a match with one of the handsome brothers. They might want to rethink their positions at this point, Kartin mused sardonically.

He returned his slinking eyes to the girl, his sloping chin resting on his chest. Even this girl of a captain enjoyed greater popularity than he did. Certainly her unit's respect. The Prince's eyes shifted to the man at the back of the room. Of course that might have a lot to do with the tall, dangerous redhead, her sergeant. And now, after capturing the Southern Prince—saving the city at the eleventh hour—no doubt her popularity would soar in the North Country. He regretted the field promotion that had elevated her to captain, but that was none of his doing, so he could not blame himself. Again, he suspected the redhead was the true brains in the unit, and responsible for her promotion.

He never felt comfortable around her. What was it—
beside the fact that she seldom addressed him as
anything other than Kartin? Just Kartin. It was insolent—
disrespectful—but he couldn't correct her publicly
without pointing up his own weakness. It was safer to
allow his captains to think she enjoyed some sort of
special favor with him. His lips twitched as he considered
this idea, confident of the assumption that would first
jump to mind.

She was all proper and respectful today, however.
Kartin's lips twitched again with sardonic amusement.
She must want this really bad. Why?

He snorted.

Whoever held the Prince, held all the cards, all the
power against Southern Khal. Not that anyone could do
anything but hold it. But if she wished to look important,
he could afford to be generous and act like he considered
it a small matter. And she was right, they couldn't allow
the Prince to die; he must be kept healthy. She had a nice
airy home on the west side of the city.

"And you have suitable accommodations," he said
finally, as she waited quietly for his decision. "Thank you
for reminding me of my intention to place the Prince
under your supervision."

The girl received this lie smoothly; he had expected
no less from her.

* * * * *

Davik was installed in a bright open viewing cell; a
tall room with smooth plastered walls that rose halfway
into the upper level of the house. A hangover from the
days of slavery and designed to hold slaves, the ancient
home would not have been complete without a viewing

cell. Although slavery in Khal was rare these days, viewing cells remained popular; women found them useful as playpens for their children, or to showcase their prized possessions. In Davik's case, the room reverted to its original purpose; to allow the cell's occupant to be observed—and guarded—from the upper level. Davik ignored the sleeping mat on the bench built against one wall and threw himself on the floor, propped his back against the wall, and brooded.

His eyes cut to the top of the wall. At the moment, no one watched but he guessed there were guards nearby. He was to have some privacy, then. He had to assume others would observe him, that *she* intended to watch him or even communicate with him, safe from his reach. Oh, it was her house, he knew. On his way in, he had seen enough to ascertain that. It was not large. Plain, clean, unadorned, and quiet, filled with the hated scent of her. And because he thought she might come to the wall at night, he took care to sleep on his stomach. More than one night, he lay awake—listening for her—but if she came, he never heard her.

At the end of the first day, a stack of books was delivered. He glared at them from across the room but didn't move to open any of them. Two days later, parchment and pen were delivered along with ink. These he glared at for a day before he retrieved them the next morning in a sudden burst of energy, carried them to his bench, and began to write. He wrote all that day and continued into the night, as lamps were solicitously lit for him. The next day his work was delivered to his hostess. It was entitled, The Harlot. The last six stanzas were devoted wholly to his revenge, wherein the fifty men of her unit were forced to rape their captain, utilizing every accommodating orifice in her body, repeatedly and — to whatever extent possible — at the same time.

* * * * *

She sat at her table, looked up from the parchment, and attempted a smile. "It doesn't say here whether or not I enjoy it. I suppose that's left to the reader's interpretation." She handed the parchment to the redhead and watched him as he scanned the last page, his eyes that riveting blue found at the hard edge of lightning.

"I think he's made it clear enough," Dye said, argumentatively. "At least, *I* don't need an interpreter."

"Neither does it mention if my men are willing."

Dye grimaced. "Well, you can count me out," he said emphatically.

She smiled her affection at him.

His lip curled in a sneer as he threw the parchment on the table. "My guess is the man can't get it up without watching someone else in the act. You'd better hope he's never returned to power."

"Is he asleep?" She watched the redhead nod. "Are you sure?"

Padding silently to the half-wall, she watched him in the dim lamplight, but he never turned over and she couldn't see his face. In the morning, she was agitated. "He's not eating," she stated.

"Not much," Dye agreed.

"Do you think he's trying to…end his life?"

Dye shook his head. "He'll eat when he's hungry."

That day Davik broke his pen and used the splintered end to scratch on the plaster walls of his cell: The Harlot, all twenty-eight verses. That kept him busy for two days. When he was done, he went back over each letter, scoring his ballad deep into the wall. Dipping the broken pen into the jar of ink, he filled in the letters so the words stood out in cruel, stark relief on the white plaster background. She sent him a jar of wine. He sat with his back against the wall and drank half the jar before he passed out in the middle of the afternoon—on his back.

* * * * *

"Are you sure?" she asked Dye.

"I'm sure," Dye told her.

Leaning on the half-wall, she gazed down at the Khallic Prince.

Like most Khals, he was a handsome man, with thick, straight, blond hair and a strong square chin. Unlike most Khals, his eyes were blue—blue-green, actually—rather than brown. Other than that, his features were perhaps not so blunt, a little finer, a little more angular than a typical Khal's. And though not as tall as his brother had been, he topped six feet—putting him a good three inches above his countrymen. Blond Khals were pretty much five-ten. Uniformly five-ten. But then, the King of Khal was a big man. Rhyssian blood. It turned up everywhere. Height—in a Khal—was usually accompanied by Rhyssian red hair and was more common in the North Country than in the South.

He was not so different from any other Khal. Until he smiled. When he smiled it started in his eyes, then flickered at the corner of his mouth. He suppressed it, like a naughty but favored child who couldn't be trusted to behave. But when he gave it rein, and he laughed! She shook her head as she surveyed his dark-rimmed eyes, his hollowed cheeks, the clothes that hung loosely on him, then pushed herself away from the wall.

"It's been ten days. He's hardly eaten. He grows thin." She strode down the corridor, Dye following her.

"He'll eat."

"I would talk to him."

Dye sighed. "I'll have him chained."

Chapter Fifteen

When she came to him it wasn't at the wall; she came through the door. But he was expecting her; why else had he been chained to the bench? The chains chimed a harsh metallic note as he gestured to the walls around him. "What do you think of my work?"

"It's fairly written," she said quietly, choosing her words purposefully.

She wore plain doeskin leggings and linen jerkin, leather vest. A loose thong of leather caught her hair behind her neck. Errant wisps of hair, dark and rebellious, escaped to sneak around her face. His eyes dropped to her feet.

The boots were the same.

How could he have ever thought she was beautiful, he wondered as he stared at her face. With her hair pulled back she appeared harder, more severe, more like a soldier. Dark smudges beneath her eyes made her look worn, like a soldier with problems.

"I couldn't decide whether to call it The Harlot or The Betrayal."

She nodded. "You were betrayed," she agreed. "Although I managed to do it without lying."

"Should I congratulate you? You never said more than ten words!"

"I didn't want to tell you anything," she admitted. "I didn't even want you to know my name. Although I had been only two years in Kartin's army, and just recently promoted, I was afraid your spies might have informed you of me. But Petra is a common enough name."

"Petra is common," he agreed. "And hard.

"*'I can submit — willingly'*," he mimicked her with mocking tone. "You just about jumped onto my dick." He gave her a look of cold detachment.

She pressed her lips between her teeth and looked at the ground. "My grandparents were of Slurian descent." She raised her eyes to his.

His eyes narrowed. "Are you trying to tell me you were controlling my—" And then he realized what she was saying. "You were...*stroking* me! With your thoughts!" His eyes flared with heat and he struggled to maintain his detachment. "What need to control a man's mind when you can control his balls?"

She returned his gaze, levelly.

"Was it," he gritted, "any of it — real?"

"It was all of it real."

His look turned to hateful scorn. "The fainting?"

"Everything. The fainting. The scars on my wrists. Five years in your father's prison. That's not why I took on the mission, but it made it easier. My...what turned into — affection — for you, and your brother. My arrivals. It was all real."

"Everything," he said bitterly. "Including Warrik's very real death. Despite your sincere affection for him," he said with poison.

She met his venomous gaze bravely and nodded. "I'd have stopped his death, if I could have," she pointed out.

"Yes," he agreed. "I believe that. That you could have stopped his death. But you didn't." He turned his face from her. "I see now, it was all real," he said, his voice like a razor. "Including the very real knife at my throat."

Her lips parted as she realized her error. She shook her head. "That was a bluff. I was trying to stop Warrik."

"You were trying to kill us," he said flatly. "I have the scar to prove it." He fingered the thin pink line that slashed his throat.

"If I'd sought to kill you with the knife, you'd be dead," she told him. "But...it was my brainchild," she admitted. "My plan from conception. It was my intention to submit to you from the start, in the hope you'd not bind me. I was to make sure you and your brother were inside the inn—and distracted—on the fourth dawn."

"Why so long!" he interrupted with agonized frustration. "Why four days?"

"I didn't know how long it would take to get into your...inside your headquarters. I had to allow myself enough time. But Warrik—"

"Warrik didn't stand a chance when you baited him with that showpiece ass of yours. He was baited and hooked from the start. And gutted in the end. You missed your calling," he said savagely.

She nodded, knowing what he meant.

"At least whoring would have been an honest profession." Davik shook his head. "When my men brought you in, you'd neither food nor water; I assumed you'd left the city in a hurry. If I'd given it more thought, it might have occurred to me you didn't plan on getting far. You didn't, did you? No farther than our camp."

She nodded.

"Mithra Fucking Andarta!" Frustrated, he raised his angry eyes to the ceiling. "That bright blue skirt," he gritted through clenched teeth. "How could I not have realized? Who would try to run the sentry line in a brilliant, blue skirt, except someone who wished to be caught?"

She pressed her lips together and took a determined breath. "I was nervous when Warrik began undressing me in your presence—it felt strange to be with two men—but I hid it, intent on my mission, determined to submit. And do it well enough that you'd keep me for at least a few days. I figured I could take it, no matter how bad it was. I never considered I might be facing the reverse situation. Could I take it, and follow through with my plan, no matter how good it was?

"I'd heard you were careful, intelligent. I was most concerned about distracting you, drawing you in. When Warrik took me on his lap, I was dry. You can't fake that. I was afraid too. Afraid of his size, but mostly afraid you'd see right through me. I did my utmost to draw you in, engage your interest." She took a breath. "And I touched you. With my mind. Intimately; to excite you. As soon as you entered me, I knew the mission was a fait accompli. That was all that mattered.

"That was all that mattered," she murmured, "up until that first arrival. That first kiss.

"I could have cried when Warrik pulled me off you in the middle of my arrival. "But then you were beside me..." her hand strayed to her face; unconsciously her knuckles brushed the side of her cheek "...kissing me." Her eyes went very distant.

She was drawing him in again, he thought with disgust. Or trying to. He gave her a cold look of distaste. "And I'm to believe you're in love with me." Her eyes snapped to focus on his face. "I hope you are," he said. "I pray you are. It will make my revenge that much more satisfying."

She nodded and continued. "I kept telling myself I could do it; right up until the point I knew I couldn't. I tried to escape to my men. To abort the mission. When I failed, you told me to find another solution. I came up with what I thought was a reasonable plan with a fair prospect of success. I thought the knife at your neck would stop your brother long enough for me to explain. In retrospect, I can see the plan was flawed. I was willing to risk Warrik's life to save yours. I mismanaged the situation."

He regarded her with narrow-eyed disgust. "And the bowman on the mountain? I was to believe your own countrymen pursued you? Or was he simply another man you'd betrayed?"

She shook her head. "He was there to kill you, not me. The man acted on his own; a man from my unit. He'd argued against the mission and was angry when I moved ahead with the plan. I didn't know he'd followed us — didn't know he was there — but when he saw us struggling together, he may have thought you were trying to force me.

"I killed him," she said with matter-of-fact regret. "When I ordered him to stop. He hesitated — automatically — out of habit."

"No," he said flatly. "*Don't* rob me of that too. I killed him. *I* killed him." Intuition kicked in and his mind made the leap. He stared at her, a mean malicious glint in his eye. "He was your lover."

She nodded. "It had been a while. I didn't know he still had an interest." She ground the heel of her palm into her temple as if searching for the next words.

"The fact that you and your brother were so often together made the two of you a enticing target. Always beside each other in battle, in the same place at night. Anyone who took out one of you was almost guaranteed to get the second. The problem was your lack of routine. We never knew where you'd be. Your schedule varied so much. Sometimes you rode the sentry lines at midnight. Sometimes you slept till near noon. But we knew we could always find you both in the same place." She smiled, but it was grim. "We thought it was because you didn't trust each other. I never guessed it was because you were so close." She looked at the ground and nodded. "Close enough to share the same woman and do it with as much tenderness as I've ever known."

"Tenderness!" Finally he smiled, but it was a smile without warmth or tenderness. "Are you that naïve? Are you really? So naïve you don't know the difference between tenderness and being fucked?" He threw back his head and laughed with pure malevolence. "I can see how you might mistake one man's intentions. But two? Two men at once? That's not tenderness, sweetheart. That's plain old spread-her-legs-for-me-while-I-ram-my-dick-up-her-cunt-and-fuck-the-slut-as-hard-as-I-can."

She accepted this tirade calmly and nodded. "I tried to convince myself I owed you nothing. That you were just two bucks rutting in the same doe. That, if either of you cared about me, you probably wouldn't be able to share me. Wouldn't be able to watch the other man take me. I admit my life has lacked tenderness in any great quantity, but yes, I thought I knew the difference."

"A life without tenderness," he mocked her cruelly. "Let me out of these chains and I'll demonstrate how I feel about you, if only to avenge Warrik. When I'm done, you'll know you've been fucked—and without tenderness."

She half turned from him then, as though she could no longer bear the weight of his gaze. "I told myself it wasn't betrayal. That I'd not be breaking your trust or friendship, when you'd offered me neither. But by then it didn't matter how you felt about me. The problem was reduced to how I felt about you." She shrugged and the action appeared to cause her pain. "I thought you deserved an explanation," she said, "from me...before...

"I'm sorry," she said, her voice hollow. "I don't expect you to forgive me, no more than I can forgive myself, but I'm sorry nonetheless." She turned back to him a last time. "Your brother would have made a good King."

Like he cared what she thought! Rage licked his temper to a point. "Who's fucking you now?" he asked with vindictive pleasantry, as though she hadn't spoken. "Kartin?"

* * * * *

"Arrange his escape," she told Dye after leaving the viewing cell.

Dye gave his head a warning half-shake. "You can't do that, Petra." He hurried to catch her up. "When Kartin finds out, you won't be *able* to get out of here fast enough. You won't be able to *run* fast enough or *far* enough."

"I'm not going to run. Kartin won't remain in power."

Dye's jaw dropped in astonishment. He grabbed the girl's wrist and whirled her to face him. "Why! Why, Petra!"

"Because Kartin is not the man to lead Khal."

Chapter Sixteen

"And *that man* is?" Dye pointed back toward the cell. "Maybe at one time, Petra. But *that man* will never get over what we did to his brother. He's sunk so deep in slogging hatred, he'll never see his boots again. He'll never see the North as anything other than the enemy."

She turned on him. "Give him a break, Dye! He loved his brother."

"And I loved mine. But I didn't allow his death to destroy me."

She took a step backward. "Don't, Dye. Don't *let* me think I've destroyed him. I can fix this. We can fix this. But you've got to help."

* * * * *

The cell door blasted open with a loud crack that left it shivering on its hinges, but Davik barely acknowledged the intrusion. The redhead slammed into the cell and threw a tray on the bench then turned to face the Prince of Southern Khal. "Eat," he bellowed. "You'll need your energy if you plan to escape."

His chains recently removed, Davik rubbed his wrists. With icy mien, he regarded the intruder. "Why should I want to escape?"

With a wide gesture, Dye indicated the surrounding walls. "So you can enact your revenge, of course. Come man, you can't expect me to do everything; show a little initiative. I'm counting on you not to faint in the middle of your flight."

Flight! Why should he wish to leave when everything he wanted was right here?

The girl.

With broad intolerance, the redhead regarded the Prince a few moments, then his eyes wandered impatiently and stuck as he stared across the room. Davik followed his gaze to the black verse on the wall. "You know, fuck doesn't rhyme with cock; not exactly."

"It's close enough," Davik muttered disagreeably.

Dye nodded. His eyes harbored a malicious glint. "You know," he said. "The men in her unit have a wager going. It's ten to one you can't get it up on your own, without watching."

Davik struggled to his feet.

"And that's the real reason behind your reven—"

With a mangled oath involving deities behaving badly, Davik threw himself across the room at the man. Despite the ferocity of the Prince's rage, the redhead was ahead of Davik, twisting his arm high on his back, crushing his windpipe beneath a hard forearm. Dye laughed maliciously. "Oh, please. Give me an excuse, man. Just give me an excuse and I'll break both your arm and your neck." When Davik ceased to struggle, Dye shoved him away. The Prince hit the wall hard and slid to the ground. "You've some life left in you then," Dye smirked. "She'll be glad to know of it."

The door slammed behind the redhead and Davik listened for the bolts slotting into place. He glowered at the tray then crabbed over to it and fed himself slowly. He was to escape then, courtesy of his hostess. He chewed and swallowed. He could go along with that. He would accommodate her that far. As far as through that door. He watched the door with cold expression. After that, he would find his way to her—along the shortest route possible.

When he woke, the sun was in his eyes. Groggily, he searched his environs and cursed. He was leagues from Veronix, south of the city. Nearby, tied to a tree, a saddled horse tossed its head and whickered. Lurching to his feet, he caught up one of the water skins hanging from his mount's harness.

Drugged. He'd been drugged and brought here. He drank thirstily and flipped open one of the saddlebags, searching for the food he knew he'd find. Tearing off a hunk of flatbread with his teeth, his eyes traveled north toward the city. No help for it, he thought, resolutely. He attempted a mount from the ground but couldn't pull it off in his weakened condition. Leading the horse to a fallen tree, he got on the beast's back and turned its head south.

From his distant vantage point, Dye watched the Prince disappear into the flatlands.

* * * * *

The Prince ricocheted through the Great Palace in Taranis, delegating in short, blunt bursts of energy. Residents and visitors, men and women alike, parted before him as he dragged a vacuum behind him that sucked up an entourage of subordinates. Servants, stewards, soldiers, guards scattered as they received their commands.

"Mother!" Davik turned a corner and came to an abrupt halt.

A long knife-edge of a woman stood before him. "See your father before you leave, Davik."

The Prince suppressed a shiver as The Queen of Khal brushed coolly by.

He was admitted to his father's bedroom where he found the old soldier propped up amidst a company of pillows. He looked small, Davik thought. He had been such a big man, a giant at one time. He wished that his father's frail condition could be attributed to the shock of losing his oldest son, but that would be attributing feelings to a man too busy being King to have ever been a father; the King had been in his bed for more than a year now. Davik bowed before the old man.

"Davik," the old man wheezed. "I won't keep you long. It's vital you resume the siege before the Rebels have a chance to re-supply. They must be punished for The Heir's death," he commanded with a rattle.

Davik nodded grimly.

The old King shook his head. "I'm sorry about your brother. You'll miss him, of course. Perhaps more than anyone. You mustn't blame yourself for his death."

The young Prince stiffened. "I was deceived."

"Has it occurred to you that perhaps you were not? That while you were betrayed, you were not deceived."

"Father?"

The old man made a face. "If you were taken in, maybe it was because the girl wasn't acting. You know how impractical women are. The girl probably fell in love with one of you—both of you! And it's entirely possible she betrayed you without uttering a single lie."

Davik didn't want to think about it. Didn't want to think about her.

"Know your enemy, son," he said curtly. "Use it against her."

"I will, father."

* * * * *

Davik pulled the door closed behind him and turned to stare at the smooth, copper-clad surface. An avalanche of unwelcome feelings scraped his raw emotions like an open wound and, for an instant, he felt utterly alone—solitary in a singular emptiness.

Ruthlessly, he shoved this weakness aside. He was behind schedule. He wanted to be on the road tomorrow, early. The corridor was dark and empty as he headed across the palace; his steps rang hollow on the flagstone walk. He hadn't asked his father about the girl who robbed Fastig. He didn't want to know anymore. What was the point, when the whore had lied about everything? Most like she wasn't even the same girl.

His steps slowed.

Even assuming his father was right, and the girl had never lied, what did that mean? Was there any reason to believe she was the girl who robbed Fastig? She hadn't actually admitted to the theft. 'You've a good memory,' was all she had said. The Prince shrugged with irritation and resumed his pace. What else? She claimed to have spent five years in Taranis prison, said she had not been raped; neither did she complain that she had suffered in any way.

He snorted.

No. She just heroically fainted in his arms when he tried to bind her wrists. And that act had drawn him in so completely. She had duped him right from the start. How could he have been—?

He stopped completely in the corridor.

Unless her fainting wasn't an act.

His guard scrambled to keep up with him as he ordered a mount harnessed. A careening ride through the city streets brought him to the cold stone building, Taranis Prison. With a gruff word to the sentries, he was escorted to the warden's office where he found a chair and waited for the man to join him.

Chapter Seventeen

The warden nodded. "Fastig's Diamond Thief." He was a seasoned man with a keen confidence and intelligent eyes. "I remember the girl.

"Petra," he said slowly and waited for the Prince's reaction. When there was none, a shield dropped before his eyes. "It's only three years or so since she escaped," he explained. "Tall for her age, dark skin, black, black hair. She was a tough young thing," he said with admiration he didn't bother to hide. "Only fourteen. I watched her receive her lashes." The man shook his head. "She pressed her lips together and never uttered a sound. No more than blinked each time the lash fell." He regarded the Prince rebelliously. "She was to have received thirty. I called it good at twenty."

Davik nodded curtly. The girl drew everyone in. "She received no other punishment?"

The man shook his head. "I received word almost immediately she was to be treated with care."

"Word?" Davik's astonishment was complete. "From who?"

"The palace!"

"Who, at the palace?"

The man shook his head. "I don't know. I never knew."

Davik stared at the wall. "Do you know why?"

He shrugged. "I assumed she was somebody's daughter. Somebody important enough to protect her, but not important enough to buy her freedom. That same Somebody sent her books though. Lots of books." The warden's eyes traveled behind the Prince.

Davik followed his gaze to a shelf stacked with manuscripts. He stood and sorted through them briefly, vaguely noting most of them were histories. He opened an ornate little collection of ballads. "All hers?"

The warden nodded.

"You kept her books. You could have sold them."

"I like to read. A man of my means can't afford many books."

Davik gave the man a scathing look.

"I thought she might be back," he admitted without apology. "Might be recaptured. Might get into more trouble."

"Were the diamonds ever recovered?"

"She gave them back. Didn't you know? That's how she was caught."

"She returned the jewelry? And Fastig still demanded her punishment?"

The warden made a face. "You know how Fastig is. And he can afford to buy the King's—." The man stopped, realizing whom he was addressing. "Well, you know how Fastig is," he finished.

"I think she only did it as a lark. According to her story, she went into the house on a dare and was to come out with one of those atrocious red scarves he wears. While she was in his room, he stumbled in half drunk. She crouched behind the bed and watched him open his hidden vault. She didn't empty the vault; just took the diamonds. Kept them a few days, long enough for him to discover they were missing and to offer a reward, long enough for her to gain some notoriety. Then she thought it would be fun to surprise him with their return — to their original location. Fastig insisted she was returning to empty his vault."

"And perhaps she was."

The warden shrugged. "She could have done that the first time she was there; of course there was nothing in the vault by the time of her return. Any thief might have expected that."

After a moment's silence, the warden continued. "You know how well guarded his villa is; she got in through his cat door." He indicated with his hands the small size of this opening. "She was just a skinny kid back then. She'd never have made it after she came into her breasts...and hips."

"And all this was revealed at her hearing," Davik said with sarcasm.

"Some of it. Some of it she spoke of while she was here."

"You visited with her?"

"My duties keep me too busy for visiting with prisoners," he said, a rime of frost on his words. "But I'm a curious man. And I oversaw every entry into her cell."

"And why was that."

"I've not so many women here. Few enough I can make sure they're not abused by their guards."

"So she was not mistreated, then?" He had to ask. "Nor was she raped?"

The man looked offended. "Not at all!"

"You're sure. Her guards—"

"Her guards couldn't have reached her if they'd wanted to; she was behind bars. I had the keys and oversaw all entries into her cell," he repeated.

"She did not suffer then," Davik gritted. The small volume of ballads crumpled in his tightening fist. He turned abruptly then halted before the door. "Her escape?" His tone was accusatory.

"I was off the night she escaped." The warden's eyes flashed. "But if I were going to help the girl, I'd not have waited five years."

The man was too clever and smug. Davik turned back to him slowly. "Did you know...one of your men jerked himself in her presence? Routinely?" The smug bastard's expression told Davik the man hadn't known.

"These things happen," the warden returned with flinty expression. "She could have told me of it."

But she hadn't. "No! Not her! She was too *fucking* noble to complain! She'd not compromise the man's position!"

The warden's eyes dropped to the elegant little book crushed in Davik's fist, as he met the Prince's fury with superior calm.

The storm in Davik's eyes died suddenly. "I'm sorry," he said coldly, "but your noble slut murdered my brother, The Heir to Khal."

The warden raised his eyes to the Prince's face. "When you put a child in jail, you run the risk of making a lifelong enemy," he pointed out; steel edged his words.

Davik slammed the door behind him. She drew everyone in.

The warden flinched as the door smacked into the jamb. For several moments, the man stared at the place where the Prince had stood, then he started out of his seat and paced over to pull the door open. The Prince was nowhere in sight. Damn. He probably should have mentioned her wrists. The girl's wrists. And ankles. It wasn't fair to say she hadn't suffered.

* * * * *

It was late by the time Davik left his mount in the stables and climbed the steps to Taranis Palace. Too late to bother his father and he planned an early departure in the dawn. His father might have some idea of why the girl was granted special treatment during her imprisonment, or he might not. Most like, she caught the eye of some sympathetic benefactor who pitied the striking fourteen year old. The girl drew everyone in.

He no longer cared to learn anything more about the whore.

What difference did it make, anyhow?

Chapter Eighteen

Mavrik took his ten paces, scanned the horizon quickly and turned to take another ten. It was a miserable, dense, black night and he hunched his shoulders as he burrowed into his clothing. With the wind behind him, he took the next ten paces more slowly. He sighed. Things were not the same since The Heir's death. The New Heir was fair and equitable; he always had been. But the tone, the mood had changed; the camaraderie lost, the laughter, humor dimmed—almost extinguished altogether. He spat on the ground and cursed the slut who had murdered his Prince, then cursed the weather equally. He turned and looked for the next sentry, but couldn't find him in the impenetrable—

Dye drew his steel across the young soldier's throat. "You're dead," he hissed in the lad's ear.

The Northman gave the boy a shove and handed him his dagger. With his hand on his throat, the young soldier goggled at the blade. "Take it," Dye laughed. "Then lead me to your Prince." Still the youth stared, then slowly drew his hand from his throat and stared at his palm. "Tell him you captured me," Dye suggested.

* * * * *

Although it was gone midnight, Davik sat at the table in the inn, staring sullenly across the room at his mat. It had taken him all of thirteen days to regroup his forces and return to the gates of Veronix. The weather was coming out of the north on the march back, unseasonably cold and biting. The army fought the stubborn headwind and slashing rain every step of the way. Even now, the weather screeched at the shuttered windows like a banshee slut.

They had lost a little ground, he thought, but nothing that couldn't be recouped. He would have the city, soon.

And everyone in it.

Her.

He would have her, and his revenge. It was just a matter of time.

Fighting the weather to close the door, a guard ducked into the inn and crossed the room to whisper in the Prince's ear. Davik nodded with sudden interest, stood and turned.

The tall, hard redhead stood just inside the door. "I've come to offer you the city," Dye said without preamble. "My unit will open the gates for you tonight and help you reach Kartin, then negotiate with his army for nonviolence. I'm confident they'll submit to you under the right conditions."

Davik stared at him quietly. Snorted. "I'm to be drawn in again," he said with disgust. "How can she think—?"

The man shook his head. "She no longer captains the unit; it's under my command. And you can keep me hostage if you wish; take me with you to the gates. My men have their orders. Although my absence may make Kartin suspicious. More suspicious than he already is."

Davik regarded him with continued disbelief.

"You needn't accompany your army through the gates. Follow them after the palace is secured."

Davik dropped into a chair and regarded Dye as he stood just inside the door. There was no reason *not* to suspect a trap. And yet the man's direct, casual manner was convincing. "And why should I believe you will betray Kartin?"

Dye shrugged. "The city can't hold out against you. We knew that before. There was nothing left; hence the plan to capture you. The success of Petra's mission made us the victors—for a time—until your 'escape'. This time you'll win. As before, I intend to be on the winning side."

"And what do you expect to gain in return for this betrayal?"

Dye regarded him quietly, without words.

"This won't buy the girl anything."

"Yes it will," Dye returned. He turned to the door, opened it a crack, and squinted outside. "I've seen your 'ballad'. It's quite a piece of work." Dye returned his eyes to the Prince. "My men don't deserve the dishonor. They were just soldiers following orders."

Davik considered this for several moments. "Two nights, hence, then."

"No," Dye countered. "Tonight. Tonight, or not at all."

"Why?"

"I have my reasons." He gave the Prince a grim smile. "All will be revealed in time."

* * * * *

Upon taking the city of Veronix, certain of its capitulation, and satisfied with its occupation, Prince Davik had only one thing on his mind, and a good many orders associated with it. "Man the gates," he instructed his captains, "the walls. Nobody gets out. Nobody. Post a double sentry line three hundred paces out. You understand? Find the girl. Round up her unit and bring them to the hall."

He would fuck her in front of her men.

Almost immediately, a disciplined, unified tramp echoed in the corridors and Davik turned to watch Dye lead his men into the hall.

Dye had marshaled his men immediately upon receiving the Prince's summons. Marching into the hall, they formed a neat array in the center of the room. A hundred Southern soldiers lined the alcove that ran the perimeter of the hall. When the Southern Prince ignored the Northern Unit, the men shuffled restlessly. These were the men responsible for The Heir's death. Although they had given his brother the city, it might not buy them his pardon. Their eyes shifted to their captain, the only man at ease in the hall. With a careless salute for the Prince, Dye threw himself into a chair. Well, if you were going to die, you might as well do it comfortably. If the Prince turned tables on them, Dye reckoned the man had just provocation. Petra had said he wouldn't. He'd soon know for himself.

"The people of Veronix have been hungry a long time," Dye reminded the Prince casually.

"Our sheep are being driven in and butchered. I've sent out hunting parties. Additional supplies are on their way from Taranis. *Don't*—tell me how to do my job, Northman."

Five Southern soldiers entered the room and saluted the Prince. Davik's captain shook his head.

Davik stepped off the dais and yanked the nearest North Country soldier off his feet. "Where is she?"

"Sir?"

"Where's your Unit Captain?"

The man's eyes went to Dye.

Dye regarded the Prince with nonchalance. "I'm their captain," he reminded the Prince. "If you mean the girl, I can tell you where she is. Can take you to her, if you wish."

A few angry paces brought the two men face to face. "Can you bring her here?" he spat with angry cynicism.

Negligently, Dye cast his eyes around the room. "If you wish."

"Do so!" The Prince motioned his five men to accompany Dye.

* * * * *

The Prince paced the silent room while the men of her unit palmed the sweat from their faces — even though the hall was chilly, the sun stubbornly absent in the morning sky. Davik's heart thundered in his chest. His throat was dry, his palms damp. His eyes met those of his guards flanking the Northern throne; their gazes were accusatory. Angrily, he turned away from them. They were the two men who had stopped her escape from the inn; the guards she had defended when he was upset about her torn skirt. He nodded to himself. The girl drew everyone in. But their attitude warned him to go carefully.

The door opened with a crash as Dye kicked it open and strode into the hall. In his arms he carried the limp rag that was Petra. When he reached the stunned Prince, he shoved the girl into Davik's arms.

The hall was dead silent as her men watched with stony faces.

"You might have to fix her up a bit, before you can revive her long enough to beat her senseless again," Dye suggested.

Chapter Nineteen

The Prince's expression, as he looked down at the girl in his arms, started out as blank denial, followed by acute loss. As though he were deprived of something he very much wanted, valued, or had looked forward to.

She was dirty, he thought at first. And she was. Filthy. But most of the dark splashes on her limbs were bruises. What remained of her clothing barely covered her. Quickly, he removed his eyes from her battered face. Her nose was broken, he realized as he stared at the floor. Her nose, the only proud feature in her winsome face. And then he couldn't think for several moments. "Who…who did this to her?"

"Kartin."

Davik shook his head blankly. "He would do this to one of his captains. One of his soldiers?"

Grumbling concurrence rumbled among her men.

Dye shrugged. "She let you escape."

Davik's eyes narrowed into hard slits. "Where is he?"

"I believe he is currently lodged in the room next to hers."

"The dungeons."

Dye inclined his head. A look of sarcasm accompanied the act.

"How the mighty have fallen," Davik whispered, still stunned. "How long has this been going on?"

"She's been in the cell since your 'escape'. Beaten every day since you arrived at the gates."

This was why her elite corps had joined him. To stop Kartin. And the beatings. This was why Dye insisted he attack immediately. She didn't look like she could have taken another day of him outside the gates.

"Shall I return her to her room?" Dye offered with a cold smirk.

Too late, Davik realized he held the girl like a bolt of priceless silk. Like a rag, he tossed her into a chair and turned to face her men. They stared beyond him, at the girl, her long body draped over the Northern throne.

"Why did you let this continue — for three nights?"

"Kartin was suspicious. I couldn't get away." Dye watched the Prince's jaw grind.

"Dismiss your men," he bit out between clenched teeth.

The Northern unit drew up into two lines and saluted in the Prince's direction, their eyes focused behind him. He watched the men troop out behind the redhead, then turned to one of his men. "Put the girl in my room," he said curtly. "Have one of my women check her injuries." He descended the dais. "Ursa," he said. "Is Ursa still with us?"

"Yes, Prince Davik."

"Have Ursa look at her."

* * * * *

He sat at the desk in his room, sulking moodily while Ursa pulled the shreds of clothing from the girl's body. As she did so, a dirty wad of parchment fell to the floor. Ursa unfolded it and scanned its contents.

"What is it?"

The old woman gave him a hard look and brought him the wadded sheets. "Filth," she said. "It's a wonder she didn't use it to wipe her ass." With ultimate distaste, she dropped it on the desk.

It was his ballad, The Harlot. Dirty and damp with sweat, stained brown in several places. Blood, he realized. Her blood. He watched Ursa bathe the girl and wrap her broken skin.

"Clothes?" Ursa questioned cynically.

He crossed the room to his saddlebags and pulled out a pair of scarlet shorts.

"Scarlet," she muttered disagreeably. "How apropos. Scarlet for the harlot."

"Tuck this into her shorts." He handed the wadded parchment back to Ursa.

She took a step backward. "No My Lord." With her arms determinedly at her sides, she stepped around the Prince and went through the door. He watched her back with frustration and cursed all women grown too old to fear men, or anything else.

He sat watching her, a long while, after Ursa left. Wishing she were healthy. He wanted his moment of revenge, wanted it now. And it was denied him. He wanted to kill Kartin. He stalked to the door and opened it. "Return her to her cell," he ordered his man. "The Northern Captain will show you. Clean it first," he said with irritation. "And Menlas? Chain her."

He walked back across the room, slapping the wadded parchment against his palm, clearly reluctant to approach the still form on his bed. Finally, taking his courage firmly in hand, he sidled up to her as a man would approach a deadly tetra and, without touching her, tucked the wad into the waistband of her shorts. Stooping to the floor, he retrieved a thin strip of leather. Her hair thong. He looked at the thong in his hand — looked at her hair — then pushed the thong over his hand and onto his wrist. Stood staring down at her for several moments, then dropped onto the bed. Her body twitched. Hesitantly, he brushed a knuckle over her broken lips. Her eyelids flickered beneath a tiny frown. "Hurt," she whispered from swollen lips. "Don't touch."

* * * * *

The Pretender Kartin was found dead the next morning, bludgeoned to death in his cell. Dye delivered this news to Davik in his rooms.

The Prince did not look up from his desk. "And I don't expect we shall ever discover who was responsible," he said succinctly.

Dye's eyes glinted and his lips curled shrewdly. "You are mistaken, My Prince. I am quite willing to bear the responsibility, assuming no one else will step forward."

"Suit yourself, then."

"You're welcome," murmured the redhead. "After all, what are captains for?" He sauntered from the room, confident the claim would do nothing to hurt his reputation — and fool no one.

Unwittingly, the Southern Prince had just won the allegiance of every Northern soldier in the city.

Chapter Twenty

Davik strode along the dim, drafty corridor. At the end of the hall, he could see Dye waiting outside his door. His captains had advised him against his growing connection with the Northern Captain. It was reckless to put his life at the man's disposal, his captains argued, but Davik was in a reckless mood. Two Northern soldiers saluted him smartly as they passed. He stopped in stunned disbelief, then turned and watched the men stride off. When he reached Dye, he flicked narrowed eyes at the Northman, let his guards open the door, then paced to his desk. Turning to face the redhead again, he speared the man with a look of hot accusation. Unconsciously, he rolled the leather thong between his fingers.

Dye shrugged. "She's a bit of a hero in these parts," he offered. "Do you remember the night you lost twenty horses?"

Davik's fingers tightened on the thong. "That was her?" He'd never understood how the theft had been accomplished. But he'd be damned if he'd ask now. His jaw clamped shut.

"Westerman blood," Dye taunted. "She can see in the dark."

Davik was silent.

"About as well as you can see on a bright, sunny day," he continued with enjoyment. "We weren't starving yet. But there hadn't been any meat for a long time."

Davik's jaw dropped. "She ate my horses? *She ate my horses!*" he exclaimed, his horror real and evident. "I knew I had cause to hate that woman," he muttered. He shook his head and stared at his desktop. "She ate my horses."

Dye laughed. "It's funny," he philosophized, "how readily popularity can be won through some small generous heroism." He stopped to enjoy Davik's expression, then ground on. "...while others die a noble death, for the same cause, unrecognized and unappreciated."

But Davik would not be baited.

"In one daring raid, she gave the people of Veronix more than Kartin ever had. She put meat on everyone's table for one night, and flipped off your Flatland Army at the same time. Ask any kid in the city about the big horse barbeque, and watch his eyes light up." Dye shook his head. "Kartin should never have touched her," he ruminated. "And now that he's dead, the man who killed him shares her popularity."

"I thought you were supposed to have killed him," Davik grumbled.

"And so I've told everyone. Only, I'm known among my men to be a great liar." Dye sighed with satisfaction. "Beaten to death. Fitting. I think the people liked that, particularly. I know my men did."

Dye's musings were interrupted when the guards announced Ursa's arrival and Davik turned his attention to the old woman as she crossed the room. Ursa tended to the girl every day in her cell, per the Prince's command. He'd allowed a week to pass before ordering the woman to report.

"She is mending My Lord. But not mended."

"Tell me when her menses begins," he said without looking at the woman.

"My Lord?"

"You heard me, Ursa. I want to know when it starts and when it has finished."

She couldn't keep the disgust from her face. "Yes, My Lord."

Davik watched the woman out the door, his mouth a determined slash in his face. He had to know if she carried a child. It would be his—or his brother's. He shot a look at Dye, but the redhead lounged in a chair with apparent disinterest.

"She should be publicly executed." His mother swept into the room, dragging a chill draft with her.

Davik's expression remained grim. His mother's recent arrival was an unwanted, unpleasant surprise. "That would turn every man in the city against me, Mother."

"That would *teach* the North Country to fear and respect you." She dropped a sheet of parchment onto his desk.

How could she think that respect accompanied fear? He rolled the leather thong down over his hand then back up to his wrist. "No, Mother. That would teach the North Country to fear and *despise* me." The tall, shrill woman snorted. "As far as the people here are concerned, she was just a soldier doing her job."

"She made a fool of you and murdered your brother, thumbed her nose at Khal. I want to see her dead, Davik."

The Northern Captain cleared his throat. "When I bought the alliance of the city's soldiers," he said with savor, "I promised them the girl would live."

Davik's mother turned her narrowed eyes on the North Country man. "Then arrange her escape, and have her murdered," she told her son.

Davik blew out a snort of annoyance. "What's this?" he said, to change the subject. He scanned the document on the desk and shook his head wearily. "I'm not much in the mood for wedding, Mother."

The woman waved a hand dismissively. "It's not a contract. It's just a document stating your willingness to wed one of The Old Queen's granddaughters, should one of them be interested."

Davik's eyes rested on the redhead in the chair before his desk. He suspected Dye was able to communicate with the girl. "I was under the impression that Tien's granddaughters were free to choose their own husbands."

His mother nodded. "By all accounts, Queen Tien doesn't believe in political weddings and doesn't meddle in her grandchildren's love lives, anymore than she interfered in her own children's. Like I said, it's just an offer. You met some of the girls when you visited Tien's court. A number of them showed a great interest in you."

Davik shook his head. "A number of them showed a great interest in Warrik."

"Only because he was The Heir."

Something tightened in the pit of his stomach. This woman who demanded the girl's death hadn't wasted a single tear on his brother. Her son! "If they showed an interest in my brother," he gritted, "it was because of Warrik's sense of humor, his giant heart, his incredible strength and kindness. Not to mention he was the best looking man on the continent."

He looked at Dye again. Did the girl still think she loved him? "Most of them are redheads aren't they?"

"The Princesses? I believe so," the Queen answered hastily. "No—I remember at least two blonds. Tien has quite a few grandchildren."

He picked up his seal and dipped it in the ink.

Dye cleared his throat again, with smirking drama.

His mother interrupted. "Davik, I can't see why you keep this man—."

"He's my liaison with the Northern forces, Mother." Impatiently, he turned his attention to Dye.

"When I convinced Kartin's army to surrender without a fight, I told them you'd wed a North Country Princess." Dye smirked at the Prince.

Davik's jaw dropped, but his mother laughed scornfully. "I wasn't aware of any Khallic Princesses living in the north!" She turned from Dye to her son. "You can't wed a Northern Princess when they don't have one! I insist on a wedding alliance with Greater Thrall, Davik. What this man has promised is not your concern."

Dye gave the Prince an uncompromising stare. "When you wed, your wife will be a Princess."

"Is he—is he saying what I think he's saying? That it matters not who you wed because she'll become a Princess upon the wedding! If you think! For one instant!

My son will wed common blood and make some farm girl a Princess!"

Davik regarded the two combatants distantly, his attention elsewhere. Finally, convinced that word would reach the girl in the dungeons below the palace, he picked up his seal and stamped the document, rolled it, and put it in Dye's hand. "Have a rider transport this to Gluthra."

The Queen rose from her chair and smirked nastily at the North Country man. "The girl dies," she reminded her son.

"I'll deal with her in my own way, Mother."

"You may *deal* with her as you wish, Davik. After that, make sure she dies. I have three other sons," she reminded him.

"You can't threaten a man with something he doesn't want, Mother."

"Then step aside Davik."

He shook his head. He couldn't do that.

Chapter Twenty-One

He got the same response from Ursa two weeks later. "She is mending, My Lord. But not mended."

He regarded the old woman with frustration. The girl drew everyone in! "When do you think she might be mended, Ursa?" he asked with mock patience.

The old woman shrugged. "Perhaps if My Lord would remove the girl's shackles…"

"That won't happen," he said without a moment's consideration. It irked him that he had to ask Ursa again, about the girl's menses, but he was relieved to know she had started two days previously.

He gave her two more weeks then went to see her. Drank a jar first, though. Well, maybe a little more than a jar. He was not so drunk he couldn't raise his cock, but drunk enough not to care what he did with it or where he put it, and anesthetized such that he knew his erection would last a long time before any feeling reached it. A long time.

He stepped into her cell carrying a chair in one hand. She slept on the bench across the room, her hands hugging her bare upper body. It was cold in the cell, he realized from beneath his protective coating of alcohol. He stopped a moment to watch her; a warm curving line interrupted by a violent splash of scarlet. Unconsciously, he ran a hand through his hair, pushing it behind his ear.

When he tripped on his way across the room, she opened her eyes and found him. He watched her eyes fill with hope. It made him angry. He would have preferred her anger or hate, or fear even.

She pushed herself up to sit on the bench. She looked thin and her arms shook from the simple effort of raising herself. Someone—Ursa, he guessed—had managed to jog her nose back into place, or at least almost. Her dark eyes were enormous in her narrowed face; a faint smudge of purple remained beneath one eye. "My Lord Prince," she started then stopped, registering the contempt on his face. "You honor me," she said quietly.

A foot of iron chain separated the manacles at her wrists.

He pulled the leather thong from his wrist and threw it at her. "Tie your hair back."

As she reached behind her neck to confine her hair, the chains lay against her throat, a slave's necklace. Her breasts lifted and his rebel dick responded with a nagging, whining twinge. His eyes closed in a moment of fury. "I have come," he announced with arrogance, "to do what I should have done when I first saw you. I should have raped you."

Her eyebrows lifted and she nodded sadly. "It won't be rape. I'll sub—"

His fist in her chains dragged her to her feet. "It will be rape," he snarled into her face.

She gasped and her eyes widened, her expression one of pain and sorrow—all without fear. "You're not that kind of man," she warned him.

"I assure you, I can be." He shoved her onto the bench. She hit it hard in a rattle of heavy chains. "I admit there will be obstacles. Not strangely, I don't find myself aroused by the whore who lied with both sets of lips." Stooping quickly he grasped her ankles and put her feet on the bench, wrenched them apart, then forced her knees to follow. With a hand at the top her shorts, he tore the silk downward and bared her sex to showcase in a puddle of blood red silk. He pulled the chair between them and turned it, straddling it backwards and resting his arms on the chair back.

"Open your cunt," he said coldly.

Her eyes widened on him.

"Pull your slot open with your fingers," he said harshly. "I want to look up your cunt. Find out where you hide your heart," he grated.

Her feet slipped to the ground; her legs closed. "No," she said.

He was on his feet as he slung the chair across the room and yanked her chains outward, jerking her off the bench. She hit her knees hard as she fell before him. With one hand, he untied his breeks and pulled himself out. Grasping his cock, he pumped himself methodically then, with one hand at the back of her skull and the other around his shaft, he forced his cock into her mouth. Both hands clamped her head in an iron grip as he pumped into her mouth. He watched the top of her head and felt her gag then choke as his hips continued their savage grinding — continued ruthlessly — knowing she struggled for every breath.

The alcohol proved to be only moderately successful as a numbing agent and he found himself peaking sooner than he'd expected. Crushing her face into his lower body, he came into her mouth. She choked and gagged and swallowed convulsively but didn't attempt to pull away.

Releasing her head with a thrust of contempt, he tucked his cock inside his breeks and calmly retied the laces inches from her face. Reaching for her chains, he dragged her to her feet and brought his face close to hers.

"That wasn't rape?"

She wiped her swollen mouth on the back of her chained hands and did not raise her eyes to him.

"It felt like rape to me. What did it feel like to you? Did it feel like love? Anything like love?"

She stared at the ground and shook her head.

He gave her chains a short jerk then thrust them into her chest. She gasped as she slid back to her knees.

"I'm sorry," she said in a voice small and lost in disbelief.

"Apologize to Warrik when you see him next. At Hadi's Gate. He has a big heart, or did before you put an arrow though it. He may forgive you. I never will."

Her shackles chinked and a small keening whine escaped her lips. Coldly, he looked down on her bowed head, pleased he had finally dented her iron self-command. Her hair had worked its way out of the leather thong and hung before her face like a mourning veil. "Warrik," she whispered and he watched a tear fall onto her steel shackles. She raised her face.

He met her eyes with horror. Her grief, keen and real—invoked in his brother's name—was like a knife in his heart. In her voice, he heard his own anguish articulated. In her eyes, he recognized the grief and sorrow he had thought he was alone with. Sorrow that even his parents didn't share.

Revelation hit him hard as his knees gave out. "Petra." His throat constricted and he choked on her name. He dropped to his knees and reached for her.

Caught a glimpse of her wrists, raw and wet inside steel manacles. Watched her hands twist.

Saw the skin stripped away beneath the steel to reveal wet pink flesh, purple where she bruised, gray where she blistered, yellow where she festered. Red where she was bleeding.

A thin line of scarlet ran along the edge of one manacle and dripped to the ground.

He jerked away from her. Fought to his feet. Backpedaled a few paces in panic, fighting to keep his balance. Scrambled backward across the room — as though fleeing a herd of demons — stumbling as he backed into the door. Wrenched it open and got himself through. The door slammed behind him and he threw his back against it then took a long shuddering breath as he staggered a step and leaned drunkenly against the wall. He straight-armed himself away from the wall and reeled down the narrow corridor, turned a corner, and found Dye waiting for him.

"Enjoy yourself?" Dye asked cynically.

Davik swallowed hard, straightened himself, and pushed past the man.

Dye's sneering voice followed him. "If revenge is so sweet, why do you look like you're going to puke?"

Unable to fight his rising gorge — and with a hand on the wall to steady his reeling world — Prince Davik of Khal leaned over and puked his guts up. With a silent smirk of appreciation, Dye stood watching him.

"Get those chains off her," Davik rasped, drawing his wrist over his mouth. "Now!" He shuddered. "Get her out of there. I want her...out of the palace. Out of...my country. Arrange her escape."

"Yes, my Prince," Dye granted obsequiously. "And would you have that accomplished with or without murder."

Davik whirled on him. "If I'd wanted her murdered," he gritted, "I'd have given the job to—someone I trust."

Holding his hands up in a signal for peace, Dye smiled ingratiatingly. "Just asking," he said.

Davik glowered at the man, disgust thick in his eyes. "Where does your loyalty lay, man? Who do you serve, Northman?"

"At the moment sir, you. Along with myself," Dye muttered under his breath.

Chapter Twenty-Two

"Well? Are you coming," Dye asked her again.

"I'm thinking on it," she said grumpily.

"If you're going to stay, I'll have to put the chains back—"

"Right," she said standing quickly. She was clad in traveling doeskins. She followed Dye from the cell.

* * * * *

From his rooms, Davik watched the foothills. A sun-shaft slashed through the sullen clouds and shot earthward, burying its head into the heart of the mountains. Once parted, the surly gray skies pulled back in shriveled defeat, allowing the golden light to pour out in a torrent over mountains and foothills. Somewhere within the palace walls a group of men were cheering. A deep muffled roar of approval reverberated through the halls of his palace. His palace!

Ah shit, he thought. Ah shit. His lips curled in an unhappy smile. The girl drew everyone in; even the gods. Footsteps in the corridor drew his attention and he turned.

Dye stuck his head in the door. "It's done," he said.

Davik nodded, pulled the stopper from a large jar, and upended it.

Dye joined him in a few cups, but couldn't keep up with the Prince. When his initial attempts at conversation were ignored, he joined the Prince in silent consumption.

"Was it your men I heard cheering?"

"They're your men too, Davik."

Davik nodded, finished a jar and reached for the next. The jar was almost at his mouth when his arm seized as though rusted in action—motionless—as he stared down at the table. The base of the wine jar had left a wet ring on the surface of the table. A blood red ring. His eyebrows drew together in sympathy as his eyes filled with pain. He put the jar down. "Did you bandage her wrists, Dye?" he asked faintly.

Dye snorted. "What do you care?"

Davik pulled his arm across the tabletop, blotting the ring with his sleeve. "I don't like rats either," he said weakly, "but I'd not watch one suffer."

Dye gave the Prince a long, hard look. "She couldn't stand to have them wrapped," he said brusquely.

"Shit." Another jar was consumed before the Prince staggered over to his bed and threw himself down on his back. Dye watched the man squeeze his eyes together. "Shit," he muttered again.

With his eyes on the Prince, Dye finished his cup, then crossed the room and opened a small shuttered window.

Long past dark, he clattered up a set of steps and stepped out onto the palace roof. A dim form shifted in a shadowed corner. He gave the girl a nod and unwound the rope looped over his shoulder.

"You're sure," she asked Dye.

"Aye. I'm sure. He wouldn't wake to attend the end of the world."

* * * * *

With the black night behind her and the distant ground somewhere below, Petra leapt from the roof and rappelled down the palace wall. Swinging her legs through the small opening, she sat on the sill an instant before lowering herself to the floor. She crept across the unlit room, stopping briefly at the desk, then continued to the bed where a man sprawled in a limp mass. Sinking to her knees, she considered the man's pained expression. She cocked her head to the side and frowned at him, then shook her head. "You should never have come to my cell," she told the comatose Prince. "You'll regret it for the rest of your life." The corner of her mouth lifted slightly. "But I've no doubt you'll get what you deserve, Davik." The melancholy smile was on her face as she stood and slipped out the window.

* * * * *

With morose disinterest, Prince Davik of Khal—both Northern and Southern—surveyed the stack of documents on his desk. For the fourth time, he opened the top drawer, shuffled through its contents and closed it again. One by one, he opened each remaining drawer in his desk and examined the interiors with lackluster interest. With his chin in his fist, he stared at the stack again.

The door opened and a man stepped inside. "My Lord Prince," Dye announced, and waited with a smirk. "My Lord Prince, your army is deserting."

No response.

"The Maydayns are on the march and approach the city walls even now."

Nothing.

"The Queen of Thrall demands your immediate response, on pain of attack, to her question about her granddaughter."

Davik opened his drawer and peered absently inside.

"Your mother's on her way down the hall."

Davik looked up slowly and tried to focus on the man. "My mother's coming?"

Dye laughed without sympathy, and threw himself in a chair before the Prince's desk. "Get enough to drink last night?"

Davik sighed. "If you're going to lecture me, Dye," he said in a broken whisper. "I pray you do it quietly or I will vomit right into your lap."

The doors swept open and Davik's tall, spare, ungenerous mother cut across the room like a knife. She slapped a document down on the desk in front of Davik, smug victory stamped on her face in bold letters. "You've been accepted," she announced.

Davik blinked at his mother blearily, then down at the document on the table. Helplessly, he pushed it toward Dye.

Dye's expression was chagrined as he read. "Queen Tien of Greater Thrall And Etc. accepts The Khallic Prince's offer of wedding…to her granddaughter, a Princess of the royal line, descended from…etc., etc…the ceremony to take place upon—" Dye looked up. "She's on her way here! Queen Tien! With a thousand men to protect her granddaughter."

Davik turned an unlikely shade of green as Dye's eyes shot back and forth down the page.

"Your bride comes with a large acreage in Northern Khal."

"How large?" his mother inquired greedily.

"A thousand." Dye continued. "…on the understanding that Prince Davik is the present heir to the throne of Khal and will remain so during his lifetime…"

"Ha!" This from the Khallic Queen. "And Tien pretends to disdain political weddings."

"…and breach of this contract to result in a break of all diplomatic relations between Greater Thrall and Khal, as well as other measures, including but not limited to…the cessation of peaceful relations…" Dye broke off in alarm. "*She's talking about war!*" Dye threw the contract on the desk and looked at the Prince's pale face. "You're to be wed, Prince Davik."

Chapter Twenty-Three

"The Queen of Thrall wants a receipt for that contract," Dye reminded Prince Davik the next morning.

"I thought you were against this wedding."

"Yeah, well a man's priorities change when the Army of Thrall is on his doorstep. Khal can't afford a war with Thrall And Etc."

Davik was looking slightly more fit today, and less morose, but his temper was climbing gears. He slammed each of his drawers shut then cleared his table with angry swipe that put everything on the floor. With a contained expression of annoyance, he crossed the room and continued his search in his trunk, his bed, then the floor. "I don't know," he growled. "War with a common foe might be the one thing that pulls this country together."

"Don't make jokes, Prince Davik. War with Thrall would devastate this country." He pointed a finger at the Prince. "It doesn't make sense to throw away a friendly alliance that's been in place for over a hundred years."

"Friendly alliance! With Thrall! Did your read that contract!" He stripped the bed completely, threw the sheets on the floor and regarded the mess with ferocity. "That contract had a distinctly *unfriendly* tone. Why?"

"Are you kidding, man? Your mother would piss anyone off." Dye put his shoulder against the wall, watching him. "You look like you're feeling better. Are you ready for your lecture?"

The Prince ignored him and continued his search.

"You probably never heard of the young man who got her out of your father's cesspool. He took an arrow in the back; they had almost cleared the walls. Mercifully, he died within the hour. That didn't stop your father's men from making his last hour a nightmare. But he revealed nothing that would help them find the girl."

"The girl's convincing when she spreads her legs," Davik grunted ungenerously. "No one knows that better than I."

Dye shook his head. "He was her brother."

The Prince's temper was short. "Like I said, she's convincing—"

Dye's steel against Davik's throat sheared the sentence short. "He was my brother too," the redhead hissed. "One more word from you about my brother and I'm taking the afternoon off." Dye grunted as he jerked up on the blade. "Going fishing. And I'm taking your dick as bait. Think you're the only man who loved his brother? At least Warrik was a man, and a soldier at that. My brother was just a kid. You want to call the girl a whore, go ahead. Mithra knows you treated her like one. But if you think a woman becomes a harlot when you treat her like one, you're mistaken."

He released the Prince with an angry shove. Glaring at the man, Davik rubbed his neck. "She's your sister?"

Dye jammed his blade back into the sheath on his belt. "You Khallic Princes have a *damn* high opinion of yourselves. You lock the girl in a dark hole for five years, whip most of the skin from her back, murder her brother. And you're surprised she doesn't fall on her knees and worship you and your brother for gang-fucking-rape!"

"Is that what she called it?"

"What do you call it Davik? Or is that just the way the Khallic nobility shows a girl a good time?

"She saved you! We had orders to kill the first man out of that inn on the fourth dawn. Preferably you. We were to kill the brains of the Southern army and hold The Heir hostage to leverage for peace. But we were to kill the first man out of the inn. Whoever survived would be The Heir. She couldn't warn you without betraying all of us! She stopped you. Threw herself on you and stopped us from carrying out our orders. Her Prince's orders! She tried to save your brother. All this after gang-*fucking*-rape!" He ran a hand through his angry red hair.

"It wasn't like that."

"No? What was it like, Davik? Because I'm from the North Country and North Country men don't share their women. What was it like? Was it anything like love?"

Davik stared at Dye. Yes, he thought. Yes. It had been a lot like love.

"And here in the dungeon? I don't suppose that was rape, either?"

Davik winced, his stomach roiled. "That was rape," he said with unflinching honesty.

"And what was the difference then, Davik? You didn't enjoy the rape?" he sneered. "Did it never occur to you that perhaps she didn't enjoy it? Any of it? That a North Country girl wouldn't enjoy being fucked by two noble *Flatland* Princes?"

Davik's eyebrows drew together as he recalled that dawn, when Warrik had pulled her away from him. She hadn't wanted Warrik.

"Shall I define rape for you then? It's when a man forces sex on a woman and *she doesn't want it*."

Ah shit. This was bullshit. "You almost make me feel sorry for her, Dye. Oh! Except for the fact that *she* seduced me and my brother so she could *murder* us!"

"Maybe that's how it looked from the South. From the North it looked like a brave young captain sacrificing herself to end the siege on her country. She joined the Northern Army because she hated the South, hated your father, hated what you had done to her and her brother. She executed her mission brilliantly, forced Southern Khal back to the fucking flatlands and, in capturing you, secured our ability to leverage for a signed treaty recognizing our sovereignty. In the opinion of the North Country, she was ready for The League of Hadi's Saints.

"And yet, she let you escape from her home, knowing you would resume your siege, knowing what Kartin would do to her, knowing she was letting her people down. Do you want to know why? Because she thought *you* were the man to lead Khal." Dye stopped for a breath. "She *gave* you Northern Khal," Dye finished vehemently.

"Aye, and Southern Khal too, when she killed my brother. Mind me to thank her for that." Davik threw himself into his chair and withdrew his gaze from the redhead's angry face. "Why haven't you killed me before now, Dye?"

"And put you out of your misery?" Dye laughed grimly. "I'd rather watch you suffer. Although," he muttered, "there are times you wear on my patience."

Patience. Davik stared at the man. "Patience? What are you waiting for that requires patience, Dye? For me to fall in love with your sister? This isn't a child's tale."

"Love!" Dye looked stunned. "Don't be an idiot, man. I'm waiting for you to be the leader she said you could be!" He shook his head and muttered. "Child's tale! No, this is no child's tale. I've heard a few. The Princess may have to kiss a frog, but she isn't generally the victim of gang-rape."

"It wasn't rape," he grated "and she's not a Princess."

Dye was a while with his comeback. "Next to you, she's a Princess."

Davik stared at the man with frustration. "Don't mince words, Dye. Do you mean compared to me or wed to me?"

"Wed to you? Wed! Don't you even use that word alongside my sister's name!"

"Your sister." Davik rose from the chair like a storm. "Like you've done such a great job of protecting your sister! You let Kartin beat the shit out of her. You let *me* put chains on her. Why!" Davik roared at the man. "Why didn't you tell me about her wrists?"

"*Why didn't I* — "

Davik was smashed into the wall.

Dye snarled into his face. "You knew about her wrists. Why else would a soldier of her caliber faint at the mere idea of being tied! And Ursa—what about Ursa! She told you the girl wasn't mending. She told you to remove her chains." Dye took an angry breath. "Don't *tell* me you didn't know! *Don't tell me!* Or, so help me man, I'll kill you where you stand!"

The redhead was fast, experienced and without scruple when it came to fighting. Generally, he didn't rely on strength, didn't have to. And it shouldn't have come as a surprise when the Khallic Prince lifted him by the lapels, so to speak, threw him across the room, and dove after him. Nonetheless, Dye was unprepared for the Prince's outburst. The two men went down in a flailing display of bad temper. Davik's head snapped back when Dye threw his elbow into the young man's face. Davik's knuckles smacked the floor as Dye avoided a blow, then failed to avoid the next several volleys. Out of habit, Dye pulled his knife and watched it beaten out of his hand. Cursing, and forced to close on the young Prince to avoid his flying fists, Dye managed a wresting move that flipped the Prince on his back. Davik took the crack to his head without pause, and apparently without feeling, as he returned to the fight with more brute strength than Dye would ever see in his lifetime. Sheer raging power put the Prince back on top. The Prince was approaching melt point, Dye realized. Complete, red-hot fury. And he'd be taking Dye out when he reached white-hot rage. "Right!" he bellowed over the Prince's curses. "Right. You didn't know about her wrists then."

Davik's fist hung in the air, halfway en route to blackening Dye's left eye. The spitting black fury that twisted his face was gradually replaced with grudging recognition and a return to his senses. With glowering reluctance, he sank back on his heels and dragged a wrist across his eyes.

Dye snorted. "Are you...crying?"

"You put your fucking elbow in my eye!"

Davik climbed off the Northman and held out his left hand, shaking his bloodied right, as tears poured down his face. "Mithra, Dye. I've really screwed things up, haven't I?"

The Northman took the Prince's hand and levered himself to his feet. "Yeah, you have." Dye dusted himself off. "You and me, both," he muttered. "Drink?"

"Anything but wine," Davik agreed. Chest heaving, eyes streaming, he leaned back against his desk and took in the Northman's flaming hair, his fair skin. "You don't look anything like her."

"She's the black sheep in the family. Most of us are redheads." The Northman shook his head painfully and glanced sideways at his companion. "I should have killed Kartin," he said with keen regret.

"Yeah, you should have." Davik gasped in a breath. "Why didn't you?"

"She wouldn't let me," Dye muttered disagreeably. "She said you had to do it."

Chapter Twenty-Four

"Warrik wasn't the meathead some people took him for."

A jug of ale had been delivered along with two wooden tankards. The two Khals sat across from each other, the Prince's desk between them. With his feet propped atop an open drawer, Davik rocked back on the rear legs of his chair.

Dye crossed his feet on the desktop and nodded with interest.

"People underestimated him. Mithra, he could be funny. But he was more than that."

"Nobody takes humor seriously."

Davik returned a melancholy nod. "He was so big...strong. You see a guy like that and you think he just powers his way through life. But Warrik was brave, daring and bright. Only..."

"Only people thought you brighter."

Davik sighed. "Not that I am, particularly. One time, when we were young...we'd boasted we could bring back lastmeal; the salmon were running and we thought we'd just kick a bunch out of the river, carry them home, and win the accolade we deserved. We were doing good too—had about twelve big steelhead on the bank—when this grizzly, *huge grizzly*, ambles out of the brush, sits down in the middle of *our fish*, and commences to devour them in bulk. Of course, by that time, we'd got up the further bank as fast as we could get. The bank was high, rocky, and steep and we might have been afraid of the climb if we'd stopped to think on it, if we hadn't been so afraid of that bear." Davik tipped his tankard to his lips then carried on.

"The bear finished off our catch and went into the river for his own. There we were, up a cliff with no fish and no way down; the bear was set smack in the middle of our way home and we were stuck there as long as he fancied salmon. Warrik wandered off down the cliff a ways, looking for I-didn't-know-what, then next thing I know, he's zinging rocks down at the biggest mammal on the continent. I'm backing away from the cliff edge, he's pitching rocks as hard as he can, and the bear is getting pissed. In an instant, the monster turns on us and starts up the cliff.

"The grizzly weighs a ton. Rocks are flying behind him—rocks the size of carts—and, for a moment, I think he's not going to make it; he's going down in a landslide. Then I realize he's getting ahead of the rocks and he's about to crest the cliff. I want to run, but I'm too proud at sixteen. At sixteen, I'm going to die alongside my brother." Sardonically, the corner of Davik's mouth curled. "Warrik's standing at the cliff edge, almost nose to nose with the brute. He's got a long, thick branch jammed into a crack—a crack running parallel to the cliff face—and he's throwing his weight back on it. Half the cliff gives way."

Davik took a long swallow. "Half the cliff goes down. When the dust clears, the bear's at the bottom of the cliff, just about dead from the fall. Warrik looks at me and laughs, pulls his steel, and we finish him off with our knives." Davik shrugged and smiled. "We had bear for lastmeal."

"How was it?"

"Not bad. A bit greasy, I thought. But nobody complained." He raised his tankard. "To Warrik," he said. "The braver brother."

Dye raised his tankard. "Braver? You'd not have done the same? Had you his size and strength?"

Davik mused on this a while. "Perhaps. If I'd thought of it in the first place, and if I were alone."

"And otherwise?"

"I'd not risk another man's life."

"You'd not have risked your brother's life."

"I guess not," Davik said slowly. He stared at Dye; the redhead's pupils were tiny black pinpricks centered on intense blue. "You're Westerman, too."

"Enough to stagger home from the alehouse on a moonless night."

"That's how you sneaked up on Mavrik."

Dye gave the Prince a slow smile.

"And do you share your sister's Slurian traits as well?"

"Unfortunately not. At least—not the kind that could drive the opposite sex crazy."

"You've no other brothers, Dye?"

The Northman shook his head.

Davik nodded slowly. "To your sister then." The Prince's face was melancholy as the men raised their cups together. "May she find happiness, despite...everything."

Dye sipped his ale and gave the Prince a sly sideways glance. "You're not going after her?"

"Why would I," he said without energy. "She's gone. And I am to be wed…to a Princess of Thrall."

"Why would you?" Dye repeated. "Oh, I don't know. Maybe because she's taken your seal of office."

Davik looked up sharply.

"You'll want it to stamp that receipt."

Davik's eyes went to the table and he cursed softly. "She was in here?"

"You knew she was a thief. And she has a few connections in the palace."

"Like you?"

Dye inclined his head.

Davik looked at the contract on the table. "I can have another seal made," he tendered without conviction.

"I imagine she knows that."

I imagine she knows that. The idea got trapped inside the Prince's braincase and reverberated, growing in strength and volume as it cycled in his mind.

She wanted to see him.

Davik turned slowly in Dye's direction, eyes wide as he stared right through the man. "Get me a tracker."

Dye nodded, his eyes crinkled in challenge. "You can take a tracker if you like, or I could just draw you a map." He dropped into a chair and drew a piece of parchment toward him.

Out of his chair and standing behind Dye, Davik watched the map grow on the paper. "How can you not hate me, Dye? After what my family has done to yours?"

"You're not your father," he replied. "Although you can do a fair imitation of him. You're not your mother either — thank the *gods* — each and every one of them." When the map was complete, Dye put the drawing in the Prince's hand. "And I have a fair idea of what you're feeling. So long as I'm within thirty feet of you."

Davik started.

Dye shrugged apologetically. "Slurian blood — Nay — don't be alarmed. Petra hasn't my talent, no more than I have hers." Dye paused a moment for effect. "And — Aye — I know how you feel about her."

With the map clutched in his fist, Davik headed for the door. "I'm expecting twenty steer driven in today," he threw over his shoulder. "Have one of my Northern units set up the pits and spits." The Prince spun around and pointed at the Northman. "The South is going to show the North how to throw a barbeque."

Dye watched the Prince through the door then stretched back in his chair — arms behind his head — and smirked. "You poor bastard," he told the ceiling.

Chapter Twenty-Five

Petra watched the Prince as he threw his leg over the gelding's neck and slid from its back. "You look tired," she said.

He nodded.

"Perhaps you should just kill me and have done with it."

He nodded again. "Either that or make you my wife."

She smiled, took a few skirting steps before him without approaching him. "A man once said that to my grandmother."

He frowned. His comeback had been somewhat cliché, an old line borrowed from one of the old ballads. Only, he couldn't place which ballad.

There was a long silence between them. How would it end, he wondered. "I made a mistake," he said quietly.

"In thinking you could be a complete asshole?"

"No," he returned ruefully. "I think I've actually done a fair job of that. No, I made a mistake in thinking I hated you. I don't hate you," he said. "I love you."

"I know."

"I wanted to. I wanted to hate you."

She nodded. "You loved your brother." Her voice wobbled a bit. "How can you forgive me, Davik?"

"I might ask you the same thing."

She was quick to defend him. "Dye told me what happened after you left my cell. It wasn't rape," she said, but her voice wobbled again and shattered. She turned from him quickly but not before he saw the tears. He watched her trembling shoulders.

If it wasn't rape, he thought miserably, it was damn close.

"It wasn't," she sobbed. "Tell me it wasn't Davik."

"It wasn't rape," he said sadly. He couldn't bear to see her broken. To see how he had broken her.

"I submitted, willingly."

Or would have if he'd given her the chance. He watched her back as her shoulders shook and her hands went to her face. "It wasn't rape," he repeated. "I was just hot for you. I'm sorry if I was rough." It was a sham, he knew, a lying façade. But it was what she wanted to hear. Somehow he had to retrieve his words; remake those words of violence into words of love. "One glimpse of your sweet, warm cunt and I went a bit berserk," he said, his eyes full of pain and hope. "Did I hurt you?"

She shook her head.

"Your wrists?"

Her back was still turned to him. "I don't know why, but I never got used to the shackles—my skin, I mean—not even after five years. Most prisoners develop calluses, but I never did. Maybe it was the metal. I've never been able to wear jewelry, other than pure gold; anything else irritates my skin. At any rate, the manacles rubbed my wrists and ankles perpetually raw. The pain kept me nauseated during the five years of my imprisonment. Just the thought of chains—makes me queasy."

He looked at her skinned wrists, crusted with open sores, and felt a bit queasy himself. How could she forgive him? "I blamed myself for Warrik's death. For being deceived. How could I have been deceived? By you?"

She caught at a sob.

"I think — now — it was because you weren't lying."

She nodded. "I loved you. It had been better if I didn't. Perhaps then you'd have seen through me."

"You tried to stop it. You did the best you could, under the circumstances. You couldn't betray your men." He took a breath and continued. "It was my fault. I should have given you my trust; Warrik would be alive today if I had." He backed up to sit on a dry stump. "Wouldn't he?"

She didn't answer.

"You'd have called off the mission and thrown your support behind my brother. With your endorsement, he'd have been accepted by your Northmen.

"Mithra," he whispered hopelessly. "I've made so many mistakes." He looked up at her, at her stiff back, her shoulders as they shuddered. "You've something of mine," he reminded her, thinking to distract her and allay her tears.

Turning, she wiped her cheeks with the back of her hand, reached inside her jerkin, and produced the seal.

He looked at the seal in her hand and shook his head. "That's not what I came for." He raised his eyes to hers. "The ballad, Petra. Give me back my song."

Hesitantly, her hands returned to slip inside her jerkin. She took the steps between them, handed him the thick wad of soiled parchment, then backed away. He opened it and smoothed it on his knee. It was creased, and stained, and damp, and smelled of the woman he loved. He read a few lines and grimaced. "Why did you keep it?"

"I hoped you might revise it…one day."

He shuffled through the pages. "It needs work," he admitted. "The ending in particular; it's a bit morbid." He attempted a smile but it probably didn't come off very well. He lifted his face to her. "How does it end, Petra." His voice broke. "Tell me how it will end."

Her eyes met his bravely while she considered her answer. "They made love," she said finally. "And that was just the beginning."

His heart soared. It soared. This despite the fact that a man's heart was never designed for flight.

She shook her head. "I'll miss Warrik," she said sadly.

He stared at her. What a time to be jealous, he thought, breathlessly.

He felt dizzy. It was the altitude, he thought, as his heart continued to spiral. He felt at that moment he could accomplish anything. And he knew what he wished to accomplish. He wanted to repair the damage he'd done when he entered her cell, wanted to restate his love for her, and he knew it was important to put it in coarse terms, for her sake; terms she would understand.

He started off strongly. "I couldn't stand it when my brother took you. Right from the start, I couldn't stand it…every time he took you. I wanted—and want—to be the only man who touches you, the only man who kisses you—your lips, your breasts, your warm, wet slot—I want to be the only man you spread your legs for, the only man you make love to and the only man you love. I admit...I admit my love for you is selfish, greedy, and even violent.

"I want to make love to you with my eyes wide open. I want to love you and worship you and fuck you to the core of your sweet warm depths, my cock buried to the hilt in your willing cunt, and hopefully do it...artfully...enough that I see love in your eyes again, just before you buck beneath me and rush to meet me. Do you understand what I'm saying, Petra?"

She raised her eyes slowly, a trace of smile on her lips. "I think it's the most poetic thing I've ever heard."

He went to her then and made love to her, gently, unselfishly, artfully; and it only got a bit violent there toward the end.

Chapter Twenty-Six

Davik woke with a shiver and raised himself on one elbow, looked down at the girl beside him. Between the two of them they shared almost no clothing. They'd fallen asleep in the comfortable twilight on a bed of grass. The near dawn was brisk. Thinking a cape of some sort should be in his saddlebag, he pulled on his breeks and headed for his horse. It was a bit of a hike as the horses had grazed off in the night. The gelding lifted its head and nickered at his approach. Anxious to return to the girl before the cold wakened her, he gave the beast a cursory pat and flipped open one of the saddlebags. Pulling out a small crumpled book, he started to tuck it under his arm before continuing his search. Frowning, he stopped in mid-action, a look of uncertainty on his face, then he started flipping through the pages of the book.

A crisp crackle spun him around. Automatically, his hand slapped his hip, but his steel lay on the ground back beside the girl. A full unit of Thralls materialized in the just-forming dawn. Fifty pair of pink eyes fixed on him. He backed up a step. Their weapons were sheathed, he noted. With growing resentment, he searched the lines for their captain and found the small man standing in Dye's shadow.

With malicious glee, Dye grinned at the Khallic Prince. "Hello Davik. You didn't think I was going to make this easy for you, did you?"

Davik continued to back away as denial filled his eyes. With a panicked glance in the girl's direction, he started shaking his head.

The company of Thralls closed around him quickly.

"The Queen of Thrall And Etc. awaits your attendance on your wedding day, Davik."

Davik looked dead horror at the tall redhead. "No! Dye. You can't do this. You can't do this to us. Let me — let us — disappear into Northern Khal. Tien's granddaughter can have one of my brothers."

Dye shook his head and laughed. "The Princess isn't interested in The Heir to Khal. She fancies *you*! Tien hasn't come all this way to see her granddaughter humiliated."

"You can't do this. You can't do this, Dye. To me. To Petra."

"Petra will understand — better than anyone. Andarta and country, and all that nonsense. I intend to see you get what you deserve, Davik, and avert a war with Thrall at the same time." Dye looked back in the direction the Prince had come from. "If you like, we can take Petra with us."

Would she do that? Would she, in the end, betray him? For the good of her country? She had proven — more than proven — she was willing to sacrifice much for Khal.

Davik shook his head. "I don't want her that close to my mother." It was only half a lie; the girl would never be safe within his mother's circle of influence. The other half, the lying half, he couldn't face. Would she stand by and watch him wed to another woman?

"So be it, then."

Madison Hayes

Davik gave Dye a look of hot-fired defiance. "I'll get back to her Dye," he said with hard confidence. "Somehow I'll find her again and get back to her."

The redhead laughed, his enjoyment absolute. "When did you become such a romantic? Did no one ever tell you, Davik, there's no room for love in political weddings? You may love whomever you choose, My Prince — for the rest of your life — but today you'll be wed to a Princess."

Dye held the Prince's horse as he swung into the saddle, then threw himself onto his own mount. Flanked by the silent Thralls, they turned toward the city.

* * * * *

Petra hugged her arms and murmured in her sleep. She was back in her cell. It was cold. She whimpered. Davik had...Davik had...

Petra awoke with a start. It was past dawn.

Davik had loved her. Last night. Most of the night, actually.

She bolted into a sitting position and gazed around her with sudden apprehension, sudden realization. "Davik?"

Then she was on her feet and moving, as she cursed with the rustic vocabulary of a soldier. " — Dye," she spat at the end of a vicious stream of adjectives. Struggling into her clothes, she whistled for her mount, threw herself onto its back, and rode hell-bent for Veronix.

* * * * *

Locked in his rooms on his mother's orders, The Heir groaned as he watched the lone rider streak toward the

286

city walls. He hammered on his door and roared for his mother. When the doors swung open, he almost hugged the woman in his relief. "I'm ready," he gasped. "Let's get on with it." His long stride took him down the corridor at a brisk pace, forcing his mother into a near-run as she tried to keep up with her formerly recalcitrant son, now evidently keen on wedding.

He was keen, alright—keen his mother should not know about the rider who had just swept inside the gates—praying that Dye would somehow find her before his mother's men did.

"...and do you know what these barbarians have planned for your wedding feast," his mother was complaining breathlessly. "Barbeque! *Barbeque!* What will Queen Tien think of us?"

He swept into the hall with all the handsome confidence of a Khallic Prince, ignored the many attendants who filled the room, and approached The Old Queen unwaveringly, took her hand and kissed it. Her black hair had long since turned white. Her skin stretched over her face, crinkled and creased everywhere, but without sagging anywhere. He looked into the old woman's eyes and was surprised. As always, her expression was solemn, but her keen gray eyes laughed.

She stood to accept his greeting and he was surprised again. She had always been taller than he; she must be shrinking with age, he thought. The idea made him melancholy; The Old Queen was a lone paragon in a world filled with deceit and self-serving avarice. And he felt guilty, knowing he would disappoint this woman—as he was sure to do—when he found his way back to Petra.

"Prince Davik," she said, and her voice did not waver or creak. "How handsome you've grown. Small wonder my granddaughter snapped up your tender for wedding." She pulled the Khallic Prince to sit beside her. "I trust you can be entertaining as well? A sense of humor is important in a wedded relationship. I hope you can rise to the challenge." She regarded him expectantly.

Damn. That was putting him on the spot. He honest-to-god could not think of anything amusing in his situation. And the Queen wasn't joking; she was serious about humor. She had wed a Westerman with a brilliant wit, overlooking entirely his horribly scarred face. "A sense of humor is required in wedding? Is that a hard and fast rule?"

Her old lips quirked upward.

"Or shall we save hard and fast to fill some other wedding requirement? On either count, I assure you I will rise to the challenge."

Queen Tien smiled her approval as a steady tramp grew outside the hall's doors. Davik braced himself, hoping the Princess was ugly—and dull—so he could start hating her right away, so he wouldn't feel bad when he left her. Inwardly, he groaned. He couldn't remember any of Tien's granddaughters being ugly, or even what you might call plain.

The Queen's murmurings interrupted his thoughts. "I've always been fond of this one," she was whispering to him. "She reminds me of myself when I was younger. I suppose that makes me a vain old woman. She takes after my father—Morghan." The old woman leaned toward the Prince. "You might like a warning, though. There's a short distance between this girl and my throne."

Davik turned to stare at the Queen and almost jumped when the doors swung open to admit a company of Thralls. Pink eyes blazing in chalk-white faces, the small men trooped into the hall and arranged themselves to form an honor guard for the Princess. Expectantly, the hall occupants turned toward the open door.

A young woman stepped though the opening. A woman dressed toe to crown in crisp red silk. She was the most beautiful creature the Prince had ever seen. He rose to his feet both breathless and wordless at the sight of her as she approached him with great dignity.

Chapter Twenty-Seven

"You look good in red," he eventually managed to croak.

"Scarlet," she corrected him. She gave him her hand and he hurried to take it. Raising it to his lips, he placed a kiss on her scarred wrists.

"I deserved that, didn't I," he said with a wince.

She nodded. "You're going to get everything you deserve, Davik. You should have killed me when you had the chance." Petra smiled sweetly at the Southern Prince.

He shook his head. "I should have made you my wife." He stopped as dawn hit his expression. "The Ballad of Chay! Erith, the Maydayn warlord said that to Chay!" His eyes got very big. "Chay, your grandmother. You're Chay's granddaughter. You're named for Petr. Petr Maghmarin."

"On my father's side."

"And on your mother's side?" he asked, knowing the answer.

"My grandmother is Tien."

Tien. The Queen of Thrall And Etc. Tien, the daughter of Morghan of Amdahl and Tahrra of Agryppa; the stuff of legends. "You're a Princess." These words were whispered in quiet awe.

She shook her head. "Only a Princess's daughter. And there are many cousins between me and the throne."

Davik smiled at her. Or so she thought.

"My parents chose a simple life in Northern Khal." He looked at her reproachfully. "It's a large farm," she admitted.

He slid his hand to her elbow and guided her to the perimeter of the room. Like a yard of sunflowers, every head in the room followed them. "A moment, Queen Tien?"

The Old Queen nodded her amused agreement.

Davik pulled the girl into the alcoved corridor surrounding the hall and started down its length. "You're the Princess from Northern Khal Dye said I must wed. Not a Khallic Princess; a Princess of Thrall." His eyes rested on one long caramel leg exposed by the slit in her dress. "Morghan was dark, I've read."

"Skraeling blood," she admitted.

He shook his head. She was not only a Princess and the granddaughter of Morghan's daughter. She was the granddaughter of Morghan's general, Chay. Not only that! She was a Maghmarin. Chay had children by one of the Maghmarin brothers, although the Maghmarin responsible had never been identified with absolute certainty.

But her last name was Maghmarin! Mithra and Donar Together at Once! *And* she was a brilliant strategist and captain in her own right. "I thought you'd read Chay." He smiled at her and shook his head again. "You were just recounting family history. I never really stood a chance, did I?"

"Not really. Although, if I were anything like Chay, that prison couldn't have held me. She'd have gotten out one way or another. Dead or alive. Dead if need be. And whistled as she strolled through Hadi's Gates. I've never been willing to sacrifice so much. I'm more like my mother, my grandmother."

"And your grandmother waits to attend our wedding. To protect you, and make sure the commitment is honored by me — and my mother."

She nodded. "When you sent the Queen your wedding offer, Dye sent my acceptance along to her at the same time. He probably mentioned something to her about your mother's wish to see me dead, as well as her threat to replace you as The Heir. If grandmother's missive was a bit threatening, it was to protect you as much as me. She can't actually go to war without the council's approval," she reminded him. "I intend to wed you — Davik — regardless of your inheritance."

He smiled faintly but sincerely as he found his mother's face across the room. "Mother will be furious." He frowned suddenly. "Do you want all this? Any of this?"

"An irate mother-in-law?"

"An irate mother-in-law. The country of Khal. The throne one day?" He paused. "Otherwise, I have three brothers," he reminded her. "It's your choice."

She lifted her chin proudly and smiled. "Actually, I've a mind to rule, Davik. Or to lead, as grandmother would say."

He was surprised, but not disappointed.

"I've a few ideas I'd like to see instituted…particularly in the area of prison reform."

He winced again and she smiled meanly.

He gave the girl a sidelong look as he considered what this meant; taking into consideration Queen Tien's earlier statement, one day Khal would probably be united with Thrall and self-rule would likely take another step west. "But. How is it my father could imprison Tien's granddaughter?"

"It was the only thing that saved me from hanging. I got the lashes before they realized who I was; before Grandmother intervened."

"She could have demanded your release."

"I had broken Khallic law. My sentence was not undeserved. Grandmother would intervene no further." His eyes fell to her wrists. "She didn't know I suffered," she said quietly.

"How do you intend to get through the binding ceremony?" he asked. "People might take it wrong if you faint away at the critical moment."

As a part of the binding ceremony, always two strands of some sort—usually meaningful, but often just slim braids of hair—were twisted together and wrapped around the couple's wrists.

She gave him a look of sudden realization and his eyes dropped to her wounded wrists, the wrists she couldn't bear to have wrapped, even in linen bandages. By now they had traversed half the hall and arrived back at the doors. Together they faced the corridor formed by her honor guard.

"Follow my lead," he whispered, then put her hand over his arm and stepped into the hall.

The Old Queen stood. A figure stepped from the crowd to join her. Tien smiled at her grandson, Dye, then turned to watch the young couple approach. Simultaneously, the pair sent the redhead their individual and personal glares of condemnation, the combination of which seemed to please the redhead no end; he returned them both an extreme grin.

Taking both of their hands, Davik's left and Petra's right, the Queen laid their wrists atop one other and addressed the Khallic Prince. "What do you take from this woman for the binding?"

"Only her hand do I take," Davik answered. "Her hand to represent Northern Khal where she was born and raised, a citizen of Khal—Northern Khal's staunchest advocate—knowing that she will bring unity to this country, wisdom and strength to the throne, to the South." He turned his warm gaze on the woman beside him.

Petra spoke up without hesitation. "And I take the Prince's hand to symbolize the South, knowing he is the man to unite this country, and that he will bring leadership and temperance to the throne, to the North."

Their fingers met, and Khal was united when their hands formed a closing circle around their wrists.

Epilogue

As Davik and Petra said their vows, Warrik let out a breath of relief and nodded. "I knew they'd be alright." He turned from Andarta's looking glass.

The goddess pressed her breasts into his back and reached around to stroke a hand across his wide chest.

Warrik put his big hand over hers. "Was there something you wanted to show me, darling?"

"Mmm-hmm," she purred warmly. "A little place on the other side of the universe. The people who inhabit it call it Earth."

"The other side of the universe? How in Hadi's name do you get to it?"

Andarta's eyes slipped to the other side of her bedroom. "Through that door."

Warrik frowned. "I thought that was a clothes closet."

"It is." She separated herself from him and crossed the room to open the door.

He followed her and found her digging through a stack of shoeboxes. "Now," she asked herself. "What did I do with it? I know I threw it in here someplace."

About the author:

I slung the heavy battery pack around my hips and cinched it tight — or tried to.

"Damn." Brian grabbed an awl. Leaning over me, he forged a new hole in the too-big belt.

"Any advice?" I asked him as I pulled the belt tight.

"Yeah. Don't reach for the ore cart until it starts moving, then jump on the back and immediately duck your head. The voltage in the overhead cable won't just kill you. It'll blow you apart."

That was my first day on my first job. Employed as an engineer, I've worked in an underground mine that went up — inside a mountain. I've swung over the Ohio River in a tiny cage suspended from a crane in the middle of an electrical storm. I've hung over the Hudson River at midnight in an aluminum boat — 30 foot in the air — suspended from a floating barge at the height of a blizzard, while snowplows on the bridge overhead rained slush and salt down on my shoulders. You can't do this sort of work without developing a sense of humor, and a sense of adventure.

New to publishing, I read my first romance two years ago and started writing. Both my reading and writing habits are subject to mood and I usually have several stories going at once. When I need a really good idea for a story, I clean toilets. Now there's an activity that engenders escapism.

I was surveying when I met my husband. He was my 'rod man'. While I was trying to get my crosshairs on his stadia rod, he dropped his pants and mooned me. Next thing I know, I've got the backside of paradise in my viewfinder. So I grabbed the walkie-talkie. "That's real nice," I told him, "but would you please turn around? I'd rather see the other side."

…it was love at first sight.

Madison welcomes mail from readers. You can write to her c/o Ellora's Cave Publishing at 1337 Commerce Drive, Suite 13, Stow OH 44224.

Why an electronic book?

We live in the Information Age—an exciting time in the history of human civilization in which technology rules supreme and continues to progress in leaps and bounds every minute of every hour of every day. For a multitude of reasons, more and more avid literary fans are opting to purchase e-books instead of paperbacks. The question to those not yet initiated to the world of electronic reading is simply: *why?*

1. *Price.* An electronic title at Ellora's Cave Publishing runs anywhere from 40-75% less than the cover price of the <u>exact same title</u> in paperback format. Why? Cold mathematics. It is less expensive to publish an e-book than it is to publish a paperback, so the savings are passed along to the consumer.

2. *Space.* Running out of room to house your paperback books? That is one worry you will never have with electronic novels. For a low one-time cost, you can purchase a handheld computer designed specifically for e-reading purposes. Many e-readers are larger than the average handheld, giving you plenty of screen room. Better yet, hundreds of titles can be stored within your new library—a single microchip. (Please note that Ellora's Cave does not endorse any specific brands. You can check our website at www.ellorascave.com for customer recommendations we make available to new consumers.)

3. *Mobility.* Because your new library now consists of only a microchip, your entire cache of books can be taken with you wherever you go.

4. *Personal preferences are accounted for.* Are the words you are currently reading too small? Too large? Too...**ANNOYING**? Paperback books cannot be modified according to personal preferences, but e-books can.

5. *Innovation.* The way you read a book is not the only advancement the Information Age has gifted the literary community with. There is also the factor of what you can read. Ellora's Cave Publishing will be introducing a new line of interactive titles that are available in e-book format only.

6. *Instant gratification.* Is it the middle of the night and all the bookstores are closed? Are you tired of waiting days—sometimes weeks—for online and offline bookstores to ship the novels you bought? Ellora's Cave Publishing sells instantaneous downloads 24 hours a day, 7 days a week, 365 days a year. Our e-book delivery system is 100% automated, meaning your order is filled as soon as you pay for it.

Those are a few of the top reasons why electronic novels are displacing paperbacks for many an avid reader. As always, Ellora's Cave Publishing welcomes your questions and comments. We invite you to email us at service@ellorascave.com or write to us directly at: 1337 Commerce Drive, Suite 13, Stow OH 44224.

Discover for yourself why readers can't get enough of the multiple award-winning publisher Ellora's Cave. Whether you prefer e-books or paperbacks, be sure to visit EC on the web at www.ellorascave.com for an erotic reading experience that will leave you breathless.